A FALL OF
SHADOWS

ALSO AVAILABLE BY NANCY HERRIMAN

BESS ELLYOTT
Searcher of the Dead

MYSTERY OF OLD SAN FRANCISCO
No Pity for the Dead
No Comfort for the Lost

ALSO AVAILABLE
Josiah's Treasure
The Irish Healer

A FALL OF SHADOWS

A BESS ELLYOTT MYSTERY

Nancy Herriman

CROOKED
LANE

NEW YORK

Copyright © 2019 by Nancy Herriman

All rights reserved.

Published in the United States by Crooked Lane Books, an imprint of The Quick Brown Fox & Company LLC.

Crooked Lane Books and its logo are trademarks of The Quick Brown Fox & Company LLC.

Library of Congress Catalog-in-Publication data available upon request.

ISBN (hardcover): 978-1-68331-966-5
ISBN (ePub): 978-1-68331-967-2
ISBN (ePDF): 978-1-68331-968-9

Cover design by Melanie Sun

Printed in the United States.

www.crookedlanebooks.com

Crooked Lane Books
34 West 27th St., 10th Floor
New York, NY 10001

First Edition: April 2019

10 9 8 7 6 5 4 3 2 1

To all my readers, whose kind words encourage me, I offer my deepest thanks

CHAPTER 1

October 1593
Wiltshire, England

*S*he was running, the uneven cobbles beneath her feet slick with damp and filth, her hair unbound and tangling in her eyes. Tears streamed down her face for the husband, dead from poison, she'd left behind in their hall. Around her, the houses closed in, leaned over her head as if they might topple to suffocate her. He was behind her, chasing. The man who had killed Martin. She could hear him, his breathing, his footfalls. "Bess," he called. "I come for you."

Shadows twisted and leapt. A torch flared. A cat darted across the lane. A lane so narrow she could touch the cob walls on either side, should she reach out. She tried to run faster, but her feet dragged as though mired in mud. She dared look back. He was not there. Instead, she saw a crone. A haggard old woman loomed out of the darkness, her skin marked and shriveled by her evil. She laughed, but it was no laugh of humor. "Bess . . ."

"Bess."

With a start, Bess Ellyott awoke, the beamed ceiling of her chamber in Wiltshire overhead. Far from the shadowed streets of London where fear stalked her.

Her brother, Robert, leaned into view. "God mend me, Bess, you sleep deeply." His eyes were a gentle brown like her own and, at the moment, filled with fretfulness. "Are you unwell?"

"I am well, Robin." Her pet name for him. "'Twas merely an unhappy dream."

"Your husband comes to you in your sleep," he said.

"Nay, not Martin." But the man who'd killed her husband had. And a witch.

Robert's forehead creased, and she lifted her hand to brush his cheek. The stubble of his beard was rough against her finger-tips. His face had many furrows. They had both suffered the sting of loss in recent years. Spouses. Children.

"I'faith, I am well," she said, smiling to ease his concerns. She would not be the cause of more furrows upon his face. Though he was several years older—were those flecks of gray among the brown hair at his temple?—Robert had always been her boon companion, her loyal champion. Her most beloved brother.

She elbowed herself upright. "What hour is it?" Robert had pushed aside her bed curtains, and save for the light shed by the candle he'd brought with him, her chamber was dark. "Do you leave so early for London? The sun is not yet up. Surely your affairs can wait a few hours longer."

"Humphrey believes it is set to rain soon. He'd not have me travel on muddy roads and lengthen an already long journey."

"Your manservant frets for you worse than our old cook used to do. Worse than I do." As if that were possible.

Yawning, she reached for her night-rail to draw over her linen shift.

"You need not arise, Bess."

"I am awake and would see you off."

Robert stepped aside as she swung her legs over the thick

feather mattress and slid her feet into the slippers that waited on the floor. A draft chilled her bare ankles.

"You travel so often these days, Robin. It seems you are not ever here any longer." Did she sound pitiful? She hoped not. But her dream had left her with a terrible sense of foreboding, and she did not want him to leave.

"You know I must go to London. My business affairs there require my attention."

"I do understand," she said, hugging her night-rail about her body. "At least take some crushed seeds of bishop's weed as a safeguard against the plague that remains in the city."

"Aye, Bess," he replied lightly. "As you command."

"Will you be gone long?"

"Long enough, I expect, for you to bring yourself into trouble." His face settled into sober lines. "Elizabeth, be careful. Do not become involved in others' problems. You are too compassionate for your own good."

He only called her Elizabeth when he sought to scold her.

However, she'd had good reason to become involved last time, as he well knew. "I'faith, you would not wish me to be otherwise, would you?"

"Be careful, Elizabeth," he repeated.

She wished she could promise that she would be careful and all would be well while he was gone.

But no promise rose to her lips when she feared the opposite.

★ ★ ★

"Here, Constable. Here."

The farm owner, his thick-soled shoes squelching across the wet meadow, scurried ahead of Kit Harwoode. Upon a nearby rise, the man's shepherd, in his coarse frieze tunic and woolen stockings that sagged about his knees, leaned against his staff and watched them. A handful of dead sheep lay nearby.

The farm owner pointed at the animals. "See? I have lost these, and near to half my flock is ailing."

Kit eyed the sheep. "It's not unusual for sheep to die from worms of the liver in late autumn, Goodman Cox," he said. "My uncle had many of his animals die at this time last year."

"But why are only *my* sheep perishing this year? The Reades have not had any of their flock die, and their farm abuts mine," he replied. "None of *your* sheep are dead, either."

True. "There has been no crime committed. I do not know why you sent for me."

The man sniffed. "'Tis the witch's fault."

Damn.

Kit thought—not for the first time—that when he'd had the chance, he should have insisted the burgesses not select him to be constable. He had his own lands and sheep to mind, and he'd not be expected to hunt down a superstitious farmer's supposed witch. Here he was, though, and he would not ever recant the promise he'd made to fulfill his duties.

Yet . . . *damn.*

"The witch, Goodman Cox?"

"Aye. She cursed my flock, Constable Harwoode." He stretched his neck above his sweat-stained ruff and frowned. "You must arrest her and see her punished."

"There are no witches in this village," said Kit.

"But there are," announced the shepherd, who'd till then been scratching his hip in boredom. "The old woman what lives in the cob cottage." He pointed his staff toward a spot in the distance.

Kit was familiar with the woman, a frail aging widow who'd

outlived not only her husband but her children as well. Dependent upon others to support her, she lived quietly. But not quietly enough for some, it seemed.

"Why accuse her?" he asked.

"Why?" asked the farm owner. "Ever since she walked along the road near my pastures two weeks ago, my animals have been weak and will not eat. And now this." He nodded at the dead sheep. He turned back to Kit with raised brows, as though he'd proved his point and expected Kit to agree.

"Walking along a road is not a crime, either," he said.

The man's face reddened. "You will not see her punished."

Kit gripped the hilt of his dagger, slung from his belt. "Tend to your other animals, Goodman Cox, and have these buried immediately."

The man's mouth fell open. Kit turned and strode toward the road.

"She must be punished, Constable," Goodman Cox called after him. "Before worse happens!"

★   ★   ★

"Such a horrid dream it was, Joan," said Bess to her servant, who was seated by the courtyard-facing hall window brushing dirt from the hem of one of Bess's gowns. Joan had been too busy all that day for Bess to tell her about the dream earlier.

I should not have burdened her with it now, either.

But she trusted Joan's counsel, for she was more friend than servant. They'd fled London together and had come to Wiltshire to begin anew in the safety of Robert's home. Joan was strong, the scar on her cheek that peeped now from beneath her coif an outward sign of what she'd endured before Bess had taken her in. Proof of the courage that Bess knew lived within.

"What do you think it means that I dreamt of a witch, though?" Bess did not ask Joan why she'd dreamt of Laurence; he often haunted her thoughts, both night and day, despite the miles that stretched between them. She'd discovered his treason, but her husband had paid the price for her knowledge.

"'Tis unchancy, I would say, Mistress," said Joan, holding up the skirt to examine her handiwork. She shifted the hem to a new spot and continued brushing. "Ill-boding."

Bess could not dispute the claim when she agreed.

"Mayhap my sleep was unsound because I fret over Robert's departure this morning, which has upset my thoughts and peace. That is all," said Bess, movement in the courtyard catching her eye.

"Ill-boding," Joan repeated above the scratch of bristles across the deep-green kersey. The gown was Bess's warmest, and with winter approaching, she'd have need of it.

Bess stepped nearer the hall window and peered through the wavy glass. A spurt of rain flowed in rivulets down the panes, further distorting the view. Foul weather had arrived at midday, spreading damp across the chalk hills and into the village. As befitted a successful merchant, Robert's two-story house was solid, with thick stone walls at the ground level and good glazed windows. The dampness seeped inside anyway.

Hugging her arms at her waist, Bess squinted past the rainfall. "What is Humphrey about in the courtyard?"

"He has been hanging crosses made from elder branches upon the outbuildings to protect his chickens."

"Protect them from what?"

Joan's brush paused. "Evil. Disease," she said. "Witches."

My dream. "Have the chickens need of such protection?"

"It is said in the market that sheep are dying, Mistress," said

Joan. "The old woman who lives off the lane past the bend has been accused of bewitching them."

Bess knew of the woman Joan meant. "Mother Fletcher is but an impoverished widow who keeps her own quarter. No one has need to fear her."

"The townsfolk are quick to mislike an old widowed woman who lives alone, Mistress."

"The townsfolk are always quick to mislike and mistrust," said Bess. Too often whispers and scrutiny accompanied her as she moved through town. A widow who made physic. Suspicious. "Mother Fletcher is harmless."

"As you say, Mistress."

Robert's manservant moved to the last door along the length of the outbuilding that stretched from the rear of the house.

"We should be thankful my sister is away." Dorothie and her daughter had left the village to visit her mother-in-law. To grieve together over the tragic murder of Dorothie's husband. The solution of that crime was the "problem" Bess had involved herself in when Robert had last gone to London. "She would be in a panic and insist Humphrey hang witch guards at her house as well."

"I can tell him you wish him to stop, Mistress."

"No, Joan. If hanging his witch safeguards makes Humphrey happy, I'll not stop him."

A rap sounded on the street-side door. Joan set down her work and went to answer the knock. She returned quickly. "You are summoned to the dairy east of town, Mistress. The family has need of your healing. The Merricks."

"The Merricks? They have never sent for me before."

Their house and its barns stood atop a low hill overlooking the road and meadows thick with cows. She had admired the whitewashed buildings when Robert had once taken her past them on their way to Avebury. They had gone to the town to marvel at its stone henge as well as to visit a distant cousin who lived there. A festive time that made Bess miss her brother afresh.

"Did the messenger say who is ill and what is the matter?" she asked.

"'Tis one of their dairymaids, Mistress. Vomiting, he says. Pains in her stomach. Some palsy, also."

"'Tis a mile walk. I should get underway if I'm to return before sunset," said Bess. "I shall need my mixture of organy and mint to soothe her, Joan. Collect it while I fetch my heavy-soled mules and my cloak."

"Mayhap you should take a bundle of rue as well, Mistress."

"Rue will aggravate the upset of the girl's stomach, not calm it, Joan."

"That is not why I suggest you do so, Mistress," she said. "You should take it for protection."

The look on her servant's face was more alarming than Bess's discomfiting dream. "Against witches."

"Sheep have died and now a girl in a nearby farm has fallen ill," Joan pointed out. "What or who might next be struck down?"

★　★　★

A handful of rue leaves tucked into the pocket slung from her tape girdle, Bess set out for the Merricks'. By the time she arrived, the rain had stopped and snippets of blue sky showed between the clouds. She climbed the path leading to their house. Its ground floor was built of sturdy stone, and the timber frames of the upper floor had faded to a soft gray made softer by the thin late-afternoon light. Barns that sheltered the cows and where the cheese was made spread out behind the farmhouse on either side. A woman stood outside the house's open front door, her hands clasped over the apron tied around her thick waist.

Spying Bess, she nodded, then called to someone inside the house. "The healer is here. And see that the children stay away from that girl's chamber."

"God save you, Widow Ellyott," she said in greeting, "for coming so speedily. I am Agnes Merrick."

The lines that creased her eyes and her mouth suggested to Bess that she was about forty years of age. The thickness of her waist came from being with child. Four or five months so, if Bess were to hazard a guess. The woman had loosened her bodice strings and sewn an unmatched fabric panel into the skirt of her gown to accommodate the coming swell, but the extra material would not prove adequate for long.

"God save you, Mistress Merrick."

The woman gestured Bess out of the wind. The shadows of the entry passage were deep, and Bess paused to allow her eyes to adjust to the dimness. A narrow beam of light streamed through the doorway between the corridor and the hall. Within the room, a scrawny servant girl dressed in blue set pewter upon a massive oak table in preparation for their evening meal. When she did not think her mistress would notice, she snuck glances at Bess.

"I apologize that I did not come more quickly," said Bess. "My brother has taken our only horse to London, so I had to walk."

"If my eldest daughter were here, I'd not have need of your help. She is far more skilled with herbs and simples than I. But she . . ." The woman's mouth pinched with annoyance. The motion deepened the lines around her lips and explained why those lines existed to begin with. "No matter. You have come, and we are grateful. I will take you to the girl. But first . . ."

Mistress Merrick gestured at Bess's mud-caked mules. Bess slipped them off her shoes, setting them atop the dense thatch of rushes that covered the entry area floor. At the end of the passage, the woman led Bess up a spiraling flight of steps, which creaked beneath the weight of their feet. The staircase opened onto a first-floor room that had been built to serve as a parlor or private hall but now held beds and chests. The minty aroma of pennyroyal, scattered about in hopes the herb would ward off fleas, scented the air.

A boy with Mistress Merrick's same blunt nose bolted from a far room and skittered past Bess. Avoiding his mother's gaze, he headed for the stairs. His arrival downstairs was met by a girl's angry shouts, followed by silence.

"I have put her back here." Mistress Merrick crossed to a narrow door that led to a series of chambers built above the ground-floor service rooms. The farther they walked, the danker and more shadowed the chambers became. "I feared contagion and sought to keep her away from the rest of the family and the other servants."

At least she'd not left the girl to suffer in one of the rooms likely to be found out in the barns. *Which might, in truth, be warmer than these chambers.*

"What is her name?" asked Bess.

"Anna Webb." Mistress Merrick guided Bess through another door. "She has only been with us a year."

"Has she been ill like this before?"

"No," she said. "I thought her a sturdy girl, which is why we took her on. Thanked be God the greatest part of the cheesemaking is finished for the year. My husband has gone off to the fair with two of our boys to sell what we produced this summer. Five hundredweight they're taking. A good year."

They entered the last chamber in the line, danker and darker than all the rest. Its regular life was as a storage room, if the stacked table boards, parts of bedsteads, tubs, and chipped crocks were any indication. Someone had placed a squat truckle bed in the corner. The young woman upon it lay on her side, her flaxen hair stuck to her damp forehead. A wood bucket, stinking from its contents, sat on the floor nearby.

"Anna," said Mistress Merrick, venturing no nearer than the doorstead. "The healer has come."

Anna moaned and peered at Bess with bloodshot eyes. "Who?"

Bess set down her satchel of physic. "Let us open the window."

"But it is most cool outside," argued Mistress Merrick. "The air will harm the girl."

"No more than the fetid air in here." Bess unlatched the narrow window. "And prithee have your servant girl refresh the bucket."

Mistress Merrick happily departed, leaving Bess alone with the girl.

"Anna, you have been unwell?" she asked.

"My stomach. I feel most poorly. I am so very tired." She pinched her lips together. Were her face not sallow from her sickness, she would be quite fair. "I was in good health this morning, but after dinner I became ill."

She grimaced and clutched at her stomach. But she did not retch. Perhaps the worst of her sickness had passed.

Bess untied her satchel and removed the sealed jar containing her physic. She poured the liquid into a small ceramic cup Joan had also packed. "I have brought you physic to ease your nausea."

"Gramercy, Mistress."

"You said you fell ill after dinner. Did any of those who shared your meal also become sick?"

She shook her head, her eyes tracking Bess's movements. "I think no one else is ill, Mistress. Only me."

The blue-dressed servant appeared at the door with a bucket in her hand. Pinching her nose shut, the girl scurried across the room, replaced the filthy bucket with the new, and dashed out again.

Bess helped Anna sit upright, taking care that the movement did not unsettle her stomach, and handed the girl the cup. "Take this. Drink it all. It shall help."

The girl did as ordered, then lowered herself back against the straw-filled pillow she'd been given. Bess tucked the thin blanket around Anna's shoulders.

"I am sorry for causing such troubles," said the girl. Her color seemed better, though it was hard to tell in the room's scant light. "Do you think Mistress Merrick will release me from service?"

"For becoming ill? That would be most hard-hearted. Surely your mistress is a more just woman than that."

"I pray so, for I need the work desperately," said Anna. "And I try to do it well, I do. But the others are not . . ." Her words trailed off.

"The others are not what, Anna?"

The girl chewed her lower lip and did not answer.

"Do you mean the other dairymaids?" asked Bess. "Or mean you the Merricks? Are they cruel to you?"

Her brows pinched together. "Listen not to me, Mistress. I am unwell and my mind is confused."

Bess thought she heard a noise outside the room like the shuffling of feet. Anna flinched at the sound.

How curious. But the girl appeared unwilling to speak of what it was that had startled her.

"I shall leave the drink with you." Bess set the jar on the floor next to the bucket. "Here. Within reach. You may drink of it as you need."

Anna nodded, indicating she'd heard.

"Also, Anna, I would have you know that you can trust me. I will help you."

"Gramercy, Mistress, but I need no help. I am simply a dizzard and full of self-pity."

"You are no fool, Anna, and it is not self-pity to desire to be treated well." Bess collected her satchel. "Send for me if you require aught else."

The girl rolled onto her side and curled into a ball.

Mistress Merrick waited for Bess downstairs. She fingered the keys suspended from her broad tape girdle. "So?"

"Anna should be well. I left physic for her to drink that will quiet her stomach."

"Good." Mistress Merrick led her back through the passageway and opened the front door.

A shaft of sunlight lit the umber-colored harvested fields, and the Merricks' cattle ambled across the hills toward their barns. An image of serenity quite at odds with the unease gripping the house.

"Gramercy, Widow Ellyott," said the woman, holding out coin.

"I do not require payment, Mistress Merrick."

She hastily withdrew her hand and the money it held.

Bess restored her mules to her feet, stepped outside, and pulled the hood of her cloak over her head. "Send a message again should Anna worsen, Mistress Merrick. I will come no matter the hour."

"I expect there will be no need for you to return, Widow Ellyott. Good even," she said, shutting the door in Bess's face.

"Well, then."

Bess glanced up at the window of the chamber where Anna rested. Bess pitied her, having such a woman as a mistress. With a sigh, she lowered her gaze. It was only then that she noticed the cross of elder nailed to the lintel of the Merricks' front door.

She closed her fingers around her pocket, the rue leaves inside it crunching.

Indeed, Joan, what or who might next be struck down?

CHAPTER 2

"**G**oodman Cox blamed a witch," said Kit to his cousin. Gibb Harwoode, cleaning his teeth with a silver pick, stood beside Kit in the great hall of a local merchant family, the Poynards. An evening of festivities had been planned, beginning with a lavish supper of smoked herring and trout, dressed salads, tarts, and dried fruits. The meal had concluded, and servants scuttled about removing the tables and arranging stools and chairs. Next to come was a play. A group of traveling actors— supposedly members of the Admiral's Men—had recently journeyed to the village. Kit wondered how the Poynards had managed to convince a prominent troupe to perform in this remote part of Wiltshire.

"Marry, Kit, the story of a witch is everywhere," said Gibb above the thud of planks being lowered to serve as a stage. The squeal and groan of musicians tuning their instruments added to the din, which echoed off the carved wooden beams arching overhead. "You shall be expected to bring her to be examined."

"What, to be pricked with needles to see whether or not she bleeds?"

The servants finished setting out the chairs and stools, and Gibb took a seat. "If that is what is required, coz."

Finished with his teeth, he stashed his pick within the depths of one of his pinked black velvet sleeves. Kit hadn't had much of an appetite. His cousin, undisturbed by the thought of witches, had eaten heartily.

Kit dropped onto the stool beside him. "Do not tell me you believe those sheep fell dead because they were bewitched, Gibb."

"You never know."

An impatient member of the waiting crowd—burgesses and a few of the more prosperous farmers from the surrounding countryside—demanded to know when the performance would begin. The fellow, red-faced and listing to one side, had apparently too freely drunk the claret the Poynards had served with their fine meal.

At the end of the hall, the eldest Poynard son, Jeffrey, stepped around a curtain, which had been hung to conceal the entrance to the screens passage and the service rooms beyond. He shouted at the servants to bring ale to appease the men and their wives. Not that the grumbling fellow needed more drink.

"I hope this fancy for accusing a witch passes, Gibb." Kit stretched his legs, his boot heels scraping across the checkerboard marble floor. Above the screens passage, the musicians seated in the minstrels' gallery finished their tuning and began to play. "In the meantime, I intend to enjoy the musicians. Even if they are only our town waites."

Servants arrived to pass out pewter tankards of ale. "At least the ale is fresh," said Gibb, taking a sip as the last of the guests took their seats.

At that moment, a tall man in a russet cloak parted the curtain concealing the entrance to the screens passage. He stepped onto the stage and the hall quieted.

"Good sirs and ladies, I beg your forgiveness for the delay," he announced, his voice booming with an educated accent. The fire roaring in the hearth, and the banks of candles and lanterns illuminating the stage showed his strong features. The light also revealed that the man's gray hair was a wig. "One of our players is late in arriving, but we should begin anon. Our play this evening will be *The Marriage of Wit and Wisdom*. I pray you find it full of mirth and worthy of your attention."

"What?" groaned Gibb after the man swept off the stage and exited the room. Jeffrey Poynard followed the actor, disappearing behind the curtain after him. "I thought we were to see *Titus Andronicus*."

"Apparently not."

"Just as well. I saw it performed in Bath earlier this year. Lord Strange's Players. Passable. By that Shakespeare fellow, I think."

"If you say so, Gibb."

Gibb sipped from his tankard and scanned the room's occupants, who had resumed grumbling and drinking. The waites started another tune, the shawm too loud. Kit drummed his fingers on his thigh, his hands itching for the strings of his gittern back at home.

"I must say, though," said Gibb, shifting to see over the man seated in front of him, "I am surprised to not see Mistress Ellyott's brother here."

"Robert Marshall left for London this morning," said Kit. He wondered how Bess Ellyott fared. Hopefully not finding herself in trouble again. However, she was the sort who attracted trouble, like a lodestone drawing in bits of iron. She was clever, though, and handsome, her eyes a warm brown like her hair—

"You *are* attending to her and her family," said Gibb, interrupting Kit's musings.

"I have not seen Mistress Ellyott in days."

"But you *do* know what her brother is about." Gibb grinned. "I warrant you also know where her sister and niece have gone."

"A pox on you, Gibb Harwoode."

His cousin burst into laughter.

The actor who'd made the announcement returned, Jeffrey Poynard on his heels. Poynard found a seat among his family in the front row of cushioned chairs. The actor once more took his place on the stage. His gaze swept the room, and he'd not erased the scowl that had settled on his face. The delayed player, Kit suspected, had not made his arrival, but the performance could not wait.

The fellow clasped one edge of his cloak and straightened to his full, commanding height. All in the room fell silent.

"Who marks the common course of youthful wandering wits," he began, "shall see the most of them frequent where idleness still sits. And how the irksomeness doth murder many a one—"

A banging door and a loud shout interrupted the fellow's prologue.

"What is that commotion?" whispered Gibb.

The actor attempted to restart. "And how the irksomeness—"

A man rushed into the hall, most likely one of the players. "Master Howlett!" he shouted at the fellow on stage.

"Back at last!" Howlett jumped down to the floor, the edge of his cloak flapping. "You have found him?"

"I need to speak to the constable," the fellow answered.

"Trouble now, coz," said Gibb.

The Poynards stood as one. Eyes turned toward Kit.

Gibb got to his feet along with rest of the crowd. Gripping the hilt of his dagger, its sheath tucked into his belt, Kit rose as well. "I am here."

The man—as tall as Howlett and with reddish-blond curls and a pointed beard at the tip of his chin—pushed through the assembly.

"What is this?" demanded Jeffrey Poynard in his most imperious voice. He was pompous, and imperiousness came easily.

"The hill outside the village," the man panted, squeezing his side. "I found him there."

"Take your own good time, sir," said Kit.

"What has happened to him?" asked Howlett, gripping the fellow's arm.

The player held up a gloved hand, a dark smear ruining the colorful embroidery that trimmed the lamb's leather. "Evil." He had an expressive face that jumped and jerked with every changing emotion. "Great evil."

A surge of fretful whispers arose among those huddled around him.

"He is dead. Upon the hill, Constable." He released a lengthy breath and straightened, the stitch in his side relieved. "He is dead."

★   ★   ★

Rooks were crying in the trees at the edge of town as Bess arrived home, their noise mournful, eerie. Thankfully, Joan had hung lanterns by the door to light Bess's way.

Joan rushed to greet her, removing her cloak from about her shoulders. "How fares the girl?" she asked, shaking rainwater from it.

"She will recover," said Bess, setting down her satchel. "Though I could not be certain what caused her illness, unless it comes from living with Agnes Merrick as her mistress. I'faith, the woman is a harsh one."

"Not every mistress is as kind as you."

"Kind or overly tenderhearted?"

"Now, Mistress," tutted Joan, folding the cloak over her arm.

"At least I had no need for the rue to protect me." Bess slipped off her mules—twice as mud-caked as they'd been when she arrived at the Merricks' farm—and greeted her brother's brown-and-white water spaniel. Quail had trotted in from the kitchen to inspect her, and she ruffled his ears in response. "I am safely returned."

"Which means the rue *did* protect you."

Bess smiled and entered the hall. A fire crackled upon the hearth. Bess settled upon her brother's chair, which was turned to face the flames. Quail chose a nearby spot atop the rush matting that covered the stone floor and kept the chill from their feet.

"Wish you to eat here in the hall?" asked Joan, gesturing at the table folded before the windows overlooking the courtyard. Beyond their glass, the evening shadows had overtaken the outbuildings, and the dying wind shook the garden's quince trees, heavy with yellow fruit. Bess must set Humphrey to harvesting it.

"It is so lonely to eat in the hall without Robert," said Bess. "I would not even mind my sister's company, to be frank."

A stark admission, when she and Dorothie fought more than they were ever companionable. With Robert also gone, Bess was left behind with two servants, one of whom did not much care for her, and a dog. She had work to occupy her, though. And when Robert finally returned from London, he might bring a wife. There would be no loneliness then.

"'Tis indeed quiet, Mistress."

"Too quiet," said Bess. "I shall have my meal in the upstairs parlor, Joan."

"There is no fire lit there, madam."

"Then here," said Bess. "And you may join me."

Joan pointed to herself. "Me?"

"Do not tell Humphrey. He might get jealous." Or grumble about the impropriety of Bess's friendship with her maidservant. Or both.

"You may be certain I'll not say a word to him!" Joan headed for the kitchen, Quail on her heels.

Bess got to her feet and wandered over to the courtyard-facing windows. Humphrey had disappeared somewhere, though a handful of his chickens still pecked among the gravel. The rest had gone to their roosts within the shed. She loved the view of the garden from these windows, the herbs and roses and quince trees slightly distorted by the waviness of the glass. They created an expanse of green, which softened the stone wall surrounding the messuage. She had much work to do in the garden, with the winter coming. Much to—

Bess squinted through the glass. Something was amiss, but she could not see precisely what. She went to the lobby that connected the hall and kitchen to the various rooms extending behind the house. Its door let out onto the courtyard. She unlatched it and pushed it open.

She peered through the descending darkness. The gate in the back wall was ajar.

How odd. Humphrey usually ensured the gate was locked when night fell. Perhaps his fretfulness over his chickens and the witch had distracted him.

"Joan," she called out. "The back gate has been left unlocked."

Hugging her arms about her body to ward off the evening's chill, she hurried across the courtyard, scattering chickens. She picked her way through the garden, its fading sweet and spicy aromas scenting the air. The lock had been knocked loose and had fallen to the ground nearby. Through the gate's opening protruded an arm.

"Joan! Come quickly!" Bess cried, pulling the gate wide. A woman lay sprawled where she had collapsed, facedown. A streak of darkness spread across the skirts of her kirtle, a light blue some called watchet.

Bess crouched next to her, pushing her brown hair away from her face. She pressed fingertips to the young woman's skin. Warm. Mayhap too warm from fever. However, she did breathe. Bess shook her shoulder, trying to rouse her but failing.

"Mistress?" called out Joan, her footfalls crunching across the stones. "'Od's wounds! Ill-boding, Mistress. Your dream!"

"My dream had naught to do with an ill young woman," Bess replied.

"Is that blood 'pon her skirt?"

"I cannot be certain in this light." Bess turned the woman onto her back. She was lovely, but her hair was streaked with the contents of her stomach, which she'd apparently vomited. *Another in one day . . .* "Fetch Humphrey to help me carry her into the house."

"I know not where he is," said Joan. "He may be at the alehouse."

"Just as well. We shall carry her ourselves."

"We'll not get far without dropping her, Mistress. Let me fetch the barrow to place her upon so we can wheel her into the hall."

Joan dashed off, and Bess considered the woman. She did not recognize her. "What are we to do with you, Mistress?"

Tend to her. Care for her. There was no other answer.

Joan returned with the barrow—a few planks nailed to a frame with a single wheel below and a pair of handles out the back.

"Take her legs while I hoist her shoulders. Carefully, Joan. Carefully."

Together, they lifted the young woman, who was heavier than she'd at first seemed. Groaning, they laid her upon the barrow, her dress dragging on the ground. She moaned but did not awaken. From within the house came the sound of Quail barking. Joan had shut the courtyard door on him, and he protested the excitement in the garden that he was missing.

"Let us take her into the hall," said Bess. "Once Humphrey returns, he can help us move her to the small chamber above the kitchen."

Joan gripped the barrow's handles. "Who do you think she is, Mistress?"

"A woman in trouble, Joan." Bess glanced at the young stranger's stained skirts. An ache of sympathy stuck in her throat. "A woman in most serious trouble."

★   ★   ★

The Poynards' hall drained as rapidly as a cask with its spigot removed. Its occupants chased after the player, whose name was Willim Dunning. He'd found his breath and scampered through the streets of town, bound for the hill with the body. Links and lanterns bobbed in folks' hands as they ran behind him.

"Kit, 'tis plain where the fellow is bound," said Gibb.

"It is?"

"The old fort hill," he muttered. "The druids' mound."

By the time they arrived at the hillock, half the town had

assembled to gape. Not one ventured too near. The tales that druids had once practiced their mystical rites atop its crest kept them away.

Superstitious lot.

"He is there, Constable." A man in a rust-red tunic pointed to the top of the hill, which rose all of ten feet high. At some time in his life, the fellow had lost half of his right ear. Perhaps after having it nailed to the pillory. "None of us have touched him."

"We dare not!" the fellow's companion declared. "Who can say what evil struck him down? I'd not have it strike me, too! Unholy place."

"'Twas the witch, Constable!" another called out.

Helpful.

"Gibb, bring a lantern," said Kit.

He gripped his dagger as he climbed the slope, his shoes slipping on its damp grass. A wind shook the branches of the trees surrounding the mound on three sides and cut through his clothing. Kit buttoned his padded doublet to his neck against the cold.

"You be careful, Constable!" someone among the gathered crowd cried.

Gibb scrambled up the hill behind Kit. "Dearest Lord."

"Just so."

The man lay crumpled at the very center of the mound. He'd been stabbed multiple times, his torso covered with gashes, most of them in his back. His knife, its blade clean, rested near his outstretched hand. Blood had soaked into the cloak he'd spread to rest upon and stained his shirt. The material stuck to the fellow's muscular body. And from the side of his throat protruded a broken reed pen.

"Now we know what caused his absence," said Kit.

Gibb bent down to remove the pen from the man's neck. The tip was extremely sharp and thick with gore. Gibb grimaced in disgust. "The weapon?"

"Not the one that killed him." That blade was nowhere to be seen.

"A vile, vengeful crime, coz." Gibb used the toe of his boot to prod a leather penner at the man's side. Quills and bits of paper spilled from the cylindrical container, and a brass inkwell had rolled some distance away. The quills had been snapped as though trod beneath a foot.

"He carried his penner with him everywhere," said Dunning, looking up at Kit and Gibb from the base of the mound. "He was not just an actor but a playwright as well. 'Fore God, how did he come to this?"

"What was his name?" asked Kit.

"Bartholomew Reade," said the player.

The name was familiar; someone had mentioned it to Kit only recently. It was familiar to everyone else as well, if the gasps among those assembled were any indication.

"Reade?" asked Gibb.

"You are familiar with him?"

"Aye. He is the oldest son of the farm owner whose land lies between here and town," said Gibb, holding the reed pen at arm's length as though he wished he'd never touched it. "But I thought he was gone from this area some time now."

"Master Dunning, how did you know to look for your friend here?" asked Kit. Though near to the village, the hillock was secluded, located a good dozen yards off the road and sheltered by a thicket of trees and shrubs.

"Bartholomew told me and the others he was to meet a woman." The player tugged the short cloak he wore tighter about his body. "At a small hill where no one liked to go. We— my fellows and I—chose several paths around the town, not knowing which such hill among the many Bartholomew meant. We are not from this area, like he was. How could we know? The others had no patience, quit early, and returned to prepare for the performance. I continued, though. And then . . ." He swallowed, the movement of his Adam's apple shifting the ruff about his neck. "And then I did find him."

"This evil hill," the fellow with the damaged ear said to the others nearby. "Used to be a druid temple here. On top of this mound, where they would hold their rites. Make their sacrifices."

"Commune between the living and the dead," added Gibb quietly.

"This fellow was not killed by a druid, Gibb," said Kit. "Nor by a witch."

Gibb surveyed the flat expanse of the mound's peak where they stood, his face lit by the orange glow from the lantern he carried. "Are you certain, Kit?"

"We search for a killer of flesh and blood. Not a mystical, magical being." Kit turned to the onlookers. "Know you who might have done this to Master Reade? Any of you?"

"'Twas the witch!" several shouted.

Another pointed at Dunning, who shrank back. "He or one of his fellows likely did! Players! You know that lot!"

Just then, a man in a bright-green jerkin crashed through the underbrush. "Constable! I found the killer! Here!" He jabbed a thumb toward the shrubs. "Here!"

As one, the crowd spun around and followed him. Kit hurried down the hill, Gibb on his heels.

A pockmarked fellow gripped the accused's elbow. Grizzled

and gray, more bones than substance, the old man he held squinted in the light of the torches carried by the mob.

"He was sleeping here." The fellow in green gestured at a cleared spot sheltered by a thick growth of hawthorn. "And I found this nearby." He picked up a belt and purse, which jingled with coins. "Taken from Master Reade."

"What?" The old man's breath stank of strong drink. "I did nothing."

"Master Reade's purse *is* missing," said Gibb, still holding the reed pen.

"There's no blood on the old man's clothing," said Kit. "And I doubt he could strangle a cat, let alone murder a fit young man."

"He be a vagrant, Constable. Trouble to the village," said a villager. The crowd nodded and shouted agreement. "He must be arrested."

Kit exhaled, a sour feeling in his stomach. "Take him to the jail. And send for the coroner to examine Master Reade's body."

They dragged the old man away, the vagrant unsteady and stumbling, leaving Kit and Gibb behind.

"That was quick," said Gibb.

"Too quick, Gibb," said Kit. "Far too quick."

CHAPTER 3

"I'm to take her to the above-kitchen chamber, Mistress?" asked Humphrey.

He pursed his lips and squinted at the woman, whom Bess and Joan had managed to lay upon a mattress by the hall fire. They had removed her stained skirt and petticoats and covered her with a blanket to hide the blood on her shift; if Humphrey noticed, his disapproval would be even greater.

"Joan will help you," she said.

"What if she be diseased?" he asked. "She looks like she has been sick."

They had also tried to clean the woman's face and hair, but had apparently not been thorough enough. "You will not contract an illness from her, Humphrey. Trust me on this. Now do as I ask."

He did not move. "She should go back to wherever she's come from, Mistress."

"As she has not awakened to tell us who she is, Humphrey, we do not know where to send her. All we know is that she needs our help, and we shall give it."

"Aye, Mistress. Move aside, Quail." He nudged the dog with the toe of his thick shoe. Quail had not left the woman's side since she'd been wheeled into the hall, and only reluctantly did he get to his feet.

Joan secured the blanket about the woman's body and, with Humphrey, hoisted her. The stranger's eyelids fluttered but did not open. Slowly, they carried her up the winding staircase at the corner of the hall. When she was finally settled upon the feather-mattress-topped bed in one of the empty chambers, Bess released a sigh of relief.

"Master Marshall shall not be happy," said Humphrey.

"I expect, Humphrey, that our patient will be recovered and safely back at her home by the time my brother returns from London."

Grumbling, Humphrey departed, and Bess took a seat on the stool pulled up next to the bed. "I still gather in the outcasts, do I not, Joan? My brother claims I am too compassionate. But I did not collect her. She came to me."

"Your skills are familiar to all."

"Even to those I do not know, it seems." Bess tucked the blanket around the woman's shoulders. "I shall sit with her for a while, Joan. Bring my mixture of sage and yarrow and salt, some cool water, and cloths so I may bathe her wrists. She remains a trifle feverish."

"But then what shall we do?"

"In the morning, if she has not awakened by then, I will need you to ask about the village if a woman has gone missing. I hope, though, she awakens before that becomes necessary." Bess brushed strands of hair away from the woman's eyes. Bess had thought her hair brown, but the candlelight revealed it to have an auburn hue. She was very lovely, her features even, her nose petite, and her lips lush. A woman who would turn many a man's head. "So we can ask her about the infant her body has expelled."

★   ★   ★

"Forsooth, I cannot fathom . . ." began John Howlett, the leader of the players. "What a tragedy."

He slumped on a stool, his gray wig dangling from one hand. He and Kit sat in a cramped chamber off the Poynards' service rooms. The players had been given the space to use as their tiring room. Bright bits of clothing were tossed over trunks and atop barrels, and theater properties were scattered about. Howlett's remaining players huddled in a nearby room.

"When did you last see Reade?" asked Kit over the clatter of pots and dishes coming from the direction of the nearby kitchen. A man had been killed that day, but the duties of the Poynards' household apparently could not stop.

"Around midday." Howlett had reddened his mouth with madder, which he'd tried to wipe off. The attempt had left a smear of color across his cheek. "When he did not return to prepare for the night's performance, I sent the others to search for him."

"Your player, Dunning, the one who found him, said Reade had gone to meet a woman. Did he often do that?"

"No more, no less than the others, Constable."

"What else do you know about him, Master Howlett?" asked Kit. "He was a local man, but I am unfamiliar with him."

"He was from this village," said Howlett. "I took him on around a month ago, in Shrewsbury. He claimed to have been with the Admiral's Men there and proved to be a skilled actor."

"I thought you'd all been with the Admiral's Men."

"No. A fib to add glister to our reputation, I confess. They are renowned."

What else did John Howlett "fib" about?

"The Admiral's Men are in need of monies, as are most of us these days," Howlett continued, setting his wig aside. "The theaters are closed in London because of plague, forcing everyone into the provinces in search of employment. They have released many of their players out of necessity. We ourselves no longer have a sponsor and hope to find one. We can only continue, though, until our warrant from the Privy Council allowing us to travel expires. At which point . . ." He shrugged.

"So Reade left the Admiral's Men and joined you," said Kit.

"He had ambitions to be a playwright, as well. He was desirous of becoming the next Christopher Marlowe."

Kit could not tell if the comment was meant to be critical or complimentary.

"Did the others find Reade agreeable, or did his ambitions cause strife?" he asked.

"There are always petty jealousies amongst players, Constable. Sober-mindedness to ever be restored among them," the fellow replied, sounding weary of his responsibility to do the restoring.

"Jealousies sufficient to wish to kill the man?"

Howlett paled, the madder he'd rubbed across his cheekbones standing out in garish red spots, and shivered. The room was clammy, the stone floor beneath their feet slick with moisture. He might be shivering from the chill. Or he might not.

"Why ask these questions, Constable? Has not the murderer been clapped in the town jail?"

"I have my reasons." From the pouch suspended from his belt, Kit withdrew the pen, its tip stained from ink and Reade's blood. He held it up to the light of the lantern he'd earlier set on the floor.

Howlett's eyes widened. "He was killed with one of his pens?"

"It was found thrust into his neck. His other quills were crushed as though in anger."

"A reed pen," said Howlett, more calmly. "A pun upon his name?"

"Mayhap so," agreed Kit. "An interesting act."

"To be stabbed with his own writing tool." Howlett shook his head. "Reade carried his quills and pens everywhere with him. Aside from his own scribbling, he was responsible for making changes to our plays as necessary. Cut scenes. Reduce dialogue if we lack the right number of actors or are in need of a change because of a new player. I'd set him to the task of trimming one of our manuscripts, in fact, as we are short a player."

Kit returned the pen to his pouch. "I have a final question for you, Master Howlett. Why did you bring your players to this particular town? As long as I have lived here, we have never had a traveling troupe perform in this part of Wiltshire."

Howlett released a sharp, short laugh. "Our visit was Bartholomew's idea. He had been in communication with the Poynards about a performance. So we came." He lifted an eyebrow. "Rather ironic, think you not?"

★　★　★

"Who let you in?" Kit asked, entering his upstairs hall to find his cousin sprawled on a chair set before the empty hearth.

Gibb straightened. "Alice. Who else? 'Tis not as though you have given me a key."

After weeks of hounding by Gibb and his father, Kit had finally hired a girl to tend to his house.

"Your father, my dear uncle, thinks you spend too much time in my company as it is," said Kit. "And clearly you have no need of a key when my maidservant gives you free rein."

Kit crossed the room, tossing his hat onto his desk and following it with his dagger. The pen thrust into Reade's neck he laid alongside the items. "Any news?"

"The coroner made his ruling of murder," said Gibb. "And his jury agree with the decision to accuse that old man. His name is Jellis, by the way. Has no home of which I am aware."

"At least he is not a witch nor wizard."

"Nor druid."

"Aye." Kit stared out the hall window. His house was located near the town's market center and overlooked the dark streets below. Here and there, lanterns or torches burned at doorways. They shed their light upon the town watchman, who tapped his staff and rang his bell as he crossed the cobbles. "The master of the troupe says it was Reade's idea to come here."

Gibb whistled. "Not the best idea."

Kit pushed away from the window. He dropped onto the chair across from Gibb. "And now he cannot repent it."

"Curious though, think you not?" Gibb hugged his short cape about his torso and gave an elaborate shudder. "Can you not light a fire, Kit? 'Tis cold as a witch's—"

"Aye, Gibb. I understand," said Kit. "Should I have Alice bring a warm posset for you to drink for your weary old bones?"

"Fie on you, Kit."

"Alice would likely faint if I went into the kitchen and made a demand," he said. "I do not know what to do with her. She fears her own shadow." But she'd come cheap, and now he understood why.

"Perhaps I should send my sister here to advise both you and Alice."

"Frances has returned home?" She'd been staying with friends in Gloucester for the past few months.

"She has done, and she would greatly delight in giving you counsel about servants."

"I do not need more Harwoode cousins minding my affairs."

"Frances would enjoy the visit."

"I know she would, and that is the problem."

Gibb chuckled, then sobered. "Think you it is true that Reade went to the hill to tryst with a woman? Many folk around here avoid the old druids' mound, which does make it the perfect place to meet. If you seek privacy and do not fear the place."

"I'll not ask if you have made use of this place yourself for trysting, Gibb."

Gibb smirked. "How you jest, coz." He peered at Kit. "*Do* you have a posset heated in the kitchen?" he asked hopefully.

"No."

Gibb groaned and rubbed his gloved hands together to warm them. "There is not ever a bite to eat or a cup to be had in this house. I truly imagined that hiring Alice would change matters."

"It has not. And you"—Kit leaned over to poke his cousin with his finger—"are ever hungry and thirsty."

"True," he said. "We have not found the weapon, though. We will search again on the morrow."

"My thanks for your help."

"But even if we discover the blade, Kit, how can we prove Jellis did not kill Reade?"

Kit dragged his fingertips through his short beard. "There, Gibb, is the question with no clear answer. As yet."

★   ★   ★

A noise roused Bess from her dozing, and she rubbed her eyes. The candle Joan had set on the floor had burned low, dripping wax onto the holder's pewter base. Light peeked through the gaps in the brocade curtain hung across the chamber's window. Morning had come.

The woman upon the bed moaned, the same sound that must have awoken Bess, and she opened her eyes.

She looked over at Bess. Her eyes were a shade not unlike cinnamon, soft and warm.

"Where am I?" She shifted to sit upright but slumped back against the pillow. "How have I come to be in this chamber?"

"Do you not recall?"

"Not clearly."

Bess bent down, her stiff back rebelling from having been seated without moving for hours. She reached for the flagon of the organy and mint steeped in wine that Joan had set on the floor near the candle and poured some into a cup. "Here. Drink this. You might feel better if you do."

Without protest, the woman sipped from the cup.

"What is your name?" Bess asked her.

"Ellyn," she said.

"Ellyn . . ." Bess prodded.

"'Tis best that I give you no more of a name than that."

"As you wish, Mistress Ellyn." Bess poured more of the wine into the woman's cup. "I am Elizabeth Ellyott, though most who know me well call me Bess. I am an herbalist and healer."

"Yes. I do know who you are. Your niece told me of you."

"My sister Dorothie's daughter? Margery?" Bess asked. "If you are her friend, then you are indeed most welcome here. I would send for her, but she is away with her mother."

"I know that as well, Mistress," she said.

Ellyn's eyes scanned the small but comfortable chamber. A bed, a pair of stools, a trunk, and a little table with a pottery pitcher and basin atop it occupied the space. When Margery came to stay overnight, she used this room.

"Where is my kirtle, Mistress Ellyott?" Ellyn asked, plucking at the blanket covering her. "And my petticoats?"

"We took them away. My servant will try to clean your skirts with ox gall and alum, but I fear the blood might have permanently stained the fabric," said Bess gently. "You have lost your child, Mistress."

"My . . . my . . ." Ellyn's voice came out a croak. Her head drooped.

"There is no need for shame," said Bess, lowering the flagon to the chamber's wooden floor. "Many young women find themselves in this situation. Your husband—"

"I have no husband."

Ah. As I'd thought. "Then mayhap it is for the best that you have lost the child."

Ellyn lifted her gaze to Bess's face. "Think you so, Mistress Ellyott?"

"Unless you wished to marry the child's father, and now that will not be as likely," she ventured.

"No. I have no need at all to marry the child's father now."

Ellyn's color was returning to her cheeks. She would need more than herb-infused wine to regain her strength, though.

"You are fortunate that you have not suffered any serious effects from your . . . your illness, Mistress Ellyn. I trust you shall fully recover," said Bess. "But I would have my servant inform your family that you are here with us, and that you are safe."

"They will not care."

"Is that why you will not give your name? You do not wish me to contact them?"

Ellyn's fingers, with their well-tended nails, curled a corner of the blanket. Though her nails were groomed and clean, her hands had not the smooth skin of a wealthy woman of leisure. She had seen work, but Bess did not imagine her to be a servant.

"They will care that I am gone, but only my brother will spare a thought for my well-being. The rest will be happy," she said.

A statement made with sad resignation. It should not be like this in the world, where a woman like her could feel so easily cast aside. But Bess well knew the world was very ready to cast aside those who might not conform.

"You may stay with us as long as you need, Ellyn. But I cannot keep you in secret here forever, hiding from whatever it is you have fled."

"I will leave as soon as I am able. I do not wish to burden you."

"You are no burden, Mistress Ellyn. Life, though, has taught me that our pasts always tend to catch us up." Bess leaned toward her. "Tell me where you have come from, Ellyn, and what happened to your child."

She would not ask if the woman had meant to be rid of the infant. The babe was gone and placing blame would not restore it.

Her eyes searched Bess's face. "Would you believe me if I said I am not certain?"

"I might."

"I am not certain. I do not recall," she insisted. "I remember getting ill and bleeding. I remember thinking of you, because of what you have done for others in the town and what Margery had said about your kindness. I remember coming here by the path along the river. But as for before . . ." She pressed her lips together. "I would not be accused of killing the child, Mistress."

"I am not here to accuse you, Ellyn." Such a charge would bring the swiftest of condemnation, with hanging as punishment.

She reached for Bess's forearm. "You must help me, Mistress. I beg you. Help me."

"You have come to me, and I shall do what I can. Certes, I shall," said Bess. "This I vow, for it is my calling. Trust me."

Ellyn gave a nod and released her grip.

Bess rose from the stool. "I will send my servant Joan to you with some thin gruel. Let her know if your stomach is not ready for the food, though."

Collecting the flagon and cup, she headed for the door.

"Mistress Ellyott, will you tell the constable that I am here?"

Bess looked back at her. "I suspect he will discover your presence, Mistress."

"But *you* will not tell him."

"I said I would help you. So, no," she said. "I shall not tell him."

But Humphrey undoubtedly would.

*   *   *

"How did you come to have the purse and belt, old man?" asked Kit, his breath clouding in the damp morning air.

He leaned through the open door to the circular building that served as the town jail. Jellis hunched in a heap against the far wall, his moth-eaten coat wrapped tightly around his scrawny frame, holding his head in his bony hands. The night had passed, but the fellow still smelled of strong drink.

"I know not," he said.

"They fell from the sky, mayhap?"

Jellis peered at Kit through the thin strands of greasy hair that hung down around his pallid face. He looked ill.

"I know not," he repeated. Half of his teeth were missing, and the half that still clung to his gums were rotted.

"They belonged to a man stabbed to death last night," said Kit. "Found dead a dozen paces from where you slept. Did you kill him for the coins within the purse?"

"Nay! I killed no one," he protested, and pushed himself upright against the stone wall at his back. "I had a little sup of beer, then fell asleep. I did hear noises, but there always be noises amongst the trees at night."

He'd drunk more than a small amount of beer. "Mayhap you do not recall what you did while you were deep in your cups," said Kit. "You were in the woods, spotted Bartholomew Reade, and thought to thieve from him."

Jellis gaped at Kit. "'Tis Bartholomew Reade who be dead?"

"Yes."

Tears formed in his eyes. They spilled down his haggard, hollow cheeks. "I knew him as a young lad. A witty boy and high-spirited. He cannot be dead, though. He left."

"He returned with a troupe of actors three days ago."

"Poor lad. Poor, poor lad." He squinted at Kit. "But could it be that woman what killed him?"

CHAPTER 4

"Tell me you have found the knife, Gibb," said Kit, wiping ink off the tip of his quill and returning it to its stand. He'd been attempting to review his farm accounts since returning from the jail, but instead had spent most of the time staring out the window above his writing desk, lost in thought.

Gibb stood at the room's doorway. "Nay, for none are willing to venture out in this fog."

It hung thick over the market square, muffling the usual sound of sellers' cries and wooden wheels over cobble. "I thought everyone believes Old Jellis is our killer. What have they to fear, out in the fog? Surely not a murderer."

"The witch?"

"Druids, perhaps?"

"Aye, Kit. Mock me if you will. I regret ever mentioning druids to you," said Gibb. "The fog is lifting, though, and I have offered to pay a pence to anyone who finds the weapon."

"We'll be brought chipped kitchen knives and rusty daggers if you're offering money, Gibb."

"Marry, coz, I know not why I assist you. Be certain I shall warn Frances of your ill temper and tell her to return with her friend to Gloucester."

"Ah, now we know the reason your sister wishes to visit me," said Kit. "A friend. A female one, no doubt."

Gibb did not refute Kit's conclusion.

"Want you that I retract my offer of a reward?" his cousin asked.

"No, Gibb, no. I am merely in an ill temper, as you say. Another murder in but a month."

"At least Mistress Ellyott is not involved in this one," said Gibb. Last time it had been her brother-in-law killed.

"Give her time. She likely will be," Kit replied.

"I spoke with Master Reade's father this morn. He was too distraught to bring forward the name of anyone who might have harmed his son. He is content to have Old Jellis accused," said Gibb. "This is a wretched, sad business, Kit."

As he well knew. Work that had soured them both, he more than Gibb. They were no longer the young, reckless men they'd once been, readily amused by life's follies.

"The old man claims he saw a woman at the mound. Can I believe a drunkard like him, though?"

"Did he give a description?" asked Gibb.

"Of typical size, wearing a dark flowing gown. She may as well have been a forest fairy, given what he saw. Or did not see," said Kit. "He was deep in his cups. I'd likely see mysterious women if I was as drunk as he'd been. But it is not just the knife we hunt for, Gibb. We search for the murderer's clothing, which should be spattered with blood. It's possible the killer discarded his outermost garment somewhere to be rid of it."

"I shall tell the lads to search for such an item, as well."

Soft footsteps out in the passageway drew Gibb's attention. He stepped aside to allow Alice to peek around the doorcase. Kit had hired a mouse, not a maidservant. "Master Harwoode, a man has come to the kitchen door to speak with you."

"Who, Alice? What is his name?"

"He says he is Humphrey Knody, and that he has come from Master Marshall's house," she said. "'Tis about the man who was murdered."

Gibb snorted a laugh. "Not much time at all for our Mistress Ellyott."

Kit stood. "This fellow has information for me?"

"Aye." Alice paled—which Kit had thought impossible, given the usual whiteness of her skin—and swallowed hard before answering. "He has brought a bloodied dress for you to see."

★ ★ ★

"Mistress, I have learned of no woman missing from any household, so we have not a name for our guest," whispered Joan, casting a glance toward the kitchen's beamed ceiling. Above them rested a recovering young woman.

"Mistress Ellyn cannot hear us, Joan. You need not whisper," said Bess. She leaned into the manchet bread dough she was kneading for Joan to take to the baker's. Robert's kitchen was well outfitted save for a decent oven.

"Though I learned naught of our guest, Mistress, I did hear most unhappy news." Joan clasped her hands at her waist. "A man's body was found yestereven."

Bess ceased kneading. *Jesu.* Last night. When a desperate young woman had come to their gate.

"What of this body that has been found?" Bess asked, despite Robert's pleas that she not get involved in matters that did not concern her. But what if this matter *did* concern her?

"The man was stabbed many times. And into his neck was thrust a reed pen," added Joan. "He was found atop the hillock that lies just outside of town, on the road to Avebury."

Bess had walked by the very hillock only yesterday, on her way to tend to Anna. Robert had once regaled her with tales explaining the mound's existence. Some said it had been the base of a fort from the time of King Arthur and much taller than it was now. Others claimed it was a holy site for the druids who had long ago practiced their beliefs in the area, while others were convinced it was a burial mound for ancient peoples. None of the tales had ever encouraged Bess to want to get nearer to the hill. The mound seemed ever cloaked in shadows and mists. Whenever she passed, she'd go by as hastily as possible.

Bess resumed kneading the loaf. "Who was he?"

"Bartholomew Reade. A son of one of the local farmers. He had left to make his fortune, but had returned a few days ago with the traveling players who had come to town," she explained. "An old drunkard sits in the jail accused of the crime, Mistress. However . . ."

Bess looked over at her. "However?"

"Could a weak, aged fellow overpower a young man like Master Reade?"

"Not likely."

"Mistress, I must also say this, for others will mark it as suspicious," said Joan. "But the same night that a man was slain, Mistress Ellyn came to our door covered in blood."

They would, were they to know. For even Bess had come to wonder.

"Mistress Ellyn miscarried a child. She was not covered in Master Reade's blood," she said. "You and I are the only ones, besides Ellyn, who know her clothing was blood-streaked. None will mark her arrival at our house as suspicious."

Joan pressed her lips into a grim line. "Her kirtle is gone from where I hid it, Mistress. Humphrey must have become suspicious of why we had so hastily removed her skirts and secreted them away," she said. "What if he has taken it to the constable?"

A bitter lump settled in Bess's stomach. "The old drunkard will not be viewed as guilty for long, Joan. They will come for Ellyn."

"What are we to do?"

"Constable Harwoode is a fair and honest man, and we must convince him of her innocence." Bess scrubbed bits of dough from her fingers. "Ellyn is a friend of Margery. I can do no less for her."

But how to convince him?

★ ★ ★

Kit rapped his knuckles against the thick oak door, the bundled kirtle tucked beneath his arm. Across the way, one of Mistress Ellyott's neighbors peered through her ground-floor window. She bobbed from side to side to see around the mullions that hampered her clear view of him. Down the lane, a man pushing a handcart halted to note that the constable visited the Marshall house. Kit nodded at the fellow, sending him bustling onward.

Mistress Ellyott's servant, Joan Barbor, answered the door. Her gaze flicked to the bloodied skirts he carried. She did not appear surprised to see him or them.

"Come into the hall, Constable," she said, offering a curtsy. She led him through the short passageway beyond the entry and turned right into the hall. The sun had burned away the remainder of the morning fog and lit the room in warming light. "Prithee, wait here while I fetch my mistress."

She departed, the jangle of the keys suspended from her girdle and the sound of her footfalls across the stone flooring becoming faint. Their brown-and-white dog wandered in from another room and came to greet Kit, tail wagging. Kit scratched the dog's ears. The dog sniffed the clothing Kit held and ceased wagging its tail.

"It's an unhappy load I carry," he said to the animal. "And I wonder what your mistress will have to say about it and its owner."

"I shall say there is an innocent, although sad, explanation for the blood upon that kirtle, Constable Harwoode."

Bess Ellyott stood in the doorway, her shoulders squared within her gown and her gaze unflinching. Gibb had once referred to her eyes as "fine." His cousin had overlooked their greatest feature—intelligence. Facing her made Kit realize how much he'd missed those intelligent eyes and their owner. Despite his efforts to convince himself he'd no room in his overbusy life for a woman.

The dog ambled over to sit at her side. Kit bowed, which caused her frown to soften a trifle.

"Good morrow, Mistress. I see you are well."

"And you also, Constable." Her frown returned. "As I said, there is an innocent explanation for the blood, though not a happy one."

"I'm prepared to hear the explanation."

"The young woman who owned the gown miscarried her child. She required my help."

"This woman came to your door?" he asked. "Why not instead call you to her house to attend to her?"

Mistress Ellyott paused. *Ah. She holds on to a secret about this woman.*

"Need I supply the obvious answer to your question, Constable?"

He set the bloodied kirtle atop a nearby stool. "Your man-servant tells me that the woman is a vagrant."

"It pains me that Humphrey sought to tattle to you behind my back," she said stiffly. "And he is my brother's manservant, not mine."

"Nonetheless, is his observation the *obvious* answer to my question? She has no home hereabouts?"

"She will not tell us where she has come from. She is afraid to name her family. Out of fear for their scorn, I suspect. And *that* is the obvious answer." She held up a hand to stay his next words. "And before you discourse upon what the law requires, I am aware that, should she be a vagrant, she must be driven from my home like a rabid cur. But she is unwell, and I will not allow you to cause her more harm by prying her from the chamber where she rests."

Bess Ellyott was a bold one. Other men, men like his father, would say she was difficult and should better know her place. Kit was not his father, though, and she both vexed him and intrigued him. She had from the moment they'd met. Why was it, then, that a fresh murder was required to bring them together again?

Perhaps because he'd chosen to avoid her. Not always easy to achieve in a town this small.

"You are certain the blood was hers," he said. "A witness claims to have seen a woman near the mound where the dead man was discovered."

"I am enough of a healer, Constable, to read the signs that a woman has miscarried," she answered. "I have heard about the man who was murdered, and that you have arrested some fellow for the crime. Why suspect my patient?"

"I have my doubts about the vagrant's guilt."

Mistress Ellyott leveled her gaze at him. "This witness . . . how did he describe the woman?"

Kit cleared his throat; time to admit the description Jellis had given was vague and likely not worth believing. "She wore a dark, flowing gown and was of typical size."

"As you can well see, Constable, the kirtle you have brought is not a dark, flowing gown but watchet-colored," she said. "Further, she collapsed at our gate, too weak to move. She would not have had the strength to commit murder."

A logical conclusion. As he would expect from her. "Mayhap I should assess that for myself, Mistress Ellyott."

*   *   *

Tying her mantle about her neck, Joan hurried out of the house. She glanced over her shoulder, back at the street-facing windows to see if any noted her passage. 'Twas not the mistress or the constable she sought to evade. It was Humphrey's prying. He lived to cause her trouble. To cause them all trouble.

"Taking Mistress Ellyn's kirtle to the constable, not trusting the mistress to do what was right. Devil take him," she said aloud, uncaring who heard.

And because of Humphrey, Constable Harwoode sought to charge Mistress Ellyn with a man's death.

It was wrong of her to have been eavesdropping at the hall doorstead, but it would be far worse if such a charge were to be made. The accusation would take hold of Mistress Ellyn like a limpet to a rock, impossible to pry free.

Joan rushed down the lane, nodding to the few who greeted her. More than a year since she and the mistress had come to this town, tucked among the chalk and the fields and the cattle and the sheep, and many still cast wary looks at her. She was a stranger and strangers were misliked, even though her mistress's brother was an important merchant. A stranger who spoke with a London accent and who bore a scar upon her face that would ache on wintry nights, reminding her of what she had suffered at the hands of a man. Joan understood Mistress Ellyn's secretiveness better than most.

We will protect you, Mistress Ellyn. My mistress and I.

At the end of the lane, Joan entered the town square. It was busy, but not half so crowded as it would be on market day. It echoed with the noise of schoolboys chattering outside the walls of the school, unmindful of their master. The blacksmith's hammer rang out as he repaired a pair of shears. The cobbler's apprentice gave a cry, soliciting business. A mother shouted at her heedless child to 'ware the costermonger's wagon rattling across the cobbles, bearing down upon the market cross near to where the child ran after a piglet escaped from its sty.

It was nothing like the streets and squares of London, clogged with filth and muck. Where the press of crowds could crush a body, or distract one from the cutpurses slipping among the masses with nimble fingers and sharp knives. Here, she rarely had to dodge the remains of chamber pots that mingled with the dung of horses and of animals being driven to market. Or hold her nose against the stench and the smoke.

At times, though, she did miss the pulsing life of the city. The grand old buildings that soared into the sky. St. Paul's. The Tower. The Thames so thick with boats and skiffs and barges on some days that a body could nearly cross the river's width by jumping from one to the next. The church bells and the accents of voices from many corners of the country and beyond. The scent of meat pies that would set a mouth to watering. The sight of the aging queen on procession through the city, in lace and jewels that twinked and sparkled, banners fluttering, brightly attired horses trotting boldly.

All was not grand and glorious, though. Intrigues and danger walked those streets as well. A man's ambition had seen the master killed and had forced her and the mistress to flee to safety.

"And, girl, 'tis best you remember how stealthily danger stalks its victim," she muttered to herself as she crossed the square.

The Poynards' house stood a distance along Church Street, separate from the houses and shops on either side. It was a large and grand building of stone and timbering, jettied upper floors, and oriel windows that caught the daylight. Far larger and grander even than Master Marshall's house. The ample grounds that stretched out back were encircled by a tall rock wall, broken only by a spare number of gates.

The house's window glass sparkled in the crisp October sunlight, the fog all vanished. Movement showed behind the panes, so she rushed past quickly. She did not want to speak to a Poynard, not that any would talk to her, a servant. No, she knew of someone in the household who would be far more willing to tell her what she wished to know.

Joan rounded the corner of the house and rushed along its side. Past its service buildings and to the nearest gate. Casting a prayer toward the god that did not always seem to hear her prayers, she pounded upon it.

After a few moments that seemed to last longer than the sermons the priest would give on Sundays, the latch clanked and the gate inched open.

She exhaled when she saw the person standing on the other side. "God be thanked you answered, Simon."

"Mistress Barbor!" he exclaimed, darting through the opening in the gate and closing it behind him.

One of the Poynards' servants, he was a boy of no more than eleven or twelve years of age. When she'd first spotted him in the market square, her heart had stopped, he looked so like the brother she had lost to the fever in a London jail. Her last remnant of family. Simon was so like her brother—gangly arms and legs, his hair curling wildly beneath a wool cap, even the way he moved—that she'd nearly cried out her brother's name, expecting the boy to turn in response. But Simon was not her brother, though he'd quickly become a friend.

She grinned that he'd called her "Mistress." Grinned, then shook a finger at him. "You call me Joan, Simon. I'm no one's mistress."

"Are you going to fish in the river today? I cannot go along and help you this time," he said, downcast. "The actors are still with us, and the masters are in an angry mood. A more angry mood than usual."

"It is because of the actors that I am here. You know that one has died."

"Aye!" He bent close to her and lowered his voice. "Have you heard that a weasel was seen near the body? Folk have claimed it was a witch's familiar."

"Where did you hear that silliness, boy?"

"The dead man was found on that hill. The one that is cursed," he answered, blushing, and she was sorry she'd scoffed at him. "But Old Jellis was arrested."

"Aye, he was," she said. "I tell you this in secret, Simon, that the constable does not think him guilty."

"Then it *was* a witch!"

His comment made her shudder. "Know you anything about Master Reade?"

"His mates did not like him," he said. "He sat alone at meals. I saw when I took the wine flagons up to the lesser hall for supper that the others sat at one end of the table and ignored him."

Aha! "His mates hated him."

"They cast gibes at him. One said he had no wit," he said. "Further, they misliked him for his boasts about women."

Taunts that gave Master Reade more of a motive to kill one of them than the other way 'round. But Mistress Ellyott was better at understanding these matters than she was.

"Were there names for these women?" *Such as Ellyn?* "Did any come to visit him here?"

"No names," said Simon. "And Master Poynard would not ever allow a woman to visit a player housed beneath his roof!"

"Did you see aught else that might explain who might have wished the fellow dead?" Joan asked.

"Mayhap so," he replied. "Yestermorn. Master Reade was shouting at someone. He was out in the yard, but I could not see the fellow he shouted at. It might have been Master Poynard he argued with, Master Jeffrey Poynard, but I'm not sure."

"What was it they argued over?"

"A woman," he said, and winked.

A woman, again. "Did they speak her name?"

"Nay. The other fellow just yelled, 'Stay away from her.' No name. Master Reade cursed in answer to him and stomped off, shoving by me on his way out of the yard," he said. His eyes widened. "And never again was Master Reade seen alive."

*   *   *

"You promised you'd not tell him I was here, Mistress Ellyott," said Ellyn in a voice raw with disappointment.

Bess glanced at Kit Harwoode, whose countenance was sterner than she'd ever observed before.

"My brother's manservant found your bloodied kirtle and took it to him," she said to Ellyn. "I am sorry."

"You are Ellyn Merrick, are you not?" asked the constable.

A Merrick? "Ellyn, you should have told me," interrupted Bess. "I was called to your family's farm yesterday afternoon to attend to one of your dairymaids. Anna Webb."

"Then you met my mother and understand why I did not give you my full name."

I'faith, she did understand.

"Mistress Ellyott tells me you have lost a child, Mistress Merrick," said the constable.

Ellyn's fingers clutched the bed's white woolen coverlet. "I have."

He did not put forward the question he might have. "Do you know Bartholomew Reade?" he asked instead.

"I do," she answered. "But I have not seen in him in many, many weeks. Why do you ask?"

"He was murdered yesterday. Stabbed."

She gasped. Tears sprang up to tremble on her eyelids. "No! No!"

"Ellyn, you must take care." Bess hastened to the young woman's side. She took Ellyn's clammy, trembling hand and sat upon the bed. "Constable, she is yet frail. Cannot your questions wait?"

"Tell me about Master Reade, Mistress," he said to Ellyn.

Apparently his questions could not wait, thought Bess.

Ellyn withdrew her hand from Bess's. "He was a good man," she said, wiping away her tears. "He desired to become a playwright in London, and had been traveling with the Admiral's Men as an actor."

Though she'd not seen him for many weeks, she had obviously followed his whereabouts.

The constable cast a glance at Bess; mayhap he shared her thought. "So you knew him well, Mistress Merrick."

"I knew him well. As did many folk hereabouts."

"Were you aware he'd returned here with the troupe visiting the Poynards, Mistress Merrick?"

"I had heard, but I had not seen him."

The constable dragged his fingertips through his short beard. It was the sign his mind was occupied with musings. *Constable Harwoode is a fair and honest man.* But how well did Bess know him, in truth? Was she so certain of his fairness and honesty?

"Do you have an answer to who might have killed Master Reade, Mistress Merrick?" he asked.

She lowered her head, and a fresh tear slid down her cheek. "There is one who would have wished him harm," she said. "Jeffrey Poynard. He was jealous of Bartholomew's past attentions to me and my feelings for him. Jeffrey Poynard wants me for himself."

"You and Master Reade were in love with each other?" Bess asked. A connection to a dead man stronger than the coincidence that she'd arrived at Bess's garden gate the same night he had been murdered. *Jesu.*

"At one time," said Ellyn.

"Mistress Ellyott, allow me to ask the questions," chided the constable.

"Forgive me," said Bess, chastened.

"So you propose, Mistress Merrick, that when Reade returned to town, Master Poynard's jealousy rekindled. Furthermore, he may have been jealous enough to remove a rival for your heart."

"Jeffrey Poynard does not readily control his passions, his wrath, Constable," she said, lifting her gaze. "He is not a man to be crossed."

"Yet Master Reade communicated with Jeffrey Poynard about a performance at the Poynards' home and chose to stay within his house," said Constable Harwoode, his eyes narrowing. "Why would he have done so if there was ill will between them?"

"I know not. I know not!" she wailed. "And now he is dead!"

CHAPTER 5

Bess closed the door to Ellyn's chamber.
"Constable, prithee wait!" she called out. His footfalls pounded on the staircase as he descended. Bess hiked her skirts and dashed after him. "Constable!"

He paused at the foot of the winding stairs. "You trust her?"

"Certes, I do," she answered. "Could she have pretended such distress? I know not how you could imagine it possible."

"Easily, for I have a rich imagination." The constable halted inside the hall. "The man she has accused was at his house the evening of Reade's death, Mistress Ellyott. I saw him there myself."

"You mean that Ellyn blames Master Poynard to deflect suspicion from herself," she answered. "I have explained that she miscarried, Constable. Why can you not believe me?"

"Because the same evening Ellyn Merrick arrives at your door bleeding, her former lover is found dead," he said. "If you have not concluded the coincidence is strange, Mistress, then you are not the clever woman I believe you to be."

Nay, I do mark it as strange, Constable.

"I have questions of my own. As it is clear you mistrust Mistress Ellyn and regard her as a suspect in this crime," she said.

"Firstly, how long did Master Reade lie dead atop that mound? And could the crime have occurred *before* the Poynards threw open their doors for the night's entertainment?"

"In daylight? Not far from a well-trafficked highway?"

"The day was overcast with clouds, Constable, with rain at times. Further, the hillock is surrounded by thickets and trees and is not so readily seen from the road," she answered. "As you likely observed when you went there. Many folk avoid the mound, too, fearing it cursed. And with the talk of a witch being afoot, they will avoid the place all the more. As best they can whilst passing."

"You have heard about the witch."

"Humphrey nails elder crosses to the animal sheds for protection," she said. "Could it be possible that Jeffrey Poynard slipped away during the commotion of the guests gathering and supper being served?"

"Gibb and I arrived later than most of the guests. Poynard might have left his house and returned," he admitted. "But before you become smug, Mistress Ellyott, I saw no blood soiling Poynard's clothing to indicate he'd recently stabbed a man."

"'Tis simple, Constable. He disposed of his outer garment."

A muscle in his jaw twitched. "I'll not debate this matter any further with you, Mistress Ellyott. But I will say this. Do not risk your own safety protecting a woman who might be guilty of a terrible crime," he said. "I beg you to be careful."

"You sound like my brother."

"It is a pity, then, that you appear unwilling to listen to *either* of us."

The constable spun on his heel and stomped from the hall and out of the house.

Joan darted into the room, Quail close behind.

"Bah!" Bess shouted. "Does he imagine he can command me?"

"He *is* a man, Mistress."

But such a man was not the Kit Harwoode she thought she'd known.

Quail ambled over to sniff at her skirt where it had brushed the constable's leg. "I will not allow him to accuse Ellyn of murder, though, merely because it might prove simple to do so."

"Mistress, I have only just come from the Poynards' and spoken to a servant there about Master Reade," said Joan. "I have news that might be of import and help prove Mistress Ellyn's innocence."

★　★　★

"Good morrow, Constable. You find me at my work." Jeffrey Poynard, seated at his carved oak desk, raised a well-kept hand to gesture at the stacks of papers spread across its surface. The rings on his fingers glinted. "However, I am pleased the news that the players disrupt our household has reached you quickly. They fight and curse and spit at each other. Prithee, haul them away."

"I'm not here to haul away the players, Master Poynard," said Kit.

"Then why have you come? You see that I am busy."

Kit dragged over a stool, flipped aside his cloak, and sat. "Master Poynard, I need your help with a matter."

Eyeing Kit, he rested one hand atop his silver inkwell and his other hand upon the peasecod-bellied swell of his doublet. His pale clothing—silver-gray doublet, trunk hose, and netherstocks—gleamed like a shaft of light amid the room's walnut paneling and red furnishings. Kit trusted that the splendid effect was intentional.

Pompous coxcomb.

"But not the matter that interests me," said Poynard.

"The matter might interest you," said Kit. "For it does concern the players."

The fingers he'd splayed across his doublet drummed. "Reade."

He might be pompous, but he was not stupid.

"Someone has accused you of killing him," said Kit.

"What?" he scoffed. "That is a ridiculous lie."

His face had reddened to the shade of the velvet covering his chair. The color was everywhere. Cushions of crimson. Bolsters of vermillion silk. Turkey carpets shot through with scarlet. Even the floor tiles were a deep brick red.

"I have been told you hated Reade," said Kit. "Jealousy over a woman."

Poynard rolled his eyes. "That stale story." He snapped shut the lid of his inkwell. The sound was sharp in the hushed silence of the space. "Old Jellis stands accused. He struck Reade down to steal from the fellow. He will stand trial at the Quarter Sessions and be found guilty, then hang. I know not why you listen to slander when the question of who killed Bartholomew Reade has already been answered."

"Jellis is frail, and there wasn't a drop of blood on his clothing," said Kit. "You are an intelligent man, Master Poynard. You see why I search for other possible murderers."

"Such as me?"

"When a townsperson makes an accusation, Master Poynard, I must investigate."

"What is the name of the one who makes such an accusation?"

"I am not free to say."

Poynard drew in a breath, and his face returned to its normal color. "I suspect I know the source, so you need not name the person. However, Constable Harwoode, any dispute I once had with Bartholomew is no longer relevant. We may not have become friends, but we had reconciled. My father and servants will speak for me. I was in this house at the time of Bartholomew's unfortunate death."

"What time was that, Master Poynard? Have I said?"

Poynard pinched his lips together.

"You agreed to welcome Reade and his troupe here, to stay within your house," said Kit. "Most generous of you."

"As I said, Constable, I carried no grudge against the man. He proposed to me to bring the troupe here. He was welcome in our house. His father and mine are old friends. I pitied Bartholomew. His plans to become an important playwright were foundering." Spoken with a touch of glee. "Mayhap, if you doubt Jellis's guilt, you might find Bartholomew's killer among his troublesome fellows. They clearly resented him. Some quarrel over a play he had written, I believe."

As much as Kit had liked the idea that the arrogant Jeffrey Poynard could be guilty, he might have to turn his attention elsewhere.

"Might I search the rooms that the players were given to use, Master Poynard?"

The stiffness in Poynard's shoulders eased. "You may do so and welcome."

"My thanks," said Kit, and he departed.

He made his way to the rooms the players were occupying and where Kit had spoken to Howlett the night of the murder. The passageway where they were located led to the kitchen, and a female servant hurried toward him from its direction.

"Do you have the key to these rooms?" Kit asked the girl, halting her.

"Me? Nay. Only our steward does," she said. "But the lock is broken on that one." She pointed at the door to the room where Kit had interviewed Howlett. "And those two have not been locked since the players come to sleep in them."

"My thanks," he replied.

She curtsied and hurried on.

The nearest room was dimly lit by a grimy horn-paned window. It held a pair of trundle beds and a trunk and not much else—a discarded torn stocking, some sheets of paper covered over with the lines from a play and notes alongside in another hand, empty cups, and a chamber pot still full of piss. He rattled the lock on the trunk, but it would not release.

Kit stepped back into the passageway. The kitchen servant stood at the end of the corridor whispering excitedly to another girl. They spotted Kit and jumped apart from each other, their cheeks flaring pink.

"Fetch any of the players here who might have a key for their trunks," he ordered.

The kitchen servant curtsied and ran off. The other girl did likewise.

The next chamber had nothing more to offer than the first one. Kit entered the storage room, stacked with the troupe's supplies. Several more trunks occupied the space. Locked as well.

"You have need of me, Constable?" asked a man's voice from the doorway. It was the player who'd found Reade's body.

"Dunning, am I correct?" Kit asked.

"That be my name, sir."

"Open these trunks."

Keys rattling, Dunning bent to releasing the locks. "There you be, good sir."

Kit hunted through the items inside each trunk. Wigs, outfits to dress as lords or peasants or maidservants. Jars of cosmetics. Baubles to wear. Three dull swords for fight scenes.

But no clothing stained with blood. No sharp knife hastily cleaned and returned to a sheath.

"What is it you search for, Constable? If I may make bold to ask."

"Any item that might offer a clue as to the identity of a murderer, Master Dunning."

Dunning swallowed so loudly Kit could hear the sound across the room. "You search among the troupe's belongings for such an item?"

The next trunk held more of the same as the first. "I have also heard, Master Dunning, that you and your fellows did not care for Master Reade," he said, restoring the trunks' contents.

"Petty problems. That is all. The sort that arise among actors."

Kit looked over at him. The fellow was tall, his head well above the lintel of the doorstead. He'd ducked to enter. "Not a quarrel over a play he'd written?"

"The play? 'Twas Howlett who . . . I misspeak. Mind me not, Constable."

"I would hear what you have to say about Howlett, Master Dunning."

Dunning cleared his throat. "Bartholomew had threatened to report to London that Howlett was stealing plays and performing them without a license."

Kit rocked back on his heels. "Oh?"

"It sometimes happens that a troupe will thieve manuscripts, sir. When a troupe cannot afford the price," he explained.

"Whose plays had Howlett stolen?"

"A few works from a minor playwright. Of late, though, Howlett had pressed Bartholomew to allow us the use of his latest manuscript. A three-act play that he had written but would not let Howlett have. Ah!" He smacked his lips as though savoring a delicacy. "It is a master work. Not as good as what Marlowe writes, 'tis true, but we could make our reputation with that play. Howlett is hopelost and fears the troupe will not long survive. At present, we have no champion, no patron."

"But Reade would not sell it?" asked Kit. "His reputation as a playwright would be made, as well."

"He'd not sell it to Howlett, no matter the price he might offer," said Dunning. "Not many nights ago, as we journeyed to this very town, Bartholomew declared that he would give it to a friend rather than allow Howlett to pollute the play with his dramatics. Howlett cursed at Bartholomew most foully, but Bartholomew had no care if the troupe survives. He meant to go to London as soon as was possible."

Kit closed the lids on the trunks. "This woman Reade planned to meet yesterday. Did he name her?" And had he come to the village to whisk her away to London with him?

"Her name was less important than her fair appearance and other attributes."

"Did Howlett also know of Reade's intended tryst and where he'd gone?"

Dunning's eyebrows darted up his forehead like two caterpillars seeking to hide beneath the curls of his ginger-colored hair. Kit began to wonder if he was being duped by a skilled actor.

"If I had discovered the location of the hill, Constable, Howlett may also have," he said. "'Od save us, he may have done."

★　★　★

"If there is gossip to be collected about aught that occurs in this village, Mistress, Marcye Johnes already has it pocketed." Joan nodded at the door to the Cross Keys. "She might have a comment about what Simon did tell me."

"Will she share that gossip and risk being punished for speaking, though?" asked Bess.

"A risk of punishment for gossiping has never stopped Marcye before."

Two men, farm laborers in frieze tunics and boots, brushed past them on their way to the door.

"Come inside and warm yourselves, ladies," one said with a wink.

Joan shot him a glare. The fellow burst into laughter and pushed open the door. The sound of heated conversation and men singing spilled out, along with the aroma of baking meat pies and ale. And other, less pleasant smells.

Bess lifted her chin, the ruff she'd chosen to wear rubbing against her neck. Dorothie always claimed that wearing a ruff made her feel powerful; Bess found them confining, stiff, and itchy. She'd worn it simply to impress the seriousness of her visit upon the daughter of a tavern-keeper. She would be rewarded with a rash on her skin.

Bess and Joan entered the tavern. The room quieted, and dozens of eyes turned their way, tankards and cards and a tobacco pipe stilling midmotion. Women were allowed inside the Cross Keys, but Bess had never been one of them.

The young woman tapping a firkin of ale noticed their

arrival. She rushed over, knocking aside an unoccupied stool in her haste to reach Bess and Joan.

"Mistress Ellyott."

She knows who I am?

"This is Marcye Johnes, Mistress," said Joan by way of introduction.

"I would speak to you," said Bess, "about an important matter."

Five or six years younger than Bess, Marcye was pretty in her youthfulness. She had a full, round face and expressive eyes. They surveyed Bess with a mixture of impertinence and unconcealed interest. "You *are* speaking to me, Mistress."

Joan grumbled.

"Mayhap we can go outside and talk," suggested Bess. "Away from the din and distractions. If you have a moment."

Bess did not await her reply, but motioned for Joan to head outside with her. As expected, Marcye followed. The girl was too curious not to.

"Aye, so we be outside. Now what?" the young woman asked.

Bess hunted for a penny within her pocket and held it out. "Tell me what you know of Master Reade, Jeffrey Poynard, and Ellyn Merrick," said Bess.

"Might be worth more than a penny, Mistress."

"Or, i'faith, it might not."

"You know the gossip, Marcye," said Joan, prodding the girl. "More than anyone else in this town."

Marcye snatched the coin from Bess's hand and pocketed it. "I hear she stays with you."

Had Humphrey told her? "Was Master Poynard jealous of her affection for Master Reade?"

"Aye, Mistress Ellyott."

Perhaps the argument Simon witnessed *had* been between Master Reade and Master Poynard. And the woman they'd argued over had, indeed, been Ellyn.

"Know you if he was angry that Master Reade had returned to the village?" Bess asked.

"'Tis true enough he and Bartholomew had sparred over many a woman. Like two cockerels, they were," she said. "The night the troupe arrived, Master Poynard came to the tavern to drink. And to beg everyone know he and Bartholomew were boon companions. All forgiven and forgotten."

Why might he have been so forward with his comments? Unless he intended to commit violence and sought to fend off any suspicion that might naturally arise.

"Did you believe his professions?" asked Bess. "For Master Reade is dead."

"Such a sorrow," she replied. "Master Bartholomew's father grieves greatly, I hear. He lost his only other son at Gravelines, fighting the armada."

What a horrible loss. Both sons gone.

"But only a harebrain would trust Jeffrey Poynard," Marcye continued.

"So you suggest that Master Poynard lied that night about he and Bartholomew being boon companions," said Bess.

Marcye shrugged. "I suppose *she* has blamed him, rather than name one just as likely."

"And who might that be?" asked Joan.

"Not Old Jellis, the harmless creature. As gentle as a lamb when in his cups, unlike half those who fill our tavern," she said. "Master Bartholomew had befriended him. He bought the fellow drink at our tavern many times. He would never have harmed

Master Bartholomew. Never. The townsmen who say he would have done are wrong."

"Master Reade's purse was found on him," pointed out Bess.

"Old Jellis did not do it," she insisted.

"Then who might be just as likely?" asked Joan, repeating her question, tenacious as a dog with its teeth about a bone.

A coy smile crossed Marcye's face. She appeared to enjoy making them wait upon her opinion. 'Twas certain they were rapt. A flock of sheep being driven to market could have rambled past, baaing and bleating, and Bess would have not have noticed.

"I forget neither of you have lived here long," said Marcye at last. "But David Merrick has reason. He might appear meek, but be not deceived by his unassured ways."

"David Merrick? What relation is he to Ellyn?"

"Her eldest brother," said the girl. "She'd seek to protect him."

They were to suspect Old Jellis, Mother Fletcher, Jeffrey Poynard, and now David Merrick?

"But why would her brother wish to kill Master Reade?" asked Bess.

"What reasons do men have for hating each other, Mistress Ellyott?" she replied, smirking. "One a bold charmer and the other twisted with envy of him. I need say no more, do I?"

★ ★ ★

What is she about?

Across the square, three unlikely women had been huddled together outside the Cross Keys. As one was Bess Ellyott, Kit suspected he could supply an answer to his question.

She is getting entangled in matters that are not her concern. Could she not learn caution? Could she not, for once, listen?

"Kit!" Gibb ran up and cuffed Kit's shoulder. "Coz, have you fallen deaf? I have been shouting."

Marcye Johnes returned to the tavern, and Mistress Ellyott and her servant hastened off in the direction of their home.

"You have my attention now," Kit said to his cousin.

"We have found it!" He retrieved a knife from the sheath on his belt where he'd stowed it. "One of the town lads discovered the weapon. Tossed into a ditch some yards down the road. Do you think it is the knife used to kill Master Reade?"

"No one discards a perfectly good knife." With a broad blade and a carved wood handle, it was an eating knife of the type many people carried. Albeit sharper and sturdier than most eating knives. "Where did you say the boy found it?"

"In a ditch between town and the hill."

"Which suggests the person who discarded the knife had been returning to the village."

"Someone will surely be missing it, Kit," said Gibb. "'Tis a fine knife. Better than the one I use."

"The person missing it will not admit to its loss, I expect."

Kit held the knife up. A trace of brown stained the spot where the blade met the handle.

Blood.

CHAPTER 6

"Sir, you are back," said Alice. She followed Kit into his ground-floor office. Before returning to his house, he'd sent Gibb to search for a possible owner of the knife while he'd gone to examine the ditch where the weapon had been found. No bloodied garment had conveniently presented itself at the ditch or anywhere nearby.

"Yes, Alice. As you can see." He unfastened his cloak and handed it to her. Letters were stacked atop his writing desk. Among the correspondence was a note from his father, his bold handwriting stretched across the paper. It would hold no kindly greetings or fond wishes. His notes never did. No matter Kit's success, his achievements were never enough for the senior Master Harwoode.

Kit tossed aside the note. If a fire had been burning in the room's grate, he'd have thrown it there.

He looked over at Alice, who lingered upon the doorstead. "What is it you need?"

She hesitated for so long, he began to think she'd forgotten why she stood there. "Sir, you cannot be thinking sad old Goodman Jellis guilty, can you?" she asked, the words tumbling out in a rush.

"Should I not?"

His cloak hung limply from her hand, and she gaped as though unable to believe she'd spoken to him.

"Well, Alice?"

"His daughter says he cannot be. He is weak and ancient. She begs mercy."

"His daughter has spoken to you begging mercy from the law."

"She is in service to the master my sister also serves. She claims someone else is responsible," said Alice, gaining courage when he did not shout at her. "One of the Merricks."

"Oh?"

"The Merricks and the Reades have a long-lived feud," said Alice. "I myself have heard whispers of it. From the gossips."

"A feud over what?"

She frowned. "I was not told, sir."

Just then, the front door opened and Gibb strode into the office. Alice curtsied and scuttled off.

"Now what have you done to Alice that has her flustered?" he asked, glancing over his shoulder at the entry passage through which she'd disappeared.

"Having a conversation with her seems to be enough," said Kit. "She shared a story about a feud between the Reades and the Merricks."

"In truth?" asked Gibb. "If there *is* enmity between them, the Merricks had to mislike that a daughter sought an amour with a Reade."

"They might also mislike that the Reade she'd been in love with had recently returned to the village." Was *she* the woman he'd sought to meet at the hillock? An intriguing thought. Kit sat at his desk, bumping it. The stack of letters swayed and toppled, spilling across the surface. "What did you learn about the knife?"

"The players say it did not come from among their belongings."

"They could be lying," said Kit.

"I think not. They seemed honest."

"They *are* actors, Gibb."

"Fie on you, Kit."

I should not tease him. He needed Gibb's help. Valued it.

"Do not mind me, Gibb. You know the temper I have been in," he said. "What else have you learned?"

Gibb dropped onto a stool. "I questioned the players again as to where they each were yesterday afternoon before Master Reade was found dead. They were together all the day, practicing. Until Master Howlett sent them to search for Master Reade, that is."

"Did they vouch for Howlett?"

"They could not. Apparently he thinks himself above them. Takes meals apart from the other players when he can. Sleeps in separate chambers. Does not game or drink with them."

Most suspicious, Master Howlett. "Did you ask anyone else about the knife?"

"I showed it to the Poynards' kitchen staff. They said it was not one of theirs. And you need not remind me that *they* could by lying, also," answered Gibb. Leaning against the paneling at his back, he stretched his legs, encased in new deep-blue venetian trunk hose. At times, his cousin could be as much a coxcomb as Jeffrey Poynard. "I will continue questioning people. The answer is out there. For all we need do is find the owner of this knife and locate his bloodied garment, and we will have our killer, will we not, Kit?"

All we need do?

Gibb made it sound so simple.

★   ★   ★

"It is good of you to come, Widow Ellyott." Mother Fletcher smiled at Bess. "Gramercy for your kindness."

Bess had returned from the Cross Keys to Humphrey's sullen mutters. The old witch, he'd said, was in need of physic and dared to request that Bess do the healing. Why could she not tend to herself? he'd questioned. She was supposed to be a healer. He had muttered all the more when Bess had replied she would go to the woman and happily.

And here she was, within Mother Fletcher's musty cottage. Of mold-streaked daub overtopped by thatch, the dwelling appeared abandoned from the outside. On the inside—rushes in need of refreshing, linens chewed by moths and rats—the cottage looked little better.

"It is not goodness or kindness that brings me here, Mother Fletcher." Bess set down her satchel. She had brought her mixture of iris root in rose water to anoint the woman's rheumy eyes. "You have need of my help and I will give it. I do not refuse anyone."

The old widow shuffled through the rushes to the room's lone chair. It was pulled near to a scarred oak table and a smoke-charred hearth, its fire sputtering from the green branches used to feed its flames.

Bess went to help her lower onto the chair.

"Nay, see? You are indeed kind," said the widow. "I ken well the villagers and countryfolk call me a witch. Though they did not always."

The chair had been placed so that sunlight from the sole window in the cottage's front room could shine upon its occupant and lend some warmth. Women like the widow were often described as deformed and ugly hags, suspected of practicing witchcraft, their ill deeds shriveling their skin along with their souls. Mother Fletcher's cheeks were withered and pale as paste, and her eyes red-rimmed and weepy. But the sunlight glimmered in their depths, the color of the cornflowers that bloomed among the fields and full of wit.

Her eyes were also filled with loneliness, as the widow sat in her two-room cottage with its pounded earth floors and rickety furnishings and waited for patients who did not come. Who had not come, Bess imagined, for many a year.

Who gives her money to survive? Someone must do. Mayhap a villager who remained grateful for a cure provided long ago or a dutiful relative gave help. She had no children to support her, for Joan had learned that they and Mother Fletcher's husband had died in a fire. Perhaps the villagers believed she was somehow responsible for their deaths as well.

Bess unbound the ties of the satchel that held the pot of iris root and rose water. She withdrew the physic along with a square of clean linen. "Those with sense do not call you a witch."

"Their sheep have died," she said, folding her bony hands atop the apron pinned to her faded brown kirtle. "'Tis easier by far to cast blame upon me than to blame their own bad husbandry. Or to wonder if their prayers to God have gone unanswered for reasons they wish not to examine."

"Their fears will subside," said Bess, soaking a corner of the linen with the physic. "I am certain."

The widow closed her eyes. "You are a good woman and

young. Certainty comes easier to such as you," she said. "Howsomever, I warrant the churchwarden will soon arrive to inspect my withered body for the marks on my skin that would prove their beliefs correct."

He might. He very well might.

Bess bent over the woman and laid the cloth atop her eyes. Mother Fletcher startled at her touch. "Forgive me if the cloth is cold, Mother Fletcher."

"Do not make an apology, Widow Ellyott. I have suffered harsher trials than the press of a wet cloth, and your touch is gentle."

Bess daubed the woman's eyes. "I do my best."

"But now the Reade lad is dead. They have found him upon that cursed hill."

The old woman, living at the distant edge of the village and too frail to regularly travel into town, knew a great deal.

"You have learned the sad news," said Bess, refreshing the cloth with the solution of iris root and rose water.

"They accuse me of his death as well."

"How can you in your frailty have killed Master Reade? 'Tis folly to suggest it."

Mother Fletcher moved aside Bess's hand and propped open one lid, the bright blue eye peeping at Bess. "Magic?"

Despite her words and assurances, despite her belief she was not prone to superstitions, Bess shuddered.

"A man has been arrested. None have come to burn you at the stake, Mother Fletcher, for the crime," she said. "Nor has the churchwarden come to examine your skin for warts."

"Not as yet, Widow Ellyott. But 'tis true that Old Jellis is mistrusted as much as I," she said, closing the eye she'd opened.

"Och, 'tis so. I am a stranger, and he is lost and wandering. They find it easy to blame me for the illness which has killed their sheep. Easier still to accuse an unwelcome old drunkard of murder, rather than consider the culprit to be one of their own."

"Know you who killed Master Reade, Mother Fletcher?"

"No. Even if I did, as a stranger to this place, my word is not to be trusted," she replied. "Mistrusted despite the fact that my husband was born here, as were my children. But they have been lost to the plague."

Bess straightened, the cloth in her hand dripping onto the rushes beneath her feet. "I thought they had perished in a fire."

"Och, aye."

"Was the burned house near the abbey ruins once your home? The house they call the plague house?"

The widow's eyelids drooped as she became lost in thought. A cloud overspread the sun, casting her face in shadow. Bess waited and began to fear the woman might not speak again. But then her mouth moved, and the faintest sound came forth.

"At one time," she whispered. "I live now because I was away tending to a woman in a difficult and lengthy labor. In my absence, my family fell ill. I returned to find them gone and our house, burned."

Bess's breath caught, a flood of memories and feelings stopping it in her throat. "Do you sometimes wish it had been you who'd died instead?"

The old woman's gaze was gentle. "You understand."

"My children died from catarrh. And my husband . . . from evil," answered Bess. Evil that had a name. The name of Laurence. He'd been like a son to them. A treacherous son. "I would do anything to have them alive in my place."

The widow lifted a gnarled hand and rested it on Bess's arm. Her fingers were as cool as parchment. "Then they would be wishing the same. That *they* had died and you were alive."

Bess contemplated the old woman who sat before her.

"You did not send for me to offer sympathy for my loss, Mother Fletcher. Nor simply because your eyes needed tending," she said. "You know the cures required to treat their rheum as well as I."

"I sent for you to warn you, Widow Ellyott." Her fingers tightened around Bess's arm with greater strength than Bess imagined the old woman possessed. "Your kindness and goodness have made you vulnerable."

"Do you mean Ellyn Merrick? How do you know about her?"

Mother Fletcher released her grip and returned her hand to her lap. "Whispers travel faster than the wind."

"So I have come to learn." Bess set aside the cloth. "But you cannot mean that I should have refused to help Ellyn. I must."

"It is what you do next that makes you vulnerable."

"I wish to do what is right," she said. "That is what I have always done and what I shall do next."

"Certes, I doubt you not. But women like us . . . we are to be suspected. Widows. Healers. At one moment we are salvation. At the next, we are accursed." The woman's cornflower eyes held Bess's. "They trust you now, for you are yet young, not wrinkled and bent like I am. But beware, madam, for one day they shall turn on you. As they have turned on me."

★　★　★

Kit stared at the old fort hill, the so-called druids' mound, its grass trampled by the feet of the dozens who'd searched for clues about a dead man. A knife had been found, tossed aside by a murderer. Its discovery had not brought Kit any nearer to identifying the person who'd discarded the weapon, however. Until he could make that identification, Jellis would rot in the jail while he awaited trial. As good a suspect as any, according to the burgesses and townsfolk who deemed the fellow a vagrant and, therefore, a criminal deserving of suspicion and punishment.

As Bess Ellyott had pointed out, the area around the hillock was a quiet spot, and hidden enough from anyone passing along the road. In the distance, a plowman led his oxen to a field to be furrowed under for the coming winter. In the other direction, two women with empty baskets beneath their arms chattered as they trudged his way, bound for town. Quiet.

He headed for the stand of trees where Jellis had been sleeping. A woodland animal scattered at the crunch of Kit's footfalls, and rooks called overhead. His grandfather had once told him that if the rooks departed a place, ill fortune was soon to follow. Well, ill fortune had descended on this place and the rooks had not gone anywhere.

Kit scanned the tree trunks and the dirt and leaves, searching for . . . only God knew what. Pale sunlight cast shadows across the golden leaves fallen to the earth. Jellis's blanket—tattered, full of holes—lay in a heap to one side. Surprisingly, none of the cottagers who lived nearby had taken it for their own use. The ground was as heavily trampled as the grass on the hill. If he sought the killer's footmarks, he'd never find them among the many imprints of boots and wood-soled shoes. The gaggle of onlookers had obliterated everything by stomping about like a startled herd of cattle.

He searched until his neck ached from examining the dirt.

"Damn!" he shouted, causing the rooks to flutter their black wings and caw at being disturbed.

He turned toward the hill. And spotted, in a sudden beam of light, a scrap of material hooked by a bramble bush. He tugged it free from the thorny branch and rubbed his thumb over the wool. A good black brocade. Not long stuck there, he'd wager, and perhaps a torn scrap from the outer garb of a killer.

Tucking the bit of material into his belt, he turned toward the Merricks' farm to ask about a feud.

★   ★   ★

I wish to do what is right.

"And that desire has caused you trouble before," muttered Bess to herself as she trudged along the road, the strap of her satchel slung over her shoulder.

She'd left Mother Fletcher's and set out for the Merricks' farm, her excuse being that she meant to see how Anna fared. However, Marcye Johnes's declaration about David Merrick had put questions into Bess's head she desperately wanted answered.

Might Anna know the reason these particular men hated each other? And could that hatred have anything to do with Ellyn Merrick's baby?

She arrived at the Merricks' farm. Cows grazed in the meadows, and washed linens had been spread atop bushes to dry. Somewhere unseen, a rooster crowed. No servants tended the animals or moved among the outbuildings, though. Bess climbed the path to the entrance and rapped upon the door. Raised voices echoed inside the house, but no one answered her summons.

Bess skirted the house and headed for the outbuildings at the rear. Inside the nearest open-sided shed, wheels of cheese sat atop shelves, but the building was empty of the girls who would attend to washing and turning them. Bess continued on, her passage accompanied by the clucking of chickens pecking among the stones of the yard outside the hogbog, where pigs snuffled in the mud beneath the coop. A bored tan dog, sprawled in the doorway to a shed, let out a muffled bark. The smells and sounds of cows greeted her as she approached another barn, a massive whitewashed timber-framed building. One of its wide doors hung ajar, and Bess went inside. The interior was warmed by the bodies of the large animals, and languid dark eyes tracked her movement.

Hearing Bess's approach, a young woman halfway along the length of the barn exited a stall and stepped into the aisle down the building's center. She'd tucked her blue skirts into the girdle tied about her waist, raising their hems off the straw and muck covering the dirt floor. About the coif she wore, she'd wrapped a linen kerchief. Her large eyes gave Bess a wary look.

"Who are you?" she asked, wiping her chapped hands across the apron she'd tied atop her kirtle.

"My name is Elizabeth Ellyott."

"How do you, Elizabeth. My name is Thomasin. Has the mistress sent you?" the young woman asked, casting a glance over Bess's attire. "You are dressed too well to work with the cows. Were you not told what to wear?"

"I am not here to work with the cows."

"If Mistress Merrick has not sent you, then I beg your leave, for I am too busy to chatter with wandering strangers. I must do Anna's work in addition to mine own."

"I came to see how Anna fares. I was called to tend to her yesterday. I am a healer." Bess pointed to her satchel. "Is she better?"

"She is not out here to do her work, is all I know."

Thomasin made to step back into the stall holding her waiting cow.

"I pray the news of that man's death has not further harmed her health," said Bess, eyeing the dairymaid.

"Bartholomew. The fool . . ." Thomasin's voice trailed off. The cow she'd been milking lowed in its stall and shuffled restlessly. The dog Bess had seen out in the yard poked its head through the open barn door to inspect what was happening but did not come nearer.

"You knew Master Reade." Well enough to refer to him by his Christian name.

"Aye," she answered. "He was known by one and all."

Bess stepped up to her. "I need your help, Thomasin," she said in a low voice. "Mistress Ellyn has come to me, ill—"

"By ill mean you mean that she has lost her child?" Thomasin interrupted.

"You knew she carried a babe?"

"Who did not? According to the housemaid, Mistress Ellyn was sick every morning and could not take breakfast. What woman does not understand the signs?"

"Did her mother also know?" And what of David Merrick?

A shadow crossed her face. "I am not privy to the conversations that pass between the members of the household, as my days are spent out here with the cows."

"Would her family have blamed Master Reade for Ellyn's condition?" asked Bess. "For she has admitted to me she loved him."

"So God mend me, I'll say no more about the Merricks. I need this work." She gestured toward the cow chewing its cud. "I would not have the mistress dismiss me or see me locked in the stocks for gossiping, especially about them. So I'd ask you to leave."

"One more question, then I shall go," said Bess. "Who do *you* think could have killed Bartholomew Reade?"

The shadow on her face did not lift, but deepened. "Mayhap it would be better to ask Ellyn Merrick than me."

"She blames Jeffrey Poynard."

Thomasin let out a sharp laugh. "The father of her dead child?"

Bess gripped the young woman's arm. It was well muscled and strong. "How can you know this to be the truth?" And what would Bartholomew Reade have made of such information?

"I have eyes. And ears," she replied. "And before you pose your next question, Mistress, I have already said too much about what the Merricks might know."

"Pray answer me this. Why were Ellyn and Master Poynard not brought before the Church court to assess their guilt and made to offer penance, if what you say is true?" Bess asked. Since she'd been living in the village, she could not recall anyone having been made to do so.

Thomasin laughed again. "A Poynard making public penance? 'Twould never happen."

"Thomasin?" a man called from the entrance to the barn.

She dropped a curtsy as Bess turned to face the man.

"Master David," said the dairymaid. "I beg your pardon. I tried to get this woman to leave but she'd not."

Thomasin scowled at Bess.

A burst of sunshine in the yard at his back cast the man in shadow, and Bess was unable to make out his features. The straightness of his shoulders and his firm stance suggested he was young and eager to show that he possessed a measure of authority. His unassured ways, as Marcye had described them.

"What is your business here?" he asked Bess.

"I came to see how Anna Webb fares, Master Merrick," she

said, walking toward him. "I tended to her yesterday. I am Widow Ellyott. Your mother may have mentioned me."

He *was* young, likely not even twenty years of age, and shorter than Bess. He had to lift his chin to level his eyes with hers. "Anna remains abed. Too ill to resume her work. As you can see, she is not out here in the barn."

He stepped aside to encourage her to pass by him and out of the barn. She kept her ground.

"I am sorry Anna is still ill," she said. "I should go to the girl and see what else I might do for her."

"That will not be possible. My mother is occupied. She cannot make you welcome."

Not that she had made Bess particularly welcome yesterday, either. "I hope Anna does not learn of Bartholomew Reade's death. I gather that many in your household knew him, had befriended him, and such news might harm her recovery."

David Merrick's eyes narrowed. "This is not your affair, Mistress Ellyott. It is not. And you had best leave. Immediately."

CHAPTER 7

Mistress Merrick rested a hand upon her pregnant belly. Feet pounded overhead, and children's voices chattered noisily in a distant room. She frowned at the commotion. "You wished to speak with me, Constable? As may be clear, I am most busy."

"I shall be brief." He crossed to a table against one of the decorated plaster walls in the ground-floor parlor and placed the knife on it. "Recognize this, Mistress?"

She stood as still as a stone. "Nay. Should I?"

"Might anyone else in the household recognize it?"

"I can name all of the items we own, Constable. 'Tis not one of ours. Besides, this type of knife is common enough," she said. "David is occupied in dealing with a person who has trespassed on our dairy, else you could ask him. If you trust not my word."

Kit had noticed the trespasser. The parlor had large mullioned windows overlooking the courtyard. Windows that had given Kit an excellent view of Mistress Ellyott charging out of one of the dairy barns minutes earlier, her cloak snapping in the wind.

"Rumors of a long-standing dispute between your family

and the Reades exist, Mistress Merrick," he said. "Is there truth in them?"

She drew her attention from the knife. "Does your question have aught to do with the weapon you have brought? If so, I would ask Master Reade's fellow players about the knife, were I you. Actors are a rough sort."

"Tell me about the feud, if you will, Mistress Merrick."

She lifted her chin. "'Tis an old tale. We no longer carry any animosity between, Constable. You will have no trouble from us. Especially at such a grievous time."

"You did not protest your daughter Ellyn's attachment to Bartholomew Reade?"

She flinched. The motion was slight but noticeable. Not fully as still as a stone.

"They had no attachment, Constable. It was a misplaced affection on Ellyn's part. She repented of it soon enough."

"Nonetheless, your family must have been unhappy to learn he was with the troupe staying at the Poynards'."

"In truth, we gave his arrival only a momentary thought," she replied. "His presence amongst them did persuade David, however, to not attend the Poynards' entertainment yester-even. My son supped with me, though he greatly esteems such performances."

Her tone was disdainful. "Many people esteem the theater, Mistress," said Kit.

"My children have no time for such folly, Constable. This dairy requires many hands."

"To make light work."

"Indeed." Footsteps echoed in the passageway. "Ah. Here is David now."

David Merrick entered the room. His gaze skipped between

his mother and Kit, touching only briefly on the knife on the table.

"Constable?" he asked. He bore a strong resemblance to Mistress Merrick—small in stature, blunt nose. He did not seem to possess her confidence, though, if the anxious way he stretched his neck to attempt to stand taller than Kit was any indication.

"The constable has been asking about Bartholomew Reade, David."

"Do not trouble yourself any longer, Mother," he said.

"As you will." She inclined her head and left.

"A sad end for Bartholomew. A good fellow. And a good playwright." Merrick shook his head mournfully. "I cannot believe. Jellis."

"Neither can I, Master Merrick. Not at all."

He stretched his neck again. "Oh?"

"Can you name anyone else who had reason to harm Master Reade?"

The muscles of his face moved but did not resolve into any particular look. "Bartholomew had his squabbles. Over women."

"He *was* a handsome fellow," said Kit.

"And had a winning manner."

David Merrick might guard the movement of his face, but his voice betrayed resentment. The resentment of a man who was neither particularly handsome nor especially winning toward one who was both.

"Did he charm your sister?" asked Kit.

"Ellyn is impetuous. But sensible, in the end."

"Was she the cause of the feud that existed between your families, Master Merrick? Your family and the Reades?"

His brow furrowed. "There is no bad blood between our families, Constable."

"I hear otherwise."

"Tittle-tattle. That is all. Those who spread it should be punished."

"Did you see Master Reade after he arrived here?"

Merrick rolled his lips between his teeth. "I am too busy with the farm. With my father and brothers at the fair. I must take charge, you see. No time for idleness with my mates."

"Ah." Kit nodded toward the table against the wall. "Do you recognize the knife there, Master Merrick?"

"Nay, I do not." Merrick squinted at it. "I am most certain I do not."

"What might your servants claim?"

"The same, Constable." He tilted his head as if straining to hear. "Ah. My mother calls to me. I have work to oversee in the cheese barn. Good day, Constable."

Kit watched him go. He'd not heard anyone calling to David Merrick.

And how telling that the fellow had not asked after his sister's health, either.

★　★　★

Bartholomew Reade is murdered. Marcye accuses David Merrick. Ellyn accuses the supposed father of her child, Jeffrey Poynard. A witness saw a woman swathed in a dark gown.

What does it all mean?

Bess followed a bend in the road, drawing near to the outlying cottages of town, her thoughts twirling like the blades of a windmill in a gust. She was so distracted, her thick-soled shoes kept miring in patches of mud.

Hiking her skirt, she slogged on. Ahead of her, smoke rose from chimneys into the sky, which clouded over with the threat of approaching rain, and church bells tolled. She marveled anew at the ordinariness of the scene. Why did not a man's murder cast a visible pall over it all?

She approached the lane upon which Robert's house was located and nodded to the baker's wife, who'd dumped a basin of wash water onto the roadway and now stared at Bess.

"Good day," she said to the woman.

"God save you, Mistress Ellyott," she replied without her customary smile.

Well, now. The gossips must be aware that a strange woman is at our house.

"It appears we might have rain soon," said Bess.

The baker's wife did not answer, and Bess hurried on. She noticed Joan standing in the lane, waving her hand frantically.

"Mistress!" she cried out. "Your good sister has returned!"

"Dorothie has come? With Margery?"

"Just Mistress Crofton," she answered. "But you must hurry! Mistress Ellyn is gone! Vanished!"

★　★　★

"No greeting for me, Elizabeth?"

Dorothie, the folds of her ruff as crisp as though freshly starched, her leaden-colored gown unsullied by travel grime—how did she accomplish such a feat?—stamped after Bess, who hurried through the second floor of the house to prove to herself that Ellyn had indeed run off. Quail danced alongside them, tail wagging.

Bess paused. "Welcome, Dorothie. You did not bring Margery with you."

"No." Dorothie held out her cheek, which Bess dropped a kiss upon. "And where is Robert? Has he left you alone again?"

To become involved in others' problems once more. "He has gone to his countinghouse in Cheapside," she said, resuming her rush through the house.

"So you are here alone." Dorothie tutted. "Then 'tis well that I have come back earlier than I had planned."

"But I am not alone. I am at home with two servants. And a dog."

"Bah. Prithee, Elizabeth, can you not halt for one moment?" Dorothie swept down the staircase behind Bess, Quail close behind. "Fie, you know how you vex me. I am weary from my journey, and you will not—"

"Then rest yourself in the hall. I seek answers as to where an ill young woman who has run away from my care has gone."

"A patient of yours has fled? Most discourteous."

Joan waited in the hall. Quail trotted over to her.

"I could not find the constable, Mistress." She bobbed the briefest of curtsies at Dorothie, who lifted a brow and went to recline on the settle. "But I did find his cousin, Master Harwoode. He will enjoin the townsfolk to search. And here. This is for Mistress Ellyn."

She handed Bess a woolen blanket.

"My thanks, Joan. She will likely have need of it." Joan had discovered a petticoat and loose jacket missing from the trunk in the room Ellyn had borrowed, along with the coverlet she'd taken from her bed. However, the items might not be sufficient to protect her from the damp and cold that rode on the wind. In her weakened condition, if it began to rain, Ellyn would suffer all the more.

"What mean you to do with that blanket?" asked Dorothie, who'd been occupied in tucking cushions around her. "Take part in the search for this woman? 'Tis best left to those in authority, Elizabeth."

"Do not fret, Dorothie. I will not ask you to search for a stranger."

Dorothie's brows rose again, arcs of light brown above her eyes. "I shall indeed *not* assist, you may be assured."

"We will return anon. Joan, come with me. Quail, stay." Her sister might take some solace in the dog's presence.

She exited the room, Dorothie sputtering her dismay that she was to be left behind without food or drink to refresh her.

"'Tis my fault Mistress Ellyn has gone off," said Joan, trailing Bess out the rear door and into the courtyard. "If I had not been sitting in the lane before the front door mending your stockings this afternoon but instead been inside the house, I would have seen her slip away."

"She may have run away before then, Joan. While we were at the Cross Keys speaking with Marcye, or while I was with Mother Fletcher," said Bess. "When did you last see her?"

"Late this morning, Mistress," she said. "After the constable left, I did try to bring her food at midday. She told me to leave it and not disturb her further."

Many hours. Too many hours. "She will not get far, Joan. She has lost too much blood and has not yet recovered."

"But, Mistress . . ."

"Humphrey should have seen her. He was to plant out the cabbages in the garden today."

"You think he would have tried to stop Mistress Ellyn if he had been in the garden to see her depart?" Joan asked, sounding dubious.

"Nay. I'faith, I do not." He'd be content to see Ellyn Merrick gone. One less troublesome woman in the house.

Bess strode across the courtyard, the gravel crunching beneath her shoes, bound for the gate set into the garden's rear wall. From the upstairs parlor window, she'd noticed that it hung open, which suggested that Ellyn had run off through the gate.

"She should not have fled," said Joan, her set of household keys jingling as she chased after Bess. "She should not."

Bess paused to allow Joan to catch her up. "One of the Merrick servants claims the child was Jeffrey Poynard's."

Her eyes went wide. "Oh! Would he not wed her?"

"I have no idea. But I must wonder what Ellyn plans now," said Bess. "What does your instinct tell you, Joan?"

"I have no need for instinct, Mistress," she said. "The penknife from her chamber is not 'pon the small desk in the room."

"It may simply be misplaced."

"The penknife was there earlier, for when I left Mistress Ellyn's midday meal on the desk, I saw it."

"If she did take the knife, 'tis dull from sharpening quills."

Joan's face sank into troubled lines. "It may be sharp enough, Mistress, for what she intends."

★　★　★

Summoned by Gibb Harwoode, those who could readily leave their shops and their farms joined in the search. Children were among their number, chattering excitedly about the grand adventure that had freed them from their work or their studies for a while. 'Twas far from a grand adventure though, thought Bess. A woman's life could be at stake. They had to locate Ellyn before she made use of the penknife she'd taken.

The searchers spread out across the lands that stretched beyond the town boundaries. It was unlikely that Ellyn would walk openly upon the road. Bess also doubted that she'd sought refuge with anyone in the village, for if she had friends willing to take her in now, she'd not have come to Bess's door in the first place. Which meant Ellyn would probably be hiding in the dense shrubbery near the river. Or perhaps within a barn or the friary ruins that loomed forlornly over the southern road. Quiet places to breathe one's last, if self-murder was what Ellyn planned.

Ellyn, do not do this. We will find a way to secure a hopeful future for you.

Somehow.

Bess paused. *Where would I go?* 'Twas a simple choice, were Bess to do the choosing. She would not huddle in a barn with dirty straw and animals or rest in the rubble of an old building. Bess would take her knife and lie down among the tall, thick grasses that grew up alongside the river, where the water burbled peacefully and birds sang among the trees.

But she was not the one taking a penknife to her wrists or throat. Might Ellyn Merrick instead seek to end her life atop a mound where another man, a man she'd loved, had so recently died?

In the distance, two men searched the outbuildings of a nearby farm. Even from where she stood, Bess could tell they were Kit Harwoode and his cousin. She drew comfort from the sight of them. Ellyn would be found.

"Ellyn!" she cried. "Let me help you!"

Off to her right, Joan crashed through a furrowed field, her skirts tucked high into her girdle. She had sharp eyes and scanned her surroundings.

"Look for blood, Joan," called Bess. "There might be a trail of it."

Joan nodded and continued her search.

Bess paused again to scan her surroundings. Several dozen yards behind her was Robert's house and their garden wall, which formed a continuous boundary with the other rear walls of their neighbors' gardens. A trampled dirt path snaked from the properties to the river ahead of her. Could she possibly spy, though, the marks of anyone who'd recently trudged from the direction of their garden? The route was popular, and many trails had been trod into the grass and dirt. Too many to discern the path of one particular woman over another.

A cottager, his tiny thatched-roof cottage situated alone past the last buildings that huddled along the town lanes, stood at his wattle fence. At his side yapped his dog.

"Good sir, did you see a woman, possibly wrapped in a yellow coverlet, run by here?" she asked him.

He scratched at his grizzled chin with filthy fingernails. "A woman? In a coverlet?"

"As I said."

"May have done. Aye, may have done." His words were accompanied by more scratching.

"Did you observe which way she went?"

"The river. I think."

The river. Mayhap Ellyn Merrick did choose to lie among the grasses, as Bess would.

Thanking the cottager, she made for the river, taking a muddy path that led to the bank. In its dirt, she did not see any spots of blood or the markings of a barefooted woman.

Joan joined her. "What had the old cottager to say?"

"He thinks he saw Ellyn headed for the river."

Joan peered over at the fellow, who'd not moved from his fence. "That old man is blind as a beetle in a cowshed, Mistress."

"We have no better idea of where she might have gone, Joan. I will accept his comment as truth and continue to search near the river."

Joan moved off in the opposite direction. Bess toed aside twigs, bent to examine dark spots that proved to be nothing. Leaves continued to drift downward, obscuring the path, and the first pattering of raindrops landed. Bess drew up the hood of her cloak.

"Mistress!" Joan called, pointing at the ground. "Here! Come!"

Bess rushed over, thistles and hawthorns snagging her stockings. "What have you found?"

"Could this be blood, Mistress?" asked Joan.

The splotches of dark red were at first difficult to see, but then they began to take form, vivid blots against the browns of dirt and twigs and golds of fallen leaves. A line that trailed toward the riverbank.

"Aye." Bess hurried forward, following where the trail of blood led. The spots were joined by the plodding footprints of the woman who had left them.

Joan followed, dodging low branches, protruding roots, and slippery patches of ground. The contour of the river came into view, blue-gray beneath the cloud-filled sky. On sunny days, the water could be clear as crystal, minnows darting above its gravel bottom or dark-speckled trout swimming.

They broke through the stand of trees. "There," said Joan, pointing.

A bundled pile, the yellow of the cloth atop it bright against the muted colors of its surroundings, lay near the edge of the river. Ellyn's long hair had come free of the braid that had restrained it to flow in waves across the grasses and mud. Her right hand was outstretched, a knife tumbled to the ground next to it.

"Ellyn!"

Bess dropped onto her knees at the woman's side. The

penknife was clean, and Bess saw no cuts on her arms or her neck. She pressed a finger to Ellyn's throat to feel for her pulse. Her skin was cool to the touch, and if her heart beat, Bess could not sense it. But then, her own fingers were numb.

"Does she live?" asked Joan, leaning over Bess's shoulder.

"I cannot say yes or no, but at least she collapsed before she used the knife." Bess gently rolled Ellyn onto her back. "And 'tis true she has lost more blood, but see? The amount is not so great."

She pointed out the red stain on the lower half of Ellyn's dirty and water-soaked skirts. A greater quantity of blood than if she had stayed in bed and rested, but not enough to steal her life from her. Even if she might have wished to lose that life.

"Think you, Mistress, that she will be grateful we have found her?" asked Joan, gathering up the wet coverlet the young woman had wrapped herself in and tucking the penknife into its depths.

"Possibly not." Bess draped the dry blanket she'd brought over Ellyn's body. "And we shall watch her more closely from now on to stop her from attempting this again." She lightly prodded the young woman's shoulder. "Ellyn? Can you hear me?"

She stirred, exhaling a low groan.

"God be thanked," said Joan. "She is alive."

"Run back to the roadway, Joan, and fetch the constable here." Bess tucked the blanket around Ellyn's body, which had taken to trembling. "I need help moving her back to our house."

★ ★ ★

Joan Barbor's cry pierced the air like the whistle of a hunter calling his dogs.

"She's been found, Gibb."

Kit took off at a run, Gibb sprinting behind him.

"There. She is there," Joan stammered, pointing toward the river.

"Joan, all will be well now. Trust me," said Gibb, in the soothing tone that always succeeded with women.

She blushed. "She is there, good sirs. Alive."

A living Ellyn Merrick, an outcome other than the one Kit had expected. "Show us where."

Joan plunged into the thicket of trees that lined the bank. Her mistress knelt in the muddy grass lining the riverbank without heed for her dress. Ellyn Merrick, draped with a woolen blanket, lay insensible beside her.

"Ah, God be thanked you have arrived so quickly. Constable, can you carry her back to my house?" asked Mistress Ellyott, collecting a muddied yellow coverlet that lay nearby. Gibb took her elbow to help her stand.

"Most certainly, Mistress." He bent to lift the senseless woman into his arms. She shuddered and moaned as he regained his feet. "Gibb, alert the others that Mistress Merrick has been found."

"Aye, Kit."

"Joan," said Mistress Ellyott, "go ahead of us and see the fire in the hall stoked. Warn my sister that we return with several others."

With care to not drop Ellyn Merrick, Kit picked his way through the trees and out into the adjoining field. Gibb had spread the news of the discovery hastily, and several of the other searchers clustered together to watch Kit pass. The Merricks were not among those assembled.

He walked behind Mistress Ellyott, who led him to the open gate in the wall surrounding her brother's garden and yard. Kit passed through, sparing a glance at the quince tree heavy with fruit, the final blooms on the flowers. Not a month ago, he'd sat in this garden with her in a more tranquil time.

"You have found her, Mistress?" asked her brother's pox-scarred manservant, slouching in the entrance to the long shed that lined one side of the courtyard. He did not sound happy.

"Bring wood for the fire in the hall, Humphrey," Bess Ellyott ordered.

Kit shifted to step sideways through the rear door, taking care to not knock Ellyn's legs against its frame. He then carried her into the hall, ducking to clear the low beam above the opening to the room. Their water spaniel rose from his nap beneath the street-side window.

"Here, Constable," said Mistress Ellyott. "Place Ellyn on the settle for now."

Joan turned away from the fire she'd been prodding into life to plump cushions for Ellyn Merrick to rest against. Linens had already been spread atop the wooden seat.

Mistress Ellyott's sister, Mistress Crofton, stood up from the cushioned chair where she'd been sitting. "Constable Harwoode." Her eyes widened at the sight of the woman he carried. "Is she dead?"

"No, Mistress Crofton," he said, lowering Ellyn to the high-backed settle.

"Well, that is a relief."

"No doubt Ellyn agrees, Dorothie," said Bess Ellyott sharply. Her sister scowled and retook her chair.

Though she resembled Bess Ellyott, Kit could not imagine two women less alike. Mistress Crofton's presence, though, might keep her sister in check. Someone had to.

Ellyn Merrick drew in a shuddering breath and opened her eyes. "What?" she asked, looking around her. "I am back here?"

"We found you in time, Ellyn," said Mistress Ellyott. "You should not have taken the knife, though."

Bloody . . . "She had a knife with her?" asked Kit.

"Later, Constable." Bess Ellyott rested a hand upon the woman's arm while Joan arranged a fresh blanket around Ellyn Merrick's body. The dog trotted over to give an inquisitive sniff. "You begged me to help you, Ellyn. I cannot do so if you run away from my house and my care. You must trust that I will help you."

"I am sorry," Mistress Merrick answered weakly.

"Joan, bring Mistress Ellyn a warm posset." Mistress Ellyott looked over at Kit. "Constable, I would speak to you alone."

He followed her out of the hall, across the entry passageway, and into the lesser parlor.

"You found her with a knife?" he asked.

"'Twas only a penknife." She folded her hands across her girdle. "Nonetheless, we—Joan and I—fear that Ellyn meant to kill herself today, disquieted by your accusations of guilt, Constable."

Or because she is guilty.

"I have warned you as best I know how, Mistress Ellyott, to stand aside of affairs that are not your concern. I will investigate Master Reade's murder. You tend to your patient."

"Because she *is* my patient, Ellyn Merrick has given me cause to care about these affairs, as you term them."

"And has your care anything to do with why you were at the Merricks' earlier today, Mistress Ellyott?"

She perked her chin. "I sought to visit a patient of mine."

"Inside the barn?"

A flush pinked her cheeks. "Jest if you will, Constable, but I have learned information you might find interesting. Firstly, that Marcye Johnes blames David Merrick for Master Reade's death. Secondly, that Master Reade was seen in the Poynard courtyard arguing with some fellow. And lastly, whilst in that barn, I was told that Jeffrey Poynard was the father of the child Mistress Ellyn has lost." Her chin went higher. "What say you now?"

Nothing.

She had struck him dumb.

CHAPTER 8

"Mean you to stay with us tonight, Dorothie?" asked Bess, closing the hall door behind her. Upstairs, Ellyn Merrick slept, the physic Bess had given to the young woman ensuring she would. "I could send Humphrey with a link to see you safely home by its light."

Inside the hall, the fire in the hearth burned low and shadows sat heavy and black in the space. On the lane beyond the street-facing windows, the watchman passed, his torch briefly shining upon the many panes.

"You may not feel alone here, Elizabeth, with your two servants and Robert's dog." From where she sat in Robert's chair, Dorothie flicked a look at Quail. He rested across the room from her; the dog had never taken to Dorothie. "But I have only my maidservant at my house."

"Then you should have stayed with Margery at your mother-in-law's house," said Bess, crossing to the hearth to prod an unburned branch onto the glowing embers. "Or brought your daughter home with you."

"I could not endure that woman's criticisms a moment longer. Blaming me for Fulke's death. As though *I* murdered her son and not our wicked manservant," hissed Dorothie. "And she begged Margery to stay. I'll not argue with the woman. My sons will inherit the property that would have gone to their father when she dies."

Money ever did explain Dorothie's actions.

Bess set down the poker and turned her back to the fire, letting it warm her. "You could go to your boys in Cambridge."

"I did ask them." She had removed her ruff, and her chin sagged onto her neckerchief. "They claim their studies occupy them too greatly to play host to their mother."

"Then you may use Robert's chamber tonight, Dorothie," said Bess. "But you will most likely desire to return to your house on the morrow. With Mistress Ellyn in our care, we cannot attend to you as you would like."

"A Merrick," said Dorothie, none too kindly.

"I'd forgotten that you know her. Ellyn did tell me she is Margery's friend."

"Ellyn is suitable enough, but the rest . . ." She shook her head. "Not long ago, the father sought to prove their connection to a noble line so they could hang a coat of arms in their parlor. Overgreedy, they are. Miscontented with their place. He found no such connection, of course."

"Know you the Reades also?"

"Not well. They are farmers," said Dorothie, a sufficient explanation for her. "Why do you ask?"

"Their son died yesterday." Only yesterday. "Murdered."

Dorothie blanched. Her emotions were ever quick to rise and to wane, but the alarm on her face startled Bess. She noticed, as she'd not earlier that day, how her sister's cheeks had thinned. How sleeplessness had robbed her green eyes of their usual sharp glint.

I must be kind to her. I must not forget that her own husband was murdered not so very long ago.

Dorothie pressed a hand to her throat. "Is the killer captured? Are we in danger?"

"An old vagrant is accused, Dorothie. We are not in danger." *I pray.*

She calmed and lowered her hand to her lap. "Good."

"But Constable Harwoode's suspicions lie elsewhere."

"Elsewhere? Well, 'tis true the Reades have enemies. They desire to rise above their station as much as the Merricks," she said. "Pish, Elizabeth. Did you spend so many years in London that you forget the jealousies and envies that simmer in a village like this one?"

"Mayhap I have," she answered. "Let me fetch you wine, sister. To settle your unrest."

In the kitchen, Joan sat before the fire. Her day's work complete, she hunched over the hornbook Bess's husband, Martin, had given to her to learn her letters. He had been such a generous and kind man. The best of masters. The best of husbands.

Oh, Martin. I could well use your counsel.

Joan heard Bess's footfalls and looked up from her hornbook. She stood and set it aside.

"My apologies for interrupting your studies, Joan," she said.

"There is no need for apologies, Mistress," she answered. "How fares your good sister and Mistress Ellyn?"

"Ellyn's adventure has not caused harm to her, so far as I can judge. She sleeps soundly," said Bess. "And Mistress Crofton stays with us this night. She will make use of my brother's chamber. Meanwhile, bring us both wine. We have need of it."

"Aye." Joan walked off and into the buttery, adjacent to the kitchen. She returned with two glasses of malmsey, one of which she handed to Bess. The wine glowed a tawny red in the firelight.

"Would you have me sleep in Mistress Ellyn's chamber tonight, Mistress?" asked Joan.

Bess swallowed a sip of wine. It burned pleasantly in her throat. "You fear she may try again to make use of that knife."

"Desperate women do not always think clearly when driven to their actions."

Joan's eyes took on a faraway look, a reverie of remembering an unhappy place and time. Was Joan aware that, whenever she became lost in her recollections, her fingers brushed the scar upon her face?

"How can I help you?" asked Bess.

Joan lowered her hand. "The time for helping me is long past, Mistress. I would not have you fret over me."

"I'faith, I cannot help but fret over us all, though I said otherwise to Dorothie just now."

"You may have cause for unease, Mistress. I should have given this to you earlier, but I did not want Mistress Crofton to see. Forgive me if I was wrong to presume so." From the pocket she'd sewn into her skirt, she withdrew a folded piece of paper with her free hand. She held it out.

"What is it?"

"My friend in London sent this to us. The letter has been many days in arriving," she said. "It arrived here just before sunset."

Joan could mean but one friend. The friend who'd been tasked with watching the man who had murdered Bess's husband.

The dread that chilled Bess could not be warmed by the kitchen fire. Setting down her wine, she took the missive and broke the seal.

"What does it say?" asked Joan, squinting at the words she could not read.

"Laurence is no longer in London. Or if he is, he is in

hiding." Bess's fingers shook. She refolded the paper and tucked it away before Joan could observe their trembling. She deserved to know the contents of the message; she need not see Bess's fear.

"God have mercy, Mistress. He is coming for us."

"Laurence does *not* know we are in Wiltshire, Joan," she said, gripping her servant's hand. He had learned, though, where Robert's Cheapside countinghouse was. *God, keep my brother safe.* "He will not find us here."

But the foreboding that her dream had brought returned with fearsome force.

★ ★ ★

Bess withdrew a key from the pocket strung from her girdle and drew the small casket, which always sat upon the table in her bedchamber, over to her. She unlocked it. Laurence's letter rested atop the others stored within the lacquered wooden box. A month ago, he had sent the note to her brother's countinghouse and Robert had brought it to Bess, unwitting of its contents. She had never told him or Dorothie the truth of what had happened to Martin. Selfishly, she'd wished to protect them from Laurence's villainy.

Bess pressed the paper flat, the flame of the candle she'd lit fluttering in the rapid exhalation of her breath.

> *I know you have someone watch me. Can you be certain,*
> *though, that I do not watch* you *as well?*
> *Take care, Elizabeth Ellyott.*
> *You are not so safe as you believe.*

The note was worn from Bess's repeated handling. He had signed it with only his initial—L—and in a flourish so grand it said much about the man who'd wielded the quill. Arrogant, was Laurence. Treacherous. Dangerous. Though more than a year had passed since Bess had last seen him, in the days before her husband had died at the man's hand, she could clearly recall the glitter of his sharp eyes. She had thought his bright gaze a reflection of his intellect. She should have known it was a reflection of his evil. She had been charmed by him, though. Had taken the very viper to her heart and brought him into their house.

Boldly—too boldly—she had replied to his note with one of her own. *I do not fear you*, was what she'd written. Such a lie. She had delayed responding for many days, and the delay was telling. He also had to have realized she lied.

Alongside Laurence's letter, Bess spread the note they had received today from Joan's friend. *He is gone.* 'Twas all the woman had written. The words, however, were sufficient to freeze Bess's bones. But to where had he gone, and what evil did he now plot? Were more people to die to conceal his treacherous schemes against the throne? To cover the evidence he left behind him like the slimy trail of a slug-snail? Did he come to Wiltshire to silence her, to bury the knowledge of his treason that Bess carried like so much putrid refuse she could not readily discard?

Bess's gaze fell upon the penknife she kept on the table. She ran a thumb over its ivory handle, avoiding the blade's sharp edge. Mayhap she should surrender to all the sorrow and the fear and use the knife to cut her wrists, as Ellyn had planned today as an end to her grief.

God help her, Bess would rather use the knife to stab Laurence.

But then she would be no better, no less evil, than he was.

★   ★   ★

"I cannot stay long. We have customers yet at the tavern, though it grows late. Those players, who have been causing such trouble for us." Marcye Johnes eyed Kit from where she stood inside his hall doorway. Eager to answer the summons he'd sent, she had rushed to his house without removing her unbleached canvas apron, spatters of grease and spilled ale soiling the linen. "Can we not be rid of them, Constable? They quarrel with each other and with our good customers."

"Your father is responsible for keeping the peace within his establishment, Mistress Johnes," said Kit, reminding her of what she was already aware. "I will be forced to fine him, if he can't."

Her eyes widened. "Prithee, do not!"

"The players will be gone soon enough," said Kit. "I sent for you about another matter."

"Oh?" she asked, sounding hopeful. She peeped at him through her lashes and smiled.

Bloody . . . "Let me be plain, Mistress Johnes, so that you may return apace to the tavern," he said. "I hear you have blamed David Merrick for killing Bartholomew Reade."

The coyness dropped away. "I am no gossip!" she shrieked. "You have no cause to punish me!"

"I want to know why you make the claim," he said. "That's all."

"'Tis not Jellis who is guilty, 'tis certain." Suddenly, she scowled. "You have heard this from Bess Ellyott."

He rested his hips against the narrow table beneath the room's window and folded his arms. "Tell me about David Merrick, Mistress Johnes."

"He despised Bartholomew," she said. "'Tis not only what I think. 'Tis well known."

"For what reason?"

"Out of envy."

"Then he must not have been pleased that his sister was in love with the fellow," said Kit.

"Ha! 'Tis truth, that! This summer, one even before Bartholomew left to act upon the stage, they fought in the Cross Keys," she said. "Master Merrick gave a swing that actually landed and left Bartholomew with a blackened eye. Bartholomew laughed it off."

"Though Merrick had been angry enough to blacken his eye, Reade returned to the village without fear."

The smile that curved her lips was tender. "Bartholomew had no fear of anyone. Certainly not David Merrick. He would have thought his return a great prank to play on his enemies."

"Reade had many enemies?"

"What man with Bartholomew's comeliness does not?"

And what woman in this village had not been swayed by the fellow? "Was one of those enemies Jeffrey Poynard, who may have been . . . well-acquainted, if you will, with Ellyn Merrick?"

Marcye's eyes lit with a speculative gleam. "You have heard the whispers. But if they shook the sheets, Constable, 'twas not willingly on her part."

"If that is so, Marcye, why has David Merrick not sought to revenge the honor taken from his sister by the fellow?"

"He is unaware the fellow dishonored his sister?" She shrugged. "Or mayhap he hoped Master Poynard's forced attentions would speed a marriage the Merricks greatly desire, Constable."

Feet thudded up the stairs, and Gibb burst into the hall. "Do I interrupt, coz?"

"My thanks, Marcye. That is all." Kit had learned all he needed from her. She offered Gibb a coy grin and swept from the room.

He waited until he heard the front door close before turning to his cousin. "What a state we find ourselves in, Gibb," he said. "Ellyn Merrick possibly pregnant with Poynard's child. A child she no longer carries. The man she loved recently returned to the village, and whose body now rests in his father's house, being prepared for burial after his murder. A brother who resented the man. Further, lest we forget, a jealous collection of actors and their master, soon to be reported to the authorities for thieving manuscripts." Kit pushed away from the table, causing it to rock back and strike the wall. "It's as though we wander lost through an ancient labyrinth, waiting to find the monster at the end."

"What part do you suppose Old Jellis played in the windings of this maze, besides the one of which he was accused?"

"Why do you ask?"

"I ask because he is dead."

★   ★   ★

The coroner clutched his robes around his gaunt frame and leaned over the old man slumped against the wall of the jail. A villager held aloft a torch to light the space, the smoke it sputtered making him cough.

"Dead," announced the coroner.

"Aye, Crowner," said Kit. "My cousin is capable of telling a dead man from a live one."

"Jellis. Dead," whispered one of the men the coroner had assembled to act as his jury. They stood about, packed into the jail like fish stuffed into a barrel for shipment. Their bodies and breaths heated the tiny space. One of them had eaten onions with his dinner.

The coroner prodded Jellis with a finger, shifting the man's clothes about. "No blood. No wounds. No obvious sign of murder."

"No one could readily have gotten inside here to wound the man, Crowner," said Kit. Only three people had keys to the jail—Gibb, himself, and the bailiff, who'd come to feed Jellis his evening meal and found his dead body.

"As you say, Constable," said the coroner stiffly. He scanned the assembled men. "Goodman Jellis perished sometime between midday and sunset. He was an old man known for his intemperate habits."

"He was a sot, you mean!" a fellow in the back shouted, to laughter from the others.

The coroner waited until the crowd quieted. "This jail is a bleak space, as it ought be. Given his habits and his age, it is my assessment that Goodman Jellis died a natural death from the short hours he spent inside it. What say you all?"

To the man, his jurors nodded or spoke aloud their agreement. But then a grumbling arose.

"'Twas the witch what killed him, Crowner!" called out a fellow wedged between the baker's apprentice and the jail's wall. He elbowed the apprentice aside to be better seen. His pockmarked face was red with anger. "That crone who is a witch!"

Silence fell for a moment before the grumbling resumed.

"Aye! That old woman!" said another.

"She cursed Cox's sheep. She killed Jellis too!" his mate agreed. "Which of us is next? She must be punished!" He looked around him. "Who be with me?"

"I will go and happily!" offered the pockmarked man. Others volunteered as well.

"Stop! Devil take you all, stop this!" shouted Kit. "Jellis died of feebleness. Not from a witch's curse."

The fellow whose breath reeked of onions stepped up to him. "You afeard of her, Constable?"

Kit gripped his dagger and glared. "If any of you, a single one, harms Mother Fletcher, I shall see *you* punished. Now, Crowner, make your pronouncement."

"A natural death," he declared, and marched away, shoving aside the men who blocked his rapid departure.

"Go home, the rest of you," ordered Kit.

They shuffled off, muttering amongst themselves. With a last look at Jellis, Kit ducked through the jail doorway and stepped into the square.

Gibb jogged over from where he'd been standing near the town well. "What was going on in there? I heard shouting."

"We must keep our ears open for news that any aim to harm Mother Fletcher, Gibb." Shivering in the brisk wind, Kit reached up to fasten the topmost button of his doublet. "Or Jellis will not be the last dead person we'll need attend."

★ ★ ★

Clouds hung thick as gray felted wool in the sky, the thinnest morning light showing Bess the way to the Merricks', her satchel of physic hugged against her waist. They might not welcome her arrival, but she still had a patient at their house whom she could not neglect.

Overnight, rain had spattered the ground, but it had passed, leaving behind puddles. She was not alone on the roadway. An aged woman carrying a basket, a clout covering the lower part of her face and hunched within the kerchief she'd tied around her neck and shoulders, hobbled toward town. Bess nodded at her as they passed each other, then hurried onward. She neared the Merricks' farm. She thought she spotted Thomasin out by the cow barn, but otherwise, no one was about.

She climbed the short path to the house and rapped upon the door. A maidservant, holding a dripping and dirty rag in her hand, answered with a curtsy. She was the same blue-dressed one Bess had noticed when she'd first come to tend to Anna.

"I am the healer, Widow Ellyott. I trust you remember me. I would see how Anna fares," said Bess, stepping by the girl. "You need not attend me. I recall where she is within the house."

"Prithee, wait for me to fetch Mistress Merrick!" the girl called after her.

As Bess had no desire to speak with the glowering and heartless Agnes Merrick—who'd sent no inquiry after Ellyn's health—she hastened through the ground-floor rooms, gripping her satchel to keep its contents from rattling together.

A voice that sounded like Mistress Merrick's shouted from the depths of the house. Bess reached the staircase, gathered up her skirts, and climbed. She listened for Mistress Merrick's voice to grow nearer, but it did not.

She tapped upon the door to the room Anna had been given and went inside. Anna sat on the truckle bed shoved into the corner, tying a garter around her stocking.

"Widow Ellyott." She slapped her skirts into place over her legs and got to her feet. "I did not expect you'd come again."

"I do not forget my patients, Anna." Bess shut the door, leaving the only source of light that from the tiny horn-paned window cut into the wall. "But I see you have recovered. My visit was not needed, after all." One small piece of good news.

"The mistress has told me to return to my work," she said,

tying the front laces of her pair of bodies. "I am most grateful to you, though."

"I did attempt to visit yesterday, but no one answered my knock."

"The household was in a furious upset." Anna paused. "Thomasin told me . . . told me . . ."

"About Bartholomew Reade's death," said Bess. "An upset to one and all, I am certain. I've been told he was well known."

She dropped back onto the truckle bed. "Aye, that he was." The girl pinched shut her eyes, tears squeezing from between her lids.

"You were fond of Master Reade, Anna?" Mayhap more than merely fond.

"He did not always take much note of me," she replied, swiping the tears off her cheeks. "But when he did, he could be most pleasant. And kind. Unlike the others, who say I am a noddy. That I have no more wits than the sheep."

"That is cruel."

"They say it anyway." Her eyes—the same placid brown of the cows she milked—lifted to Bess's face. "Bartholomew was so kind, this time. When I heard the troupe was in town, I thought he had come back for her. Instead, he wished to speak with me! So he did tell me, when I went into the village and saw him in the square that first day he and his fellows were here."

"How did he seem to you? I only ask because I wonder if his outward actions suggested he was troubled."

"Because he had fought with someone? The person who . . . who killed him?"

"Aye, Anna," said Bess. "That is what I mean."

"Nay, he did not seem troubled at all. Sweet-tempered and

full of good humor." She smiled softly. "He even gave me a gift that proved his regard, though it was taken from me."

"Who took the gift, Anna? Mistress Merrick?"

"It matters not, for it is gone," she said. "I have naught to remember him by. Just the memory of when we last spoke, and my happiness at our plans to meet at the old druids' mound. But then I became ill. I sent him a message, yet he did not heed it. And now he is . . ." She sobbed again. "Oh, Bartholomew."

If Anna had been well enough to go to him, would she be dead, too? "You know not what he wished to tell you, though."

"He'd not had time to explain when I saw him in the square. For the master of the troupe came upon us." The dairymaid clutched her skirts. "He shouted at Bartholomew to return to his practice. That the play was more important than dallying with women. The fellow's face was so black with rage, it was. Such rage as though he despised Bartholomew."

Old Jellis, Mother Fletcher, Jeffrey Poynard, David Merrick, plus the master of the troupe? Who was *not* to be suspected?

"I have heard whispers of others who may have despised Master Reade," said Bess. "Including someone within this house."

The girl chewed her bottom lip. "That night, I thought I saw . . . but it could not be . . ."

"Who, Anna?" prodded Bess. "What did you see? And where? From your window here?"

"No. No. I saw naught of import, Widow Ellyott. I was ill and my brain muddy." She shook her head, and fear darkened her eyes. "God mend me, 'twas nothing at all."

CHAPTER 9

A newly hung cross fashioned from elder twigs had been affixed to the lintel of Robert's front door. Frowning, Bess passed beneath it and unlatched the door, stepping inside.

Joan met her in the entry passage. "How is the girl this morn?"

"She is recovered." Bess handed off her cloak and satchel. "But I feel she has important information about Master Reade's murder. Unfortunately, she will not share it. I could not force her to tell me. She is too afraid."

"Has she heard the news already, Mistress?"

"As I said, she is aware of Master Reade's death."

"Not that, Mistress," said Joan. "About the drunken, frail fellow accused of the murder. He has died. The people of the village are rumbling louder about the witch's curse."

Jesu. "How did he die?"

"Of a sudden. His heart failed him."

"Not murder, then. But it is troublesome that the villagers continue to want to blame a witch. Humphrey will be hanging more elder crosses." Bess entered the hall and glanced over at the staircase. "Has Ellyn arisen yet? I would tell her that Anna has recovered."

"She was yet abed when I looked in on her earlier," she answered. "Mistress Crofton came down to break her fast, but when she heard that another man has died, she retreated to your good brother's bedchamber with head pains."

"We should leave Dorothie in peace," said Bess. "Let me know when Ellyn awakens. In the meanwhile, I have work to do in the still room. Mayhap it will calm my mind."

She crossed the hall and entered the room where she prepared her physic, which stood off the lobby behind the kitchen. The day's clouds cast the room in shadows, and she lit the lantern inside. The flame flickered off the jars arrayed atop the room's shelves, her supply of copper alembics set near the brick furnace in the corner, the herbs that hung from the ceiling beams. She inhaled deeply, hoping the aromas that scented the space would calm her, as they usually did.

This time, they failed.

Quail poked his head around the edge of the doorstead.

"Ah, Quail," she said, tying an apron around her skirts. "How do we find ourselves in such a muddle once more, hmm?"

The dog had no answer and tapped off to visit Joan in the nearby kitchen.

Bess unsealed a small jar of powered hound's-tongue and pepper she had previously prepared and poured a quantity into a waiting bowl. She was reaching for another jar containing caraway seeds when she heard the rap of feet against flagstone outside the room.

Ellyn Merrick stood in the doorway, a thin robe covering her shift.

"Good morrow, Ellyn. I asked Joan to alert me when you arose, but here you are," said Bess. "Did you sleep well?"

"I stole past her watchful gaze, I suppose," she answered,

wrapping her arms about her waist. "And yes, I did sleep well. Thanks to your physic."

Bess tipped out a quantity of the caraway seeds into her heavy bronze mortar, then resealed the jar. "How do you feel this morn?"

"Better. Foolish. I regret that I caused you to fret for my safety when you have been so kind," she said. "And you have been kind. Kinder than I deserve."

"We shall leave your actions in the past. What say you?"

Ellyn nodded.

With her pestle, Bess ground the seeds into powder. "I should tell you that Anna is well. I went to visit her not a half hour ago."

"I am pleased to hear that."

Finished with grinding, she set down the pestle and added the powdered seeds to the bowl. "She is frightened, though, after what happened to Master Reade," she said, looking over at Ellyn. "I cannot shake the feeling that she might have witnessed something important."

"I would presume everyone in the village and countryside is afraid, Mistress," she replied smoothly. If Ellyn had any suspicion that a member of her household had been involved in Master Reade's death, neither her face nor her voice betrayed the sentiment. "I know I am."

"You are safe here, Ellyn," said Bess with a reassuring smile. She turned to hunt through her various herbs until she found the dried betony she sought. "The man accused of killing him has died."

"Oh!"

"I am told he was frail," said Bess, retrieving her pottery jar of clarified honey. "His heart failed him, surely from the shock of his arrest and all that has occurred."

"God be thanked that this dreadful business is concluded," said Ellyn. "What do you make there?"

"A simple for the catarrh," answered Bess. "The barber's wife is afflicted. The physic she has made for herself has not succeeded in relieving her thick cough."

"I have used sugar in aqua vitae as a cure," said Ellyn.

Bess looked over at her. "Have you?" She had a thought. "Mayhap when you are stronger, you can help me. I would greatly enjoy teaching you what I know of simples, and perhaps learn from you as well."

"That would be most pleasant, Mistress." Ellyn smiled, her gaze taking in the room. "You have many fine spices and herbs."

The betony and honey went into the bowl with the rest of the ingredients, and Bess picked up a spoon to mix all together. "Thanks to my brother, who brings them from London on his travels there for business. He is most generous, for I could not afford them without his support."

"Your niece has always spoken lovingly of Master Marshall. He sounds a good man."

"He is indeed. My sister is here, by the way. Without Margery, unfortunately," said Bess. "You may encounter her."

"I look forward to hearing news of Margery."

The mention of family gave Bess the perfect excuse to broach the subject of David Merrick. A man she was definitely curious about. "I met your brother David yesterday."

"You did?"

"I did," said Bess. "A most serious sort of fellow. At least, that is my impression of him."

"He can be most serious. When my father is away, David is responsible for the dairy." She sounded proud.

Bess finished mixing and lifted the spoon to let the thick syrup drip back into the bowl. "What did your brother think of Bartholomew Reade?"

"They had been schoolmates."

"Friends." Not what Bess had been led to believe. Mayhap Marcye had been wrong about David's hatred for the man. Bess set aside the spoon and selected a clean jar from among the supply waiting on a shelf. "He must have been pleased his friend had returned with the troupe."

For the first time since she'd come to stand in the doorway, Ellyn's steady regard faltered. "He did not speak of Bartholomew of late. I know not my brother's feelings about his return."

"Did he imagine Master Reade had returned to take you to London with him?" asked Bess. "I have heard of his plans to go to the city."

"You have been asking questions?"

"There has been much talk, Ellyn."

"My parents desire me to marry Jeffrey Poynard," she replied. "A union that could bring us all wealth and standing. My father has promised him a portion, should we wed."

"But you do not want him, even though you carried his child," said Bess softly.

Ellyn went ashen. "You have heard a great deal."

"Did he know about the child?"

"*I* did not tell him," said the lovely woman who stood before her. A woman both strong and frail at the same time. A woman Bess could not help but pity.

"Why do you not wish to marry him?" asked Bess. "He would provide well for you."

"Have you ever met Jeffrey Poynard, Mistress Ellyott?"

"No, I have not." *But I feel I should.*

"Should you ever, you might discover why wealth and standing are insufficient."

"I already understand why, Ellyn," Bess replied, her heart filling with every emotion she'd ever felt for Martin. "I married for love."

"I would that my family would allow me to wed for love. But now . . ." She swayed and reached for the doorpost.

"Ellyn!" Bess rushed to her side as she slid to the ground. "Joan! Come now! Quickly!"

★　★　★

"Constable, forgive me if you waited long at the door," said Bess Ellyott's servant. She dipped a curtsy. "Come inside the hall, sir."

Kit followed her, ducking into the room. It was empty, save for Robert Marshall's dog, which briefly lifted its head to give Kit a look.

"I will fetch my mistress," said Joan, scurrying off.

After a short wait, footfalls sounded on the staircase set between this room and the parlor on the other side. Bess Ellyott entered the hall, an apron tied over her gown and strands of her brown hair springing loose from her coif.

He tapped the brim of his hat in greeting. "Good morrow, Mistress. Do I interrupt?"

"No, Constable," she replied, tucking the hair back beneath the linen covering her head. The spicy scent of herbs rose from her clothing. "But if you wish to speak to Ellyn again, she truly is not well enough. She fainted from weakness and distress and should be permitted to rest."

"I'm not here to speak with her."

"And I presume you are not here to speak with my sister,

who swoons upon my brother's bed upstairs, or my servants. Which leaves me." She lowered herself onto the room's settle. Her brother's dog sauntered over to lay at her feet and nap. She gestured for Kit to take the large chair before the hearth. "Is there fresh news?"

"Have you heard that the man held in the jail for killing Bartholomew Reade has died?" he asked, dropping onto the chair.

"I have." She lifted her brows. "Are you here to ask if I also believe a witch cursed him?"

"I noticed the elder above your door."

"My brother's manservant hung it there. Prithee, Constable, protect Mother Fletcher. Her life is in jeopardy if the townsfolk insist on these accusations."

"They have demanded that the priest inspect the old woman's skin to search for evil marks, Mistress," he said. "Master Enderby volunteered his services instead." The venerable churchwarden, quick to root out sin and guilt, even where it didn't exist.

"Mother Fletcher will receive no kind treatment from him. I must go to her." Bess Ellyott made to rose.

Kit lifted a hand. "Stay, Mistress. Stay. Gibb and I will do what we can to protect her." She retook her seat, and he glanced around, searching for ears attached to prying servants. "Mistress, you know a great deal about physic. Is it possible for someone to have poisoned Jellis, killing him but leaving no visible evidence?"

"I presumed his heart . . . was he ill before his death?"

"Not that I'd heard," he said. "But could it be possible?"

"It is not *impossible* to have poisoned Goodman Jellis," she replied. "Though I cannot name, I confess, a poison he might have consumed without his stomach rebelling and leaving proof inside the jail. Further, would the true murderer—if Goodman

Jellis was not actually responsible—seek to be rid of the fellow? The goodman was accused of the crime and, sadly, would likely have hung for it. Why alter the course of destiny?"

Kit buffed the back of his knuckles along the length of his chin. She was right. If Reade's purse had been left with Jellis to implicate him in the murder, the true killer had succeeded— Jellis had been taken to jail. Why kill him now?

"I'faith, if he was old and frail, I am surprised his heart did not fail him earlier," said Bess.

"The burgesses want me to stop any investigation," he said. "The man responsible, according to them, has died."

"But you will not stop, will you? For you are rigorous in the execution of your duties, Constable."

"You think too well of me, madam." He'd not always been the man who sat before her. Reasonably prosperous. Adequately respected. Responsible and rigorous.

"I know a good man when I see one, Constable Harwoode," she said with a gentle smile, which lit her eyes. "But what do we now?"

"'We,' Mistress?" he asked, as he'd asked her before. "It's clear I cannot convince you to stop involving yourself."

"You came to *me*, Constable, with your question about poison."

"So I did."

Her smile broadened, and his gaze dwelled too long upon the curve of her mouth.

"The knife the killer used has been found, but no owner for it," he said, drawing his attention back to the task at hand. "Mistress Merrick says David Merrick supped with her the night of Reade's death. The players claim that the master of the troupe,

John Howlett, feuded with Reade over Howlett's theft of a play. And Jeffrey Poynard—"

"Ellyn has admitted he was the father of her child," she interrupted. "But she would not wed him, loving Bartholomew Reade as she did and despising Master Poynard."

"Poynard insists that any number of his household can account for him the day of Reade's death," replied Kit. "Further, he claims he no longer had a dispute with the fellow."

"According to Marcye Johnes, the night of the troupe's arrival, he came into the Cross Keys to declare he and Master Reade were boon companions."

"Suspicious."

"I have learned more. One of the Merricks' dairymaids, Anna Webb, saw the master of the troupe with Master Reade. She tells me he appeared to be most furious," said Mistress Ellyott. "Perhaps he is our murderer, Constable."

"Perhaps so."

"Anna also told me that it was *she* who was to meet Bartholomew Reade at the old fort hill. However, she fell ill that morning and was unable to go."

A coincidence he did not care for. "You are certain she was truly unwell."

"I tended to her. She did not feign sickness as an alibi, Constable." She leaned her head against the high wooden back of the settle and stared at the beams overhead. The dog at her feet took to snoring. "Unlike Master Reade's fellow players, Anna is no actor."

"I trust your judgment, Mistress Ellyott."

"Anna attempted to inform Master Reade she would not meet him, but . . ." She shifted her head to look at him, her brows tucking together. "I wonder who she entrusted the message to? I did not think to ask."

"It matters not, Mistress. Obviously that person did not complete their task, as Master Reade went to the trysting spot."

"True." Footsteps tapped across the flags of the lobby that led from the rear courtyard into the house, and she waited until the person making the noise moved away. "But I must tell you this, Constable." She scooted to the edge of the settle and leaned toward him. "I think Anna observed someone at the Merricks' house acting most strangely that even, which caused her to mistrust what this person was doing."

"Did she give you a name?"

"No," she whispered. "'Tis but a suspicion of mine, but I must conclude she spied one of the Merricks. 'Twould explain why she will not give me a name. Any servant would be reluctant to accuse a master or mistress of a crime. I wonder, though, if it was David Merrick she observed."

"His mother has vouched that he was with her at supper, Mistress, and I cannot act upon a suspicion alone," he said. Though Mistress Merrick would have every reason to lie to protect her eldest son. "I need two witnesses before I can accuse him of the crime."

"Sadly, the man most likely to have seen the murder and its perpetrator has perished in the town jail."

Kit's mouth lifted with a wry smile. They had returned to the curious, sudden death of an old drunk. "Jellis was most accommodating, wasn't he?"

★   ★   ★

Bess stood in the street doorway of Robert's house. She watched the constable stride off down the lane, skirting a bundle of thatching in readiness to repair a roof and startling a cat that had been stalking mice among the pile. The house owner tipped his cap at Kit Harwoode, who gave him just a fleeting glance. Unlike the overcurious stares of the kitchen servant of Bess's neighbor across the way. She sat on the doorstep plucking feathers off a dead chicken, her gawping split between the constable and Bess.

"Good morrow," Bess called out to her, making the girl flush over her inquisitiveness.

Bess went back inside and met Joan in the hall. "We are to be the gossip of the village again, if the constable keeps paying us visits."

Joan peered through the street-facing window. "That one, Mistress, knows not when to mind her own business."

"Come now, Joan, I'd be curious also," said Bess. "And though the constable was here, he brought only more questions, no answers."

"Mayhap Simon will have an answer," said Joan. "While you were with the constable, a servant from the Poynards' house brought a message urging you to come tend to the lad and his fever."

"He is ill?"

"Nay, Mistress. 'Tis the signal he and I decided upon, should he have aught to tell you."

"Can he not come here and tell me his news?"

"He finds himself in trouble for wandering off, of late, and dare not leave the grounds," said Joan.

"Then fetch my satchel and place a bottle with my water of sorrel inside. We must make my visit to Simon appear as authentic as possible." A visit that would also permit her, perhaps, a chance to observe Jeffrey Poynard.

"Aye, madam," Joan said, and hurried off.

Bess headed for the entry door. She encountered Humphrey, who'd come in from the street with a bundle of branches in his arms.

"They charge a great amount for firewood again, Mistress."

"I will make note of your complaint and tell my good brother when he returns," she answered.

"Mayhap you might tell the constable, as he could see them fined," he said, his gaze narrowing. "He be here often enough."

"I will consider your recommendation, Humphrey."

"'Twould also be best for Joan to use less wood, Mistress."

Bess smiled stiffly. She'd no time for servants' quarrels. "I will speak with her."

Grumbling, he stomped into the hall.

Joan returned and handed Bess her satchel. "What did Humphrey want, Mistress?"

"To complain. As ever," she said.

"Should Mistress Crofton arise from her bed and ask, am I to tell her what you are about?" asked Joan.

"Most definitely not, Joan. Tell my sister anything except that I go to hear what news your friend Simon has gathered. Dorothie would not be happy with me involving myself in this affair."

Satchel in hand, Bess went out into the street. The neighbor's kitchen servant pretended not to notice her, but no doubt squinted after Bess as she hurried along the lane toward the market square. Marcye was out sweeping the cobbles in front of the Cross Keys, her gaze tracking Bess's passage. The girl spent more time, it seemed, outside the tavern than inside helping her father with his customers.

Outside, observing.

Bess redirected her steps and strolled over to Marcye. "Good morrow," she called out.

"Good morrow, Widow Ellyott." She leaned against her broom. "Have you more questions for me?"

"I may. About Goodman Jellis."

"Sad fellow," she said. "Now he's dead, the burgesses have demanded that the constable cease his inquiry."

Marcye Johnes appeared to know a great deal about Kit Harwoode. More than made Bess comfortable.

"The constable told me about their demand, but how did you learn of it?" she asked, wondering if she sounded jealous. *Fie, Bess. Do not be a goose.* Besides, Marcye was reaching above her station. Kit Harwoode was kinsman to the lord of the manor.

"Several of the burgesses were in the tavern yestereven, after the coroner had made his ruling," she said. "They complain that Kit . . . that the constable would likely continue as he pleased despite Old Jellis being accused and then dying. They mislike him, you know. For being headstrong. But I admire him for his stubbornness. And courage."

Oh, do you?

"You can see the jail from here, albeit not too clearly." Bess turned to point toward it, just visible around the corner of the weaver's shop.

"Aye."

"Perchance, did you observe a cause that might account for Goodman Jellis's sudden death?"

"I cannot see through stone walls, Mistress."

"Let me be more plain," said Bess. "Did anyone visit him and, mayhap, distress the old man? Perhaps cause his heart to fail him?"

Marcye tapped a broken fingernail against the broom handle

and stared in the direction of the jail. "Jeffrey Poynard came to speak with him," she said, a knowing smile curling her lips as though gleeful to be in possession of such a fact.

Was that the information Simon also wished to share?

"Are you certain it was him and not Master David Merrick?" asked Bess.

"Master Poynard owns a bespangled doublet of silvery velvet," she replied. "I would know that doublet and the stride of the man wearing it anywhere."

"Did they argue?"

"I did not stand about and pry, Widow Ellyott," she answered without irony. "There was the ado over Ellyn Merrick having gone missing, which dragged us all away to search."

A commotion that offered a perfect distraction from the fellow who visited Goodman Jellis. A visit that had ended in the fellow's death.

CHAPTER 10

"I am Widow Ellyott," said Bess to the Poynards' maidservant who had answered her knock. "A servant named Simon has sent for me."

"Come to the garden gate at the side, Widow Ellyott," said the girl. "He be in his room at the end of the outbuilding."

She shut the door on Bess, forcing her to find the gate that must be somewhere along the length of the stone wall. Bess passed the windows of the Poynards' ground-floor offices but caught no glimpse of a man in a gray velvet doublet. She saw another fellow, possibly a clerk, but not Jeffrey Poynard. Besides, what might a glimpse gain her? Would guilt be writ upon his forehead? She needed more than a glimpse.

The maidservant was waiting for Bess at the open garden gate, located halfway along the wall that enclosed the large rear garden and grounds.

"Here, Mistress."

The girl hurried across the broad courtyard, Bess taking long strides to keep apace with her. Ahead stood a long outbuilding. A series of small windows and doors at either end of its length broke the building's expanse of whitewashed cob walls. To her right, a gardener trimmed the lavender, rosemary, and winter savory of a knot garden. The steady clip of his shears accompanied his humming, audible over the burble of the garden's central fountain. Beyond stood a small orchard of fruit trees, and land stretched all the way to the river at the far end of the property. A summerhouse had been built atop a small rise. From beneath its roof, the views guests would have of the garden and fruit orchard would be magnificent.

"Simon took to shivering so, Mistress, though he was hale earlier this morn."

The girl's comment broke through Bess's reverie; she was not here to admire the Poynards' garden. "It is good I was sent for, then."

The maidservant stopped a distance from the outbuilding and pointed. "He be in the room at the end."

She did not blame the maidservant for not wanting to get any closer to a supposedly ailing Simon. So Bess proceeded the rest of the way on her own, which also meant she and the boy might have privacy.

She pushed open the room's door, its hinges squealing. "Simon?"

The space stank of moldering straw and the unseen animals that occupied the range of stalls beyond an opening in the wall at her left. Not only did the room stink, it was dank and windowless. Bess squinted into the shadows and made out a stool in one corner and a pile of rags in the other.

"I am Widow Ellyott. Simon, are you in here? I received your message."

The pile of rags in the corner moved. "Mistress?" a voice uttered feebly.

Mayhap the boy was actually ill.

She set her satchel on the earthen floor and bent over him.

"How do you feel?" she asked, resting the back of her hand against her forehead. It was slightly warm but not hot to the touch.

He shifted into the light cast by the open doorway. His head was covered by a mass of curling brown hair, and his eyes were the color of the moss that grew along the trunks of trees. If he were to grin, Bess expected a dimple would form in his cheek. He was very young, though. Still a child.

"Are you alone?" he croaked. "You have not been followed?"

"Aye, Simon," she said. "I have not."

"Are you sure, Mistress?"

"I will go see," she said.

Which she did, assuring herself that no one listened outside the doorway.

"We are quite alone," she said, returning to his side with the stool and taking a seat on it. "What is it you want to tell me? For my touch informs me you are not ill."

He elbowed himself upright from the straw mattress he was lying on. "I saw someone at the jail yesterday," he said, leaning against the cob wall behind him. "Afore Jellis died."

"Marcye Johnes . . . do you know Marcye, Simon?"

He flashed a grin, his cheek dimpling as anticipated. Two of his front teeth were chipped. "Everyone knows Marcye Johnes, Mistress."

Even the constable, it seemed. "On my way here, I spoke with her. She told me that Master Jeffrey Poynard had visited Goodman Jellis at the jail."

"Aye, he did, Mistress. I saw him there too."

"Know you why he would have done so?" she asked. "Goodman Jellis does not seem the sort of person Master Poynard would care a fig for."

"Old Jellis used to work for the Poynards," he explained. "Before I came here. But he drank too much. Bungled up his tasks when he was cup-shotten. Then they blamed Jellis for stealing from the mistress, when she was still alive, and were rid of him. Or so I hear."

"Did you observe Master Poynard do anything that might have hurt Goodman Jellis?"

"He weren't there long enough to have hurt him," he said. "Peeped in, jumped back in a fright, and run off, his face white as whale's bone."

"Could the old man have already been dead?" she mused aloud.

"Must have been."

"Why has he not told the constable, I wonder."

"He'd be blamed, would he not? For killing Jellis."

"Not if he told the truth about what he'd discovered. Master Poynard is a wealthy man." And wealthy men were never to be doubted.

"Master Jeffrey is afeard of the witch, Mistress. If he spoke out, he'd draw her curse upon himself!" Simon declared. "I have no fear of her, though. Not like my mates. This morn, they went to the old fort hill to look for that weasel what come from a witch somewheres. Wish I could have gone, but I couldn't. They did not find one, though, because they turned tail afore they could."

"They should not be hunting about for familiars or witches that do not exist, Simon."

"But I saw her myself!" He lifted his chin, unhappy to be reproved. "Not a quarter hour afore Master Poynard was at the jail. Wrapped in her cloak, hiding her face."

"If you mean to claim you saw Mother Fletcher, she is too

frail to journey into the village," said Bess. "And do not tell me that she rode a broom to get there; she is no witch. Furthermore, though Marcye made note of Master Poynard at the jail, she did not notice this woman you describe."

He set his jaw stubbornly. "I know what I saw, Mistress. And the churchwarden *will* find warts on her shriveled skin when he goes to look."

Prithee, Constable, stop them from their madness.

Bess pulled in a steadying breath and smiled at Simon. "My thanks, lad. You have given me much to think on," she said. "If any should stop and ask me, I shall say that I gave you a physic to speed you to good health. That is our story."

"Aye, Mistress."

Bess rose from the stool and collected her satchel. "Take good care, lad."

"It *was* a witch what killed Jellis, Mistress."

"Take care," she repeated.

She departed, closing the outbuilding door behind her, and strode across the courtyard. The gardener had moved on from the knot garden to harvest pears from a tree growing by the far wall. No other servants were in sight, which hopefully meant that her conversation with Simon had not been overheard.

She regretted, though, that she could not rid the boy of his belief that witchcraft was responsible for two recent deaths. The idea had seized hold of the townsfolk like the shaking sweats of a deadly disease; Bess only endangered herself by attempting to contradict their certainty. But she could not step blithely aside and allow them to harm the old woman.

She'd almost reached the gate when a man called out to her.

"Mistress Ellyott," he called again.

He walked with great ground-eating strides, the short cloak

he'd tied over his broad shoulders—and a silvery doublet—flapping behind him. A tall hat overtopped his black hair, and a groomed beard drew attention to his well-shaped jaw.

"Ah, Mistress Ellyott," he said once more when he reached her.

"You have me at an advantage, sir, for you know my name but I know not yours."

He offered a leg. When he straightened, a smile sat on his mouth. "I am Jeffrey Poynard."

Your identity was past question, truth be told.

"Good morrow, then, Master Poynard."

"How is Simon?" he asked. "I heard you were called to tend to him."

"He improves already, for he is strong," she answered. "I did ply him with a physic, though, to ensure that his recovery continues apace. He should be ready to return to his work by this evening."

He waved off the suggestion. "Let him rest. I'll not ask him to rise from his sick bed until necessary. Tomorrow at the earliest."

"That is most generous of you," she said. "He is a good lad."

He grinned, which made his dark eyes sparkle. "But an overcurious one, at times."

Alarm prickled along Bess's skin. "I find most servants to be curious about their masters and mistresses. Our lives intrigue them."

"Are you intriguing, Mistress? I think so," he said, sending a flush across her skin to displace the prickles of alarm. She knew she was not unhandsome, some might even call her pretty, but she had not the sort of wealth or connections that might attract his interest.

"I am but an herbalist and a healer, Master Poynard. Not in

the least intriguing." Out of the corner of her eye, Bess noticed that the maidservant who had answered the door watched them from the rear porch of the house. Proof of servants' curiosity.

"Think you so?" he asked. "Your brother speaks well of you."

"Robert?" He had spoken to Jeffrey Poynard about her? "When he returns from London, I shall chastise him for gossiping about me."

"He frets over you. I believe it was some matter concerning the murder of your brother-in-law that caused him to fear for your well-being," he said. "You discovered who the killer was."

"Nay, 'twas the constable who discovered the killer. And I try to put that event out of my mind, Master Poynard." However, she had not, to this point, succeeded.

"And now Mistress Ellyn Merrick receives your care," he said, as though Bess's involvement in the search for her brother-in-law's killer and her tending to Ellyn were connected.

"I turn no one away."

"Ah." He drew fingertips down the length of his beard, much as Constable Harwoode was inclined to do. The many rings he wore sparkled in the hazy sunlight. "Her illness does astonish me. I spoke with her but a few days past, and she was well at that time. To be stricken so suddenly . . ."

Bess returned his scrutiny with a bland face. If he did not know about Ellyn's pregnancy, she'd not reveal it. "I am thankful that I could help her."

"But then to flee your help . . . most curious, that."

Careful, Bess. "Her good reason is muddled by the distress caused by the death of her friend, Master Reade."

"He was more than a friend to her, Mistress Ellyott," he said.

"As are you, I have heard," she blurted out. "Or, I should say, you have hoped to be."

"Ah, Mistress Ellyott, you are indeed intriguing." He was smiling again. "Ellyn Merrick and I intend to wed."

Sourness rose to think of Ellyn tethered to this man who'd have his way. Who'd not called upon her to assure her of his affection and concern for her well-being, yet wished to take her as his wife. Was she but a possession he longed to own, her resistance only serving to make her all the more desirable? Was the portion her father had promised so great an enticement that Ellyn's disgust for Master Poynard was insufficient to dissuade him?

"I offer you my congratulations, Master Poynard," said Bess. 'Twas impossible for her to impart any warmth to her words. The sentiment would only be a lie. "However, I beg you to wait to marry until she is well healed and her mind at ease over this recent tragedy."

"You have my word on it," he said, offering a bow.

"Though surely Master Reade's death distresses you as well, sir. When it came at the hand of one of your former retainers," she said. "You must have been surprised that Goodman Jellis could have committed such a foul crime. Did you have a chance to speak with him to beg an explanation?"

His eyes darkened, as if a heavy cloud had passed over the sun and cast them in shadows. *Careful, Bess. Careful.* Her query had been too obvious, and she had shown her game.

"I required no explanation, Mistress Ellyott. Jellis was a drunkard and a thief," he replied smoothly. "I did speak with him, however. To tell him I would pray for him. His foul habits finally brought him the sorrow I always feared they would."

To pray for him?

"I also have offered to pay for his burial on the morrow," he added. "His daughter cannot afford the cost of the pitiful ritual a wrongdoer such as he will be allowed to receive."

"That is most kind of you."

"You act amazed that I could be kind, Mistress," he said. "I am aware someone has been witless enough to speak out of turn about me. I advise you to ignore their words. Or, mayhap, to think closely as to why this person casts suspicion on me. 'Tis not because *I* am the guilty one. Now I bid you good day."

He inclined his head, turned on his heel, and strode off.

She watched him walk back to the house, the maidservant who'd been spying on them gone from her spot upon the porch. Bess hugged her arms about her body as a sudden blow of wind scattered dust across the courtyard and sent the kitchen's chimney smoke streaming. She had learned nothing of import from Jeffrey Poynard.

A suspicion occurred to her that he, however, had learned what he'd wanted from her.

★ ★ ★

"Ah, here you are, Master Howlett," said Kit.

He signaled to the alewife to bring a tankard. He'd sent Gibb to confront the churchwarden over his plan to examine Mother Fletcher. Now to confront John Howlett about his dispute with Reade.

Howlett looked up from his tankard as Kit straddled the bench Howlett sat on, facing him. The alehouse window shutters had been let down, indicating the proprietor was serving drink to be enjoyed outside by those who'd no wish or time to crowd inside the cramped single room. An inquisitive townsman, who'd been waiting to be served, leaned through the opening and stared.

"Where else might I be in this benighted town, Constable?" asked John Howlett. He was without cosmetics today and looked to be younger than Kit had previously thought him.

The alewife brought over a pewter tankard and a blackjack of ale, pouring out a quantity before bustling off to her other customers.

"I hope you do not mind if I join you," said Kit.

"If you come to tell me that Jeffrey Poynard is at last willing to pay us the ten shillings we are owed, Constable Harwoode, then I welcome your company," he said. "We earn no money by staying in this dismal town full of farmers and dairymen. I wish to be on our way to Bath before our warrant to travel expires. God save us if we are trapped here!"

The inquisitive townsman had been joined by the smith in his heavy leather apron. Where were the prying eyes, Kit wondered, when a man had been murdered?

Rather than squeeze against the window to gawp, a handful of farm laborers tromped inside. They plodded over to a set of unoccupied stools, loose floor rushes clinging to their muddy, scuffed boots. A whiff of manure drifted behind them as they walked past Kit and Howlett.

"'Tis not an unpleasant part of Wiltshire, Master Howlett," Kit said, and swallowed some ale.

"I would expect you to think so, Constable, as you live here," said Howlett. "And I might agree, were the Poynards willing to offer us another opportunity to perform and earn some money. I have bills. Or, at the least, pay the fee we had already agreed upon."

"You did not present your play," said Kit.

"Am I to be blamed for that?" he asked. "'Tis not my fault that Bartholomew Reade got himself stabbed to death. Bah."

"Ah, yes, about Master Reade . . ."

Howlett eyed him over the top of his tankard. He set it down. A skim of foam clung to his upper lip. "Why do you and your assistant continue to question me and my men? We have explained where we were the night of Reade's murder. Willim Dunning found his body. He did not see one of his fellow players murder the man, and he did not kill Reade himself, else he'd not have admitted to finding him," he said. "Besides, that old sot was accused."

"An old, frail, harmless sot, Master Howlett. So I remain uncontented and continue to ask questions," said Kit. "Such as, could it be you are eager to depart this benighted town because you do not want me to conclude you desired to be rid of Bartholomew Reade?"

"I have just explained why I am eager to leave, Constable," said Howlett. "And I had no cause to be rid of Reade."

"Did you not?" asked Kit. "What about a quarrel over a play that you wanted from him but which he'd not allow you to perform?"

The expanse of neck above Howlett's ruff turned red. "A quarrel? That is a lie," he hissed.

"Is it also a lie that Reade had threatened to contact officials to report that you were putting on plays for which you did not have a license?" Kit asked. "Your days as the leader of a troupe, Master Howlett, would come to an abrupt end if those officials were to find you guilty."

"Would I murder for that?"

"I know not, Master Howlett," said Kit. "But it's easy to imagine—many would agree with me—that you followed Reade to his tryst on that hillock and struck him down. You were gone from the area before Dunning happened upon the body."

"I did not kill Bartholomew Reade!" He slammed a fist onto the bench, startling the alehouse mongrel, which began to bark from its spot in the corner of the room. The alewife hushed the

animal. "If you do not believe that harmless drunk was responsible, why not question the fellow who argued with Reade in
the Poynards' courtyard? Forsooth, they fought most violently
over some woman."

The argument Bess Ellyott had also mentioned. "Perhaps I
will question him. Who was he?"

"A clean-shaven man. Short of stature. Plain in appearance,"
said Howlett. "Know you such a man?"

"I may, Master Howlett."

And his name was David Merrick.

CHAPTER 11

"Mother Fletcher?" Bess rapped upon the woman's rough and unpainted front door, catching a splinter in her ungloved hand.

"Ouch," she muttered, and plucked the sliver of wood from her knuckle. A drip of blood squeezed from the tiny wound.

She stepped back and squinted for any sign of life. No smoke rose from the opening in the far end of the thatched roof. The lone window on the front of the cob house was shuttered.

Hiking her skirts to slog across the uneven ground, Bess went around the side of the building. The wattle fence that surrounded the messuage was in disrepair, sections completely absent. Bess passed through a gap, stepping over the broken remains of the twigs and branches that had been woven to form the fencing. In the rear yard, a solitary chicken pecked in the dirt. The remnants of an herb garden drooped and rotted in a far corner of the yard. Along the back wall of the cottage, another window was also shuttered, the adjacent door closed tight.

Bess pounded on it anyway. "Mother Fletcher? 'Tis Bess Ellyott. I have come to see how you are."

She rattled the handle, but the door was latched and locked. With care for more splinters, she leaned an ear against the wood.

She heard nothing. Had the woman perished overnight? Was Bess too late to warn her about the danger she faced from the angry townspeople? She could detect no sign that anyone had forced his way into the house and harmed her, though. Perhaps the widow had already fled, having heard of the churchwarden's intentions and realizing she was no longer safe in this village.

Beware, madam, for one day they may turn on you. As they have turned on me.

Those had been her words to Bess. But to where had she gone, and who might have helped her? For the old woman had no horse or cart by which to travel.

"I pray you are unharmed, Mother Fletcher. Wherever you are," whispered Bess.

Gathering her skirts once more, Bess trudged back to the lane and headed for the highway. She was but a dozen yards from it when she heard the sound of a horse at full gallop. The rider and his animal charged up the road away from town, the horse's hooves flinging dirt and stones.

Where, I wonder, is Jeffrey Poynard going in such suspicious haste?

★   ★   ★

"Christopher!" cried a female voice.

Kit, who'd been striding across the market square intending to go to the Merricks', halted. Only one woman, besides his mother, called him by his given name.

He waited for her to join him. "Good day to you, Frances."

Gibb's sister hurried over, her sea-green dress, held wide from her hips by a thick bum roll, swaying. No, she did not hurry. Frances never hurried. She took her time to do everything, every action planned with the care of a general going into battle, and that included stopping Kit in the square.

"Come now, Christopher, do not frown at me so." Leaning past her ruff—dyed a paler shade of the green of her gown—she raised on her toes to kiss him on the cheek. The scent of nutmeg and other sharp spices drifted from the silver pomander slung from her girdle. "You have not come to the house in months. Gibb says you are most busy."

"My regrets to you and your father, my good uncle, over my absence," he said. "I only just learned from Gibb you were back from Gloucester, though."

"You should have come to visit anyway."

"Gibb isn't mistaken, Frances. I *am* busy."

"And I am your most beloved cousin, whom you should desire to pass away an afternoon with," she said, smiling winsomely. She was an attractive woman, and after losing her merchant husband to a severe attack of dropsy, Kit had expected her to find a fresh one to replace him. But she seemed content to live in the Harwoode family home with a doting father and equally doting brother. Happy to enjoy the freedom that came with being a widow. Like another widow he knew.

"Has Gibb informed you of my hope you will agree to host a small supper as a welcome for my friend tomorrow?" she asked.

"What?"

"Goodness. He did not, I gather."

"No, he did not," he said. "I am too busy, Frances. There has been a murder—"

"Ah, that," she said. "Father says you waste your time. He thinks you should not meddle in the affairs of the Poynards and the Merricks."

"Does he now?" asked Kit. "And does he forbid Gibb to assist me?"

"Not as yet," she answered. "Come now, Christopher, this

supper requires almost none of your time or effort. You have Alice to help, do you not? And I shall send one of our servants over to assist her. I would host the gathering at our house, but the damage from our kitchen fire last week has yet to be fully repaired."

"Alice is no help," he said bluntly. "She will likely burn down *my* kitchen while trying to cook some supper of yours, no matter how much assistance she gets from one of your servants."

"There is no need for you to be so dramatic," she said. "And Alice is keen to learn. I rather like her."

"How much time *have* you been spending with my servant, Frances?"

"You are not ever at your house when I come by, Christopher, so I speak with her instead."

And plot. "I repeat, I am too busy to entertain your friend, Frances."

"Certes, you are none so absorbed in your work as you pretend. I would have her meet all of the family," she said. "She tires of my company and that of Gibb's."

"I can understand being tired of his company."

She laughed, a sound both gentle and hearty at the same time. He could not dislike Frances. She was indeed his favorite cousin, and he cared for her dearly. As greatly as he would care for a sister, if he had one. He merely wished she did not try to control his life like she controlled all the other male Harwoodes' lives.

"I have even less time, Frances, if you intend to see me wed to this friend of yours," he said.

Frances's eyes widened in a display of false innocence. "Would I wish any of my friends to wed you, Christopher? I pity any woman who would have you. You are changeable and surly."

"Then why introduce her to me? I sound wretched."

"Because she might tame you."

"So you do plan on wedding her to me."

"You see through my feeble ruse." She kissed him again, and he thought of another woman he'd once loved long ago and lost. Whose kisses had been equally soft on his face. "I take my leave of you. And do not mistreat Alice so. She means well."

"I do not mistreat Alice."

"Pish, Christopher. 'Tis certain you do." She smiled and strolled off, back the way she'd come.

Out of the corner of his eye, he noticed that Marcye Johnes had been watching through the windows of the Cross Keys. A different location than was usual for her to spy on the square. Her gaze shifted to a spot behind him, and Kit looked over his shoulder at what had drawn her attention. The answer was exiting All Saints church.

Kit trotted toward the church, dodging a girl dragging a cart overladen with the last of the season's apples. One tumbled from the pile to roll across the cobbles. He stooped to retrieve it, tossing it to her as he angled to intercept David Merrick.

"Ah, Master Merrick," he called out. "I was about to go to your farm to speak with you, but you have saved me the journey."

"Constable," said Merrick, raising himself to his fullest height.

Kit nodded toward the church. "Praying for mercy, were you?"

"We all need mercy, Constable."

"Some more than others," replied Kit. "Why did you not tell me about the fight you had with Bartholomew Reade the afternoon of the day he was murdered? In the Poynards' courtyard."

He flushed. "Who claims this?"

"A reliable witness."

"The fight was of no import. A trivial disagreement."

"The description I have heard did not sound trivial," said Kit. "You make me reason that you hide something, Master Merrick."

His flushed cheeks gained dark splotches of red. "I hide nothing!"

"My witness also informs me you shouted at Master Reade to 'stay away from her.' Who did you mean?"

Merrick blinked rapidly. The bell of All Saints clanged the hour, which made him blink all the more. Kit was not proud that he was finding pleasure in the man's discomfort. He was becoming as loathsome as the queen's master interrogators.

"One of our dairymaids," he said. "Bartholomew plagued her with his unwanted attention."

"The warning had naught to do with your sister Ellyn."

"No."

Kit considered him. "Remind me where you had gone the afternoon of Reade's death and into the evening, Master Merrick."

"I thought to go to the Poynards' entertainment. Changed my mind. Instead, I supped with my mother. I believe she told you this as well."

Indeed, she had. "You should have informed me of your argument with Master Reade."

"I erred. I regret that," he said. "Might I go now, Constable? I must return to the farm."

Kit extended an arm and bowed over it. "Do not let me detain you, sir."

Merrick scuttled off, resisting the obvious temptation to glance back.

★　★　★

Bess attempted to keep the suspicious-acting Jeffrey Poynard in sight without letting him realize that she was chasing him. If he noticed her, he might deviate from his intended course. Which appeared to be the Merricks' farm.

He paid no heed to the old fort hill as he passed it. Did he avoid looking at the mound out of guilt? Or out of disinterest? She did not find it as comfortable as he did to pass by the hillock, and Bess crossed to the far side of the road.

She crested a low rise in the road. Up ahead, Jeffrey Poynard had halted his horse shy of the walkway to the Merricks' front door. A spot oddly distant from the house itself. He tossed the reins over the fence that bordered the front yard and strode up the hill. But he did not go to the house. Instead, he skirted the building and headed for the outbuildings at the rear.

Crouching, Bess gathered her skirts out of her way and hurried forward. She chose a path that hugged the shrubs and fading grasses filling the ditch alongside the road. They provided a screen between her and the furtive Master Poynard.

The Merricks' dairy cattle grazed in the meadow nearest the outbuildings, and smoke drifted from the kitchen chimney, a lazy curl of white. Bess crept between the stone wall edging the yard and an adjoining field, where a trod-way had beaten down the grass and weeds. The back of the house and the area behind it came into view. Two women were outside the dairy barn, just beyond its open door. They both wore the blue of servants. Bess was not near enough to clearly identify them, but she thought they were Anna and Thomasin. They stood very close to each other, deep in agitated conversation.

Just then, Jeffrey Poynard appeared around the far side of one of the barns. The women noticed him and stepped away from each other. He spoke to Anna for a moment, and she dashed into the dairy barn. He next went over to the woman Bess thought was Thomasin and began to talk to her. Not calmly, though, given Thomasin's vigorous responding gestures.

How curious. What could he possibly want with a Merrick dairymaid?

Hunched low, Bess padded forward, along the fence which followed the curve of the yard and drew closer to the barns and sheds that sprawled behind the house. Without hopping over the barrier, she'd never get near enough to hear what they said to each other.

Hoping the breeze might send a scrap of conversation her direction, she raised up to peep over the top of the stones. Master Poynard, his body taut, took hold of Thomasin's elbow. He dragged her around the far side of the barn, where neither the occupants of the house nor Bess could spy on them.

She shifted her stance in hopes of bringing them into view again, and heard the loud crack of a branch breaking beneath her shoe at the same moment she realized she'd stepped upon it. The noise was as loud as a gunshot, and she dropped to her knees. Her pulse pounding in her head, she clapped hands to her mouth to silence the rasp of her breathing. Someone had to have heard. Any second now, the person would charge down the incline of the yard and find her hiding behind the fence. She could not run off without being spotted, though. She could only wait and meanwhile concoct a story that would explain why she crouched in the muck.

I am here because I'd chosen to walk across the fields toward the house and twisted my ankle. I am here because I thought I saw Anna out with the cattle and I wished to speak with her, but twisted my ankle. I am here because my servant told me I could find mullein growing in the disturbed patch of ground along the stone fence and I am in need of some for my physic.

God help her. She was there because she suspected Jeffrey Poynard of murdering Bartholomew Reade and sought proof.

Voices carried on the breeze, more voices than just the two belonging to Jeffrey Poynard and Thomasin. Did their owners come close to where she hid? A raven cawed in a nearby tree as if mocking her. Further, her ankle ached from her foot having twisted as it slipped on the breaking branch. She'd need to hobble homeward. Presuming no one dragged her from her hidey-hole.

The voices did not draw near, but instead grew fainter. After a few moments, Bess risked straightening enough to easily see over the top of the fence. Thomasin and Jeffrey Poynard were gone. More importantly, no one was headed her direction to examine the source of the noise she'd made. A dog barked, and the thrum of hoofbeats sounded. She dropped down again as Jeffrey Poynard galloped his horse toward town. Intent upon controlling his animal, he did not look her way and see her watching his passage.

Once he'd gone by, Bess straightened. She took another look at the house and its outbuildings. It was then that a small object caught her eye. It lay on the other side of the low stone wall, having come to rest beneath a clump of thistle as though tossed there. Mindful of her ankle, she lifted up on her toes and leaned over the fence. Her eyes had not been mistaken.

Bess glanced around. Though she was in clear view of the barns and house, no one appeared to mark her presence. Hastily, she stretched out a hand and grabbed the item, drawing it back over the wall.

It was a figure made of brown holland stuffed with straw and feathers, its length no greater than the width of a man's splayed fingers. Wrapped in a pale cloth, it had a head and a torso, but no arms or legs. Nonetheless, she could tell the tiny effigy was meant to portray a person.

A shiver danced across her skin. It was an evil thing, meant to bring harm to someone.

For into its head and sides were stuck dozens of thorns.

Chapter 12

"Should you have touched it, Mistress?" Joan stared balefully at the effigy, which Bess had set atop her servant's worktable in the kitchen. The hearth firelight danced over the figure, causing the shadows cast by the thorns jabbed into it to jig as though alive. "Should we even have it inside our house? 'Tis cursed."

"It is but a poppet made of straw and wrapped in pale-blue cloth."

Quail padded over to the edge of the table and sniffed at the object, then slunk away to sit on his haunches by the hearth. If both Joan and the dog were wary of the poppet, then mayhap Bess should be afraid as well.

"'Tis a witch's creation, Mistress." Joan picked up a nearby spoon to prod the item. One of the thorns fell out to land upon the table. "The person whose name has been given to it will die within the week."

"We should not be superstitious, Joan," said Bess. "It may be merely a jest devised by some mischievous person, wishing to frighten someone at the Merricks' farm."

Her comment did not appear to appease Joan. "Mayhap Simon spoke true about a weasel lurking nearby Master Reade's body. An animal known to be a witch's familiar," she said. "This is evil, Mistress. We must be rid of the foul thing before Humphrey spies it and has yet one more excuse to make complaints to the master when he returns from London. Or before your good sister sees it and falls truly ill."

At the moment, Dorothie sat at an early supper in the upstairs parlor, unmindful of the presence of the poppet.

"I shall take it to the constable." Who would likely lift an eyebrow and peer at Bess as though questioning the soundness of her mind.

"Mother Fletcher will be accused."

"It matters not if she is accused," said Bess. "She has fled the village."

"The mob that would seek to hang her has chased her off, then," said Joan. "What if they accuse you instead, Mistress?"

Bess had no answer to that.

Joan frowned at the poppet. "When you take this thing to the constable, Mistress, tell *him* to be rid of it."

Bess fetched a basket from the corner of the kitchen. She took the spoon from Joan and used it to slide the poppet into the basket. Joan's disquiet had spread to Bess and made her unwilling to touch it again.

"Also tell the constable that another will soon die." Joan's gaze met Bess's. "For there is nothing which can be done to break the curse."

★　★　★

"I persuaded the churchwarden to delay his visit to Mother Fletcher, coz." Gibb leaned against the paneling of Kit's hall and stretched out his legs. "But I know not how long he shall stay persuaded."

Only so long as it suits him, thought Kit, listlessly plucking the strings of his gittern, which rested atop the room's table. "Any news about the bloodied garment we seek?"

"No. I am sorry, Kit. We still have not found it."

"No need to apologize, Gibb." Kit twanged the gittern's strings, the sound echoing loudly in the hall. He pushed the instrument away.

"Marry, we turn in circles, and I become dizzy from it all." Gibb gazed longingly toward the open door. "Will not Alice bring up food for us? I am starved."

"We should go to the tavern, if you want anything to eat," said Kit. "Alice frets over your sister's plans to descend on my household tomorrow with you and her friend. It's all she thinks about, as far as I can tell, and she overlooks what she needs to do today."

"Frances's friend is rather pretty. You might like her."

"I do not require a wife, Gibb," said Kit. "You forget I used to be quite content living here alone before you and your family pressed me to hire Alice."

"But your house was a great deal filthier back then as well, coz," said Gibb. "Before long, you'd have perished from disease because of the grime."

"Your efforts to throw Frances's friend at me are rather obvious, Gibb," said Kit. "The four of us at a quiet supper together. The girl will be expecting a proposal by the end of the evening."

A grin stole across Gibb's face. "Then invite Mistress Ellyott. Three women, two men. Intentions confused."

Kit stood, grabbed up his hat, and slapped it atop his head. "I just might."

Gibb rose as well. "I dare you," he said, and exited the hall, laughing.

His laughter was suddenly cut short. Kit went out to the stairs to learn the reason why.

"Ah, Mistress Ellyott," he said to the woman standing on the step right below Gibb, who wore a bigger grin than before. "I did not hear your knock upon the door."

"Your servant was quick to answer." She hoisted a basket. "I have come with a gift for you, Constable."

★ ★ ★

"I have heard of witches' effigies, but have not ever seen one." Gibb Harwoode examined the poppet much as Joan had done, making a long neck but keeping any part of his body from brushing against it.

The constable had balanced Bess's basket and its contents on the deep ledge of the room's window to better see by its light. His regard, compared to his cousin's, was far less apprehensive and far more skeptical. The exact look she had been expecting.

"Where did you find this?" he asked Bess.

"Ah . . ." A flush heated her cheeks. "Along the stone fence at the side of the Merricks' farm."

Kit Harwoode looked over at her, a scowl lowering his brows. "What, might I ask, were you doing out by the stone fence at the side of the Merricks' farm?"

"I was following Jeffrey Poynard—"

"You'd been following Jeffrey Poynard?"

"I was worried about Mother Fletcher and had gone to her cottage. She did not respond to my knock, and I made to leave. 'Twas then I saw Master Poynard ride past along the highway in great haste. His manner was so strange that I thought to see what he was about," she replied. "And before you chastise me yet again,

Constable, there was little harm in walking along the road behind him in the middle of the afternoon. And well you know it."

"So, what *was* he about?"

"He made a visit to the Merricks'," she said. "But not the Merricks themselves. In fact, he avoided the house and its occupants most carefully. I saw him speaking with one of their dairymaids. The one named Thomasin, I believe."

"Did you hear what was said, Mistress Ellyott?" asked the constable.

"You wish that I'd crept near enough to have eavesdropped on them?" Did Kit Harwoode want her to be careful or not?

"As you went to the trouble to slink after him to spy upon his actions, you may as well have."

His cousin was pinching his lips tightly together to keep from chuckling.

"I do not know what they said," she replied. "All I know is that their conversation was brief and agitated. 'Twas then I noticed the poppet beneath a clump of thistle."

"This thing means to tell us that a witch did indeed play a part in Reade's death," said his cousin.

"Someone may wish us to believe that, Master Harwood, but do not blame Mother Fletcher for its creation," said Bess. "She is innocent. Furthermore, as I said, I went to her cottage but she was not there. I could be mistaken, but she appears to have abandoned her home and departed the village."

Gibb Harwoode frowned. "Mayhap she left the effigy at the Merricks' on her way."

"The widow limps and shuffles," replied Bess. "She would have had need to walk a considerable distance to the rear of their grounds without being seen in order to do so."

"A Merrick or one of their servants, then, left this thing where you found it, Mistress," said the constable.

"I crept behind the wall without notice, Constable Harwoode," she said. "Anyone hale enough to do likewise could have tossed it over."

"Hmm." The constable lifted the poppet, which caused his cousin to gasp.

"Kit! Leave it be! 'Tis dangerous!"

"It does not bite, Gibb." He turned it about in the window's light. "What do you make of the material it is wrapped in, Mistress Ellyott?"

"What do you mean, Constable?"

"The fineness of the fabric."

A prickle of wariness creeping across her skin, she fingered the material. "A good linen of a fine weave," she said. "Dyed this pale blue by woad."

"A common material that any person might have a scrap of?" he asked her.

"Not everyone in this village and the surrounds, no. 'Tis more costly than a simple buckram, for instance." She looked up at him. "Which means that we might assume none of the cottagers made this, for they'd not possess such good linen. But, Constable, we have excluded a mere handful of folks from suspicion."

He returned the poppet to Bess's basket. "'Tis better than suspecting the entire town."

"Not by much," she replied.

"Who do you think it is meant to be?" asked Master Harwoode.

"Its clothing could represent either a man's tunic or a woman's gown." The constable shrugged. "We would have to find the person who left it in the Merricks' yard in order to discover the answer to that question."

"It cannot have been there long," said Bess. "We had a smattering of rain yesterday, but the cloth is dry."

"So today sometime." He picked up the basket and handed it to his cousin. "Gibb, take this around and see if anyone has anything of use to say about it."

"Now? It is time for supper."

"On the morrow, then."

His cousin gingerly took the basket and held it at arm's length. "The witch's effigy will alarm the citizens, Kit. If Mother Fletcher has fled, it will secure her guilt in their minds. They will hunt her down and see her hanged or burned for certain."

"Constable, there must be another explanation than she is the one who crafted this object," said Bess.

"Which is why I'm having Gibb ask questions about it," said the constable. "Be cautious with anyone you speak with, cousin. Choose only those who can be trusted to remain quiet."

"In this town, can *any* be trusted to remain quiet?" he asked.

"Threaten them with jail, if need be. Whatever works." He turned to Bess. "I thank you for your help, Mistress Ellyott."

"Be grateful for his kind words, Mistress," said his cousin, the basket still held at a distance. "Kit never thanks me for my help."

"Because of the endless trouble you cause me."

"I see, Kit, you intend to torture me forever about Frances's plans."

Who is Frances? thought Bess.

Kit Harwoode shot a look at his cousin. "Ah, Mistress Ellyott, my cousin's comment reminds me that I have a favor to ask. What are you plans for tomorrow evening?"

★　★　★

"He requested that you join him and his family at a supper tomorrow?" Joan set the plate of parsnips and boiled ling on the table unfolded before the hall windows. The sun cast long shadows across the courtyard, and Humphrey was encouraging the last of the chickens to return to their shelter before night fell.

"He did," said Bess, draping her table napkin over her left arm. "I wonder if I should have refused."

"You did not?"

"No, I did not. Not after his cousin added his voice to the request. Further, I find I am most curious why he wishes me to be there. He chose to not explain." Thinking she heard the sound of feet on the winding stairs, Bess looked up from the steaming food toward the doorway that led onto the lobby and the staircase. But no one appeared at the entrance. "Joan, you did tell Ellyn that she is welcome to come down to join me, did you not?"

"Aye, Mistress, but she has been most downcast today. She would not eat the dinner I prepared for her this noontime and said she'd rather remain in her chamber. She begs your understanding."

"She is not sick-feeling again, is she?"

"No, Mistress. Merely dispirited," said Joan, refilling Bess's mug of weak ale. "And I have removed any sharp objects from her bedchamber."

"Most wise."

Bess ate in silence while Joan tended to the hall fire, the branches crackling and popping as they burned.

"She must dread leaving us, Mistress, for she has to suspect she cannot stay with us much longer." Joan set aside the iron poker and got to her feet. "She has ceased bleeding, and she is now strong enough to go."

"Mayhap we can allow her to stay. For a short while, at least." Though it was not Bess's place to extend the invitation; 'twould be Robert's. "She has a keen interest in herbs and simples. I would like to teach her, and help her find a place with someone in need of a woman with such knowledge. Presuming, that is, she can convince Master Poynard to relinquish his plan to wed her."

"Methinks, Mistress, the wrong man died." Joan collected Bess's empty bowl and returned to the kitchen.

Bess ate but did not taste the food as she pondered what could be done with Ellyn Merrick. Finished with her meal, she did not wait for Joan to fetch the dishes. Her servant was not in the kitchen, so she placed them near the sink used to wash the plates and pots. On Joan's worktable, the thorn that had fallen from the poppet yet laid atop its surface. Joan would never discard it, for that would require touching the thing.

Bess picked it up and returned to the hall, retaking her seat at the table. The spine was from a hawthorn and quite long, the length of her thumb. She tested its sharpness with the tip of her finger and was rewarded with a prick of blood. When she was a child, a hawthorn had grown near the door of her family's house in Oxford. Her father had wished to remove the plant, as Bess and her siblings were ever slicing themselves on the thorns. Her mother, though, would not allow him to tear out the shrub. She loved its white, sweet-scented blossoms and argued that it was well known that digging up a hawthorn brought ill fortune. So it stayed and continued to cut them until Bess and the others learned better to avoid the plant.

Bess turned the thorn in her fingers. "If this were any longer, it could make a weapon."

Her grandmother's book of recipes for simples had warned against using any part of the hawthorn to concoct cures, though, for infusions made from the plant could cause some folks' hearts to beat erratically.

"Whom were you meant to harm by being thrust into that poppet, thorn?"

This time when Bess heard steps on the staircase, she glanced up to see Dorothie entering the hall. Having no gown other than the one she'd arrived in yesterday, she had pulled it on again to wear. She had removed her bum roll and petticoats, however, leaving the skirt to drag on the room's woven rush matting.

"Dorothie, you look so tired," said Bess, setting down the thorn. "You should return to your home where your servant can tend properly to you."

"You fret for me, Elizabeth?" She lowered herself onto the chair opposite Bess's. "When have you ever done so before?"

"You are my sister. Certes, I fret for you," she said. "Are you hungry? I can fetch Joan to bring you food."

"No need. I have no appetite." Dorothie eyed the thorn. "What have you there?"

"A spine from a hawthorn."

"Whyever have you that? They are like daggers." Dorothie flicked it with her fingernail. "I do so hate them. Father should have been rid of that shrub at our old house, but Mother's pleas could not be ignored."

"I found the thorn in a most curious place, and I was intrigued by it."

"They are dangerous. But what care you about warnings from me? You do not ever listen."

"Come now, Dorothie, I do."

"When? When do you listen? Bah," said Dorothie. "But see-ing that thorn makes me recall an aged fellow here—'twas years before you arrived in this village, Elizabeth—a cottager who suf-fered greatly from the prick of a hawthorn spine. The skin around the wound swelled and turned red, and he was in such pain. 'Twas only through the aid of a local healer that he recovered."

"How intriguing," said Bess, her thoughts swirling.

"To think that the fellow's illness was caused by the pricking of a thorn," mused her sister. "Almost like a poison, it was."

★ ★ ★

"Mistress Grocer, it is late." Kit had left the tavern with Gibb after their supper and had spotted the rotund shape of the town grocer's wife pacing before the doorstep of his house.

"I must speak with you, Constable," she said.

"Come in from the street, Mistress."

Kit opened the door and showed her into the entry passage. The various items that hung from her girdle—keys, a small mirror, a brass toothpick on a long chain—clanked together as she walked.

"How can I help you at this hour?" he asked.

She pressed her hands together at her waist. "The fine you have levied against my husband, Constable, cannot be paid. We have not the funds."

"Then perhaps you should tell your husband that the weights he uses should not be lighter than indicated by the marks upon them," answered Kit. "He cheats your customers."

"'Tis not my good husband! 'Tis our apprentice. The vile, dishonest creature," she exclaimed. "He pockets the profits."

"It is your husband's responsibility and yours, Mistress Gro-cer, to govern your apprentices."

She jutted her heavy chin. "The boy has been soundly beaten."

Kit could just imagine. "Pay the fine by sunset tomorrow, Mistress Grocer, and I'll not increase it." Kit brushed by her and went back outside. He waited for her to follow; she halted at the threshold of his front door.

"Have you another concern, Mistress?"

"My husband and me . . . we did wonder when you will be bringing in the witch to be hung."

Not this again. "There is no witch hereabouts, Mistress Grocer."

She lurched forward with a clanking and clattering of the items on her belt. "But there is! I saw her myself by the market cross. Not long afore Old Jellis was found dead! Creeping about. The hag. Bent over and wrapped in her cloaks and clouts."

"Merely an aging countrywoman, Mistress Grocer. We have a few of those around here."

"Nay! 'Twas the witch. Only a woman with wicked intents would be creeping about as she was."

Someone shouted his name. A young woman in a blue kirtle was running at full tilt toward him, skidding on the damp cobbles.

"Constable!" she shouted again.

"Excuse me, Mistress Grocer."

The woman made no move to leave his side.

"God have mercy, Constable," said the girl, halting before him. Tears streamed down her thin cheeks. "Anna. 'Tis Anna!" She pointed toward the lane that wound away from town and past the Merricks' farm. "The old red cow. I do not understand how, but . . . Anna!"

CHAPTER 13

Bess eased wide the door to the chamber Ellyn borrowed. Curled on her side, she appeared to be asleep, but her eyes opened and she smiled weakly.

"I did not mean to disturb you," said Bess. "I only wanted to know if you needed anything."

"I am well, Mistress," Ellyn answered. "The constable was here earlier today. Is not the matter of Bartholomew's death resolved?"

"I have learned, Ellyn, that Constable Harwoode is not easily satisfied," said Bess. "If you are well, I shall leave you to your sleep. I give you good night."

Bess closed the door and retreated through the upstairs rooms, weariness bringing on a yawn. She had so much, too much, to fret over. Ellyn's future plans and the resolution of Master Reade's murder. The meaning of the poppet and its intended victim. Mother Fletcher's safety, wherever she had gone. The safety of Bess's family, the threat Laurence posed—where had *he* gone?—looming. During the daytime, she could put his letter and the message they had received from Joan's friend out of her mind. But as evening approached, her fears crept nearer as well.

A steadying hand pressed to the staircase wall, Bess descended the winding steps. In the hall, the hearth fire crackled.

Dorothie slouched in Robert's chair, which she had drawn as near to the hearth as she dared without risking that her skirt might be set alight by an errant spark.

"You should go to bed, Dorothie," said Bess, crossing the room.

"You seek to tell me what I ought do?"

Why must she ever be so tetchy? "So be it. I merely thought you would be more comfortable abed than slumped upon the cushions of Robert's chair."

Dorothie exhaled and hauled herself to her feet. "I will leave on the morrow, Elizabeth. You are correct. I will be more content at my own home."

"Give you good night, sister."

"I pray I can sleep for all the troubles that attend my dreams."

Bess watched her go and turned back to the hearth. She retrieved the poppet's thorn from her pocket where she'd tucked it after supper. She tossed it into the flames, hoping the fire would consume it and its evil. However, Dorothie's words returned to haunt Bess, and she could not toss them into the flames.

To think that the fellow's illness was caused by the pricking of a thorn . . . almost like a poison.

Could Goodman Jellis have been the cottager Dorothie had remembered? If he was, as Bess's sister had recalled the prior ill effects of a hawthorn spine, so might others in this village. However, to link his recent death to an earlier affliction brought on by a thorn seemed a most far-fetched idea. And an even more far-fetched means by which to commit murder. Yet . . .

A fist pounded on the front door. Joan rushed into the passageway from the kitchen and unlatched it.

"I need Widow Ellyott," announced a young woman's voice. She hiccuped upon a sob. "'Tis most urgent."

"Joan, show her in," called Bess.

The Merricks' servant, the gaunt one, hurried into the room behind Joan. Her nose was red-blotched from crying.

"You must come, Mistress. I am afeard that Anna is dying. Might already be dead."

"Did she fall ill again?" asked Bess.

"Nay. 'Tis not her sickness," she answered. "Anna was out in the barn, tending to the last of the day's milking. And the old red cow kicked her." She paused to scrub tears from her eyes. "Anna must have fallen, and the cow . . . The cow trampled her in its frenzy. Thomasin found her when Anna did not come for the evening meal. The master sent me to fetch you and the constable, Mistress. Constable Harwoode has gone on to the farm, but I know not if Anna lives, or if she is . . ."

She burst into tears, and Joan gathered her close. She gazed at Bess over the top of the girl's coifed head, her eyes dark with dismay.

"The poppet, Mistress," said Joan quietly. "It did bring wickedness to its victim."

A victim who wore the blue clothing of a servant, just like the color of the material that had been wrapped around the figure.

★ ★ ★

An abundance of lanterns had been brought into the barn and hung from overhead beams and stall partitions. The light flicked and danced, making Anna Webb's chest appear to move with indrawn breaths. But Kit had already knelt alongside her and touched a hand to her face, which was round like an innocent child's. Her skin had been cold, a dribble of blood leaking from her mouth, and no warm breath exhaled from her nose. For a reason he might not ever be able to explain, he'd removed the bits of straw that had become entangled in her coif and felt a deep sorrow.

Do not blame yourself, Kit. Her death isn't your fault.

"Who found her?" he asked the crowd of servants and numerous Merrick children who had collected inside the barn. Mistress Merrick was not among their number.

"I did," said a young woman, pushing her way forward. She wore the simple and sturdy clothes of a servant. She pointed to her chest with a chapped hand. "I am Thomasin. A dairymaid for the Merricks."

The woman Bess Ellyott had spied with Jeffrey Poynard. "Tell me what happened as best you can, Thomasin."

Her shoulders were back and her gaze direct, confident despite her lowly position. "The cow trampled her."

"I want to know *all* that happened," he said. "When she was last seen. If any of you noticed someone lurking near this barn or mayhap a stranger on the grounds."

The crowd whispered. Thomasin's brow furrowed. "I do not understand, Constable. 'Twas an accident."

"If you would."

"I decided to go look for Anna when her supper sat uneaten on the table where the servants gather for meals," she said. "I could hear the old red cow lowing and shuffling in the stall. When I reached it, I saw Anna upon the ground."

Thomasin gave Anna's body a hasty glance. The girl's milk pail lay on its side in the corner. The straw that covered the floor was scattered widely, even out into the aisle. Kit did not think the disorder typical. The rest of the barn was carefully maintained.

"I dragged the cow out of the stall and put the animal in the empty one at the far end of the barn," she continued, returning her attention to Kit. "I must have cried out loudly, for Master David came running from the house."

David Merrick stood at the edge of the crowd, near to the barn door. Heads swiveled to look at him, and he stretched to his full height.

"I did hear Thomasin's cry, Constable Harwoode," he said. "I ran to the barn. I saw that Anna had been gravely hurt. Thomasin was disquieted. I sent our house servant to fetch you and Widow Ellyott."

"Has this cow ever hurt anyone before?" Kit asked.

"She can be uneasy, at times. When unfamiliar folk are near," Thomasin answered. "Anna was known to the cow, though, and should not have caused the animal to be affrighted. Unless . . ."

"Unless what?" asked Kit.

"Unless she was uncareful," she said. "Anna was not fully well after her sickness. And she was not pleased that the mistress had roused her from her bed to return to her work." She looked over at David Merrick. *Why?* "The mistress had called Anna a slugabed, which vexed her. Further, Mistress Merrick said she'd not pay Anna her wages if she did not earn them. Which is only sensible. Mayhap Anna did not well heed her tasks. Mayhap she angered the cow somehow."

"But Anna was *never* uncareful," said a lad huddled among the children. His resemblance to David Merrick was such that Kit presumed the boy to be his young brother. "And if she was mispleased, 'twas because of something *you* said to her."

The older girl at his side kicked him, causing him to yelp in pain. She then grabbed his elbow and hauled him from the barn.

Kit waited until the murmur his words had created eased. "When was the last time anyone saw Anna Webb alive?"

Those who remained in the barn exchanged glances. A handful shrugged.

"I had to have been the last one, Constable," said Thomasin. "An hour or so before sunset. When I had finished my work in here and went to the cheese barn."

"Did you notice anyone enter or depart this barn during that time? Or see someone in the yard who shouldn't have been there?"

"No one killed Anna, Constable. What an idea to think so!" David Merrick attempted a disdainful chuckle, which faded when none of the rest joined him.

"My thanks, Thomasin," said Kit. "Master Merrick, I would have you send for the coroner, if you have not already."

"He be coming soon, Constable," said one of the servants. "I ran to tell him meself."

Just then, Mistress Ellyott swept into the barn. Her gaze took in the others gathered inside, then moved to meet Kit's. "I am too late. Jesu, I am too late."

* * *

Constable Harwoode had ordered everyone besides Bess to leave the barn. To her surprise, they had all rapidly obeyed.

She knelt in the straw next to Anna. The constable leaned against the enclosure's wall, buffing the knuckles of his right hand down the length of his clipped dark beard.

"Well?" he asked.

"She does have injuries on her torso," she said, securing the ties of the dairymaid's bodice, which she had undone. "It could be just as you say Thomasin described. The cow became agitated, kicked out, and trampled Anna when she fell."

"Nonetheless, I mislike this," he said.

"Joan thinks the poppet I found was a curse meant for Anna. The blue material wrapped around it is like the kirtle she wore." The common color of a servant's dress. "Further, I did find the figure not far from this very barn."

His fingers stilled their motion. "Or Anna was meant to *believe* she was cursed. A distraction while she milked a peevish cow."

Anna's left arm sprawled across the straw, and Bess moved it to the dead girl's side. Anna had rolled up her sleeves to prepare for milking, and her skin's chill made Bess tremble. She had touched others who'd died before; her husband and two young daughters were just three among too many. However, each time Bess felt the cold of death upon another's flesh, she would shudder anew.

I shall never become accustomed to the feeling.

"What is that?" asked the constable, who'd bent down while Bess was contemplating her miseries.

"What?" she asked.

"That mark. On her arm."

Bess searched for what he meant and spotted the line of red across Anna's forearm.

He knelt beside her and lifted the girl's arm. The line of red was longer and darker than Bess had first noticed in the light of the lantern hanging from the wall.

"It does not look like the mark from a cow's hoof," he said.

"Are you certain, Constable?" she asked, though the line was too broad for what might be left by the edge of a hoof.

"I knew a man who'd returned from war with a healed wound on his forearm," he said, gently resting Anna's arm at her side once more. "He'd received it while defending himself against an opponent wielding a sword. Luckily for him, the sword was dull and his surcoat was thickly padded. His scar was much like her bruise in size and shape."

"You believe someone hit her, Constable, and that she raised her arm to fend off the blows?"

"I do," he said. "It wasn't an accident with a cow that felled her, Mistress."

He rose and left the stall. Bess leaned through the opening and watched as he scanned the contents of the barn.

"Ah." He bent to retrieve an item in the far corner near the door. He lifted a long, thick wooden rod for her to see. "A prod."

Such as the dairymaids would use to move the cattle between fields or to encourage them to return to the barn.

"Think you that is the weapon that made the mark upon her arm?" she asked.

"Let me demonstrate." He gripped it with both hands and swung. "He swings and strikes her. She lifts her arm to fend off the blow, but the impact staggers her and she falls to the ground near to the cow. The animal, startled, treads on her, killing her."

"This does make good sense, Constable. But another murder . . . it does not bear thinking." How many might there be before they saw the end of this?

He rested the prod at his side. "I could believe a witch's curse struck Anna down," he said, the look on his face somber. "Would you prefer that to be the cause of her death, Mistress?"

★ ★ ★

Early the next morning, Kit stood before the out-jetting window of the Merricks' parlor, his hands clasped behind his back. His impatience at being made to wait was raising his ire. When he'd been shown into this drafty room instead of the hall, he should have realized neither Mistress Merrick nor her son intended to make him welcome.

The window, though, did have a beautiful if glass-distorted view across the vale and onto the hills beyond. Clouds cast a patchwork of light and shadow on the fading green. He unlatched the central casement and pushed it open. From here, where the Merricks' home stood atop a knoll, the highway was readily visible in both directions. If he leaned through the opening, he could even make out the stand of trees that surrounded the old fort hill. The druids' mound.

A breeze rattled a bundle of leaves nailed to the topmost wooden transom of the window. He reached around the casement and grabbed them. The leaves of an elder tree. He'd noticed a similar bundle nailed to the lintel above the front door as well. Some believed elder leaves kept witches' charms from entering the house. Had they been nailed there before or after Anna died?

Children's voices shouted in a nearby room, then fell quiet. Soon after, Mistress Merrick stepped into the parlor.

"I do not mean to cause you to wait, Constable Harwoode." She glanced at the leaves he held. "My husband and sons have yet to return from the fair, and all the work and discipline fall to me."

"And to your son David," he said, tossing the leaves out the window.

"And to David." She crossed the room, more quickly than many women heavy with child might, reached for the casement latch, and shut the window. "My son thought you might return to speak with us."

"I have more questions about Anna Webb."

"The girl is to be buried in the churchyard tomorrow. The

deodand fee will be paid to the Crown, as is required to atone for the cow bringing to pass her death," she said. She had a way of pressing her lips together that wrinkled her skin, aging her. "We have done our duty."

"So you have," he said.

"What more, then, need you to know?"

"There were marks on Anna's body. Fresh marks." Last night, Bess Ellyott had searched for more and found another on Anna's shoulder. "From being struck with the cattle prod, I believe."

She momentarily pressed her lips together again. "Anna angered the cow and it trampled her. It caused those marks."

"Had the animal harmed anyone before?"

"God did not give cattle sense and reason, Constable. They are easily startled and act without thought," she said. "And yestereven . . .'twas most strange. An unrest hung over the house like a thick cloud. I could sense its evil. Mayhap the animal did as well."

"Is that why you hang elder leaves on your lintel and windows?" he asked. "Do you think the cow was cursed by a witch? Mayhap the same one who left a poppet in your yard not long before Anna died?"

"A poppet in our yard?"

"Just so."

"I heard nothing of a witch's effigy. God protect us," she said.

"Since I persist in my belief that Anna's death was no accident," said Kit, "I must ask if you saw anyone near the barn around sunset, near to the time the girl died?"

"Our house sits alongside the highway. 'Twould be simple enough for anyone with malicious thoughts to creep onto our land."

"*Did* someone with malicious thoughts do just that?"

"I was occupied in the dairy-house inspecting the milk pails, as I always do at that time of day," she replied. "I had instructed that they be scalded clean and set out in the air to sweeten. This must be done daily lest the pails sour and corrupt the milk. Great care must be taken, Constable Harwoode, and servants cannot always be trusted."

"Where was Master David while you were occupied with your milk pails?"

"He was in the office, attending to the farm accounts," she said.

"If you were occupied in the dairy-house, how can you be certain he was in the office?"

"I did not hear him attacking Anna in the barn, Constable, if that is what your question suggests," she replied sharply. "The dairy-house is hard by the barn. I heard no cries, no screams. I inspected the milk pails, returned to the house, told our cook to serve supper. Soon after, David joined me in the hall along with the other children. Like every evening, Constable."

"The dairy-house is hard by the barn, and yet you heard no screams. Even if Anna had been innocently trampled by an enraged cow, you should have heard her cries," he pointed out. "You could not have been nearby when the girl died, Mistress, or you lie about what you saw or heard."

"My son did not cause Anna's death, Constable. He came to supper composed. Until we heard screeching coming from the farmyard, that is," she said. "Jennet had just served us our stewed trout. The noise came from Thomasin, shouting that she'd found Anna. My youngest girl screamed in terror and spilled her food onto the floor."

"Which of the servants knew Anna best?" asked Kit.

"Jennet."

"I would like to speak with her."

She strode off to collect the girl, returning moments later with the whey-faced servant who had fetched him to the barn last night.

She curtsied. Her eyes were watery, red. "Constable?"

"I would like to speak with her alone, Mistress Merrick."

Mistress Merrick opened her mouth to protest but decided against it. "No lies now, Jennet," she said to the girl before leaving them.

Jennet sniffled and eyed him warily.

"Anna was your friend, I'm told," said Kit, once Mistress Merrick's footsteps had faded.

"She was like a sister to me." Tears sprang to her eyes. "Neither of us have a body to care about us. And now she is gone."

"Did you see anyone out by the barn near sunset, Jennet?"

"I may have done. The crooked-legged fellow who tends the mistress's pigs and chickens, I think," she said. "But now I cannot be sure."

"No strangers."

"I had to help Cook prepare supper. I was not in the court-yard near sunset to see who came or went. I am sorry, Constable. I cannot help you."

A house full of servants and children and none had noticed anything unusual. Or were willing to admit to noticing anything unusual.

"Of late, did Anna seem fearful?" he asked. "Anxious?"

The girl chewed her lower lip. It was chapped and began to bleed. Kit wished Gibb were here with his soothing manner. Women happily revealed their deepest secrets to him.

"Jennet, I will not tell Mistress Merrick what you say. Trust me."

She squeezed her eyes shut, and when she reopened them, she seemed calmer. "Ever since the players arrived in town, Anna was a fever of changeable moods. Gladsome, then mirthless," she said. "When Bartholomew was found killed, she was greatly distressed."

"Fearful?"

"We have all of us been fearful, Constable. All the servants. Since the neighbor's sheep died. Before that was the child whose family lives near to the mill. The girl was hale in the morn and fell sick in the fields that afternoon," she explained. "Cook said a witch cursed them. That we were to watch for signs of one. The mistress came upon us talking and said for us to mind ourselves, lest we be next. Then Master Reade died. Now Anna . . ."

Tears spilled from her eyes. She dabbed them away with the corner of her apron.

Kit let a few seconds pass so the girl could collect herself. "Did Anna believe a witch had killed Master Reade?"

"She was affrighted, but I do not think of a witch."

"Someone in this household, perhaps?"

Her eyes, narrow-set but a pretty hazel color, would not look into his. "I know not, Constable. I know not."

Kit considered her. "I have one final question for you, Jennet. Yesterday, midday or so, one of the town merchants came here. Jeffrey Poynard is his name."

"I know who you mean."

"Did you see him?" asked Kit.

"I did. I'd been in the dairy barn with Anna, asking how she fared after her sickness, when Thomasin called her into the yard. Thomasin is fond of ordering the other dairymaids around," she said. "'Twas then that Master Poynard arrived."

"I am told he came to speak with her. Did you hear what he had to say?"

"'Twas not Anna he sought, nor Thomasin," she said. "He was looking for Master David."

"Why?"

She chewed her cracked and bleeding lip again. "He took to shouting that Master David was making the foul claim that Master Poynard was a murderer. He made threats against Master David. That he was to keep quiet if he valued his health," she said. "Anna and I cowered in the barn until Master Poynard left. She was so afraid. Though my place is in the house and not in the barn, I do so wish I'd stayed with her, Constable. She might be alive if I had done."

CHAPTER 14

Bess paced the ground floor parlor of Kit Harwoode's house. Occasionally, she paused to look out the window at the street as though her gaze could summon him to appear. But her gaze did not summon him. How long was he to be at the Merricks' that morning? Had he made a discovery without her?

"Fie, Bess, you are not his assistant," she muttered in frustration.

Just then, she spied the constable striding across the square toward his house. He flung open the door and charged inside. Bess intercepted him before he climbed the stairs at the rear of the entry passage.

"Constable!"

"Bloody . . . Mistress Ellyott, do not leap at me from shadowed rooms," he said, halting halfway down the passageway. He'd drawn his dagger, which he carefully returned to its sheath.

She raised her eyebrows and nodded at the weapon. "I shall not forget in future, Constable."

"That would be wise," he said. "And why are you not in my upstairs hall, where I usually encounter you?"

"Your servant would not allow me to go up there. She said the hall is untidy."

He rolled his eyes. "She prepares the space for the supper I have been coerced to hold," he replied, extending his hand in a gesture suggesting Bess should return to his parlor. He followed her into the room. "Alice has thrice moved the table and remains dissatisfied. Even though I have told her that my cousin's gathering must be delayed."

"The supper is not to be tonight?"

"Disappointed?" he asked.

She would not examine her feelings in that regard, lest she find her answer to be yes.

Bess took the chair the constable moved into place for her and changed the subject. "What did you learn at the Merricks'?"

"That Agnes Merrick would doubtless provide an alibi for her son if she witnessed him committing a crime directly in front of her." He placed a stool across from Bess and sat. "And that Jeffrey Poynard was at their farm yesterday because he was furious David Merrick was supposedly spreading the story that Poynard had killed Reade."

"I should have accompanied you and spoken to Thomasin. I would hear her version of events," said Bess.

"And you, Mistress Ellyott, should remember that to continue to ask questions risks accusations against you that I can't protect you from."

She held her back straight within her pair of bodies and placidly returned his regard.

He frowned. "You're not going to heed my warning, are you?"

She knew better than to answer.

"I have not come to your home solely to hear what you have learned from the Merricks, Constable," she replied instead. "I am here because of Goodman Jellis. Before I received the sad news about Anna, I was puzzling over the manner of his death. I would like to examine his body."

"He is set to be buried today, Mistress Ellyott," he said. "And I cannot fathom what you hope to find on the old man's body."

"I look, Constable, for the pricking of a thorn."

★ ★ ★

"You would have me suppose, Mistress Ellyott, that a hawthorn killed him?" asked Kit Harwoode.

They strode across the market square bound for the Poynards', the usual attention on them both. The constable had learned that the old man's body was being held in a room at the Poynards'. He'd died a supposed criminal, and thus his body was not to be given to his daughter to be stripped and washed and wrapped in a shroud as was proper for a good Christian. Instead, his burial would be hasty and ignoble.

"I have heard a tale from my sister about a local cottager gravely affected by the scratch of one," she said, her strides lengthening to match his. "What if Goodman Jellis was that cottager?"

"And someone chose to prick him and gravely injure him once more. Interesting," he said. "Though I expect the burgesses shall see you pilloried for this."

"Why? What crime do I commit by wishing to examine Goodman Jellis's body?"

"The crime of defaming the coroner by distrusting his findings," he said.

"Which you have also done in the past," she pointed out. "You have not been pilloried for distrusting his findings."

"Aye, but *I* am the constable."

And *she* was but a woman who did not stay confined to her proper place.

"I will take the risk, Constable. 'Tis too important," she said.

The grocer's wife, the mirror she always slung from her girdle glinting back the morning sunlight, nodded at the constable—but not at Bess—as they passed her. The cobbler's apprentice paused in calling out for custom to squint in their direction.

"Pilloried, Mistress," he repeated.

She hoped she would merely be tied to the pillory, should the coroner take offense. Rather than having an ear nailed to the post to be cut off when the punishment had concluded.

Reaching up to rub her fully intact ear through the cover of her coif, she cast a look at the pillory. It was located near the church at the far end of the market square. Blood had stained the length of the wood, a reminder of past petty criminals who'd suffered justice there.

"I do not intend to defame the coroner, Constable," she said. "I merely wish to understand the truth."

"If finding a scratch on Jellis's body will provide the truth," he replied. "I have no great stomach for your task, Mistress."

"Your stomach must be stout enough to have agreed to allow me to inspect the fellow's corpse."

"I do not recall agreeing."

"You have not stopped me, have you?" she asked, looking over at him. "Nay, you walk alongside me full of curiosity."

"You'd find a way to examine Jellis whether or not I agreed," he said. "Nonetheless, I remain wary that this venture will not end well."

"And I remain resolved." Martin would have called her obstinate.

They arrived at the Poynards'. The servant girl who answered the constable's knock perked her brows at his request to see

Goodman Jellis's body, but she allowed them entrance through the gate in the garden wall.

"The old man is there." She pointed at the room where Bess had visited Simon, the moldy former byre of some forgotten animal, and skittered off.

The constable watched the girl depart. "I give you a spare few minutes to inspect the body, Mistress, before a Poynard comes stamping into the room to interrupt us."

"I'd best prepare an excuse for what I am about, then, ought I not?"

They crossed the courtyard, and the constable pushed open the door, its hinge again squeaking. Goodman Jellis was stretched out upon a warped plank of wood set atop trestles. Someone had covered his scrawny frame with a length of canvas. The strong tang of rosemary, tucked beneath the cloth, battled against the stink of death's encroaching decay.

"Mistress?" asked Simon, rising from the stool he'd occupied. He doffed his tattered cap. "Sir."

"Simon, this is Constable Harwoode."

"I know," said the boy, returning his cap to his head.

"What are you doing here?" asked Bess.

"Master Poynard orders me to sit with the body, since someone has to." Simon eyed the constable, who returned his gaze just as keenly. "To watch for the old man's bedeviled soul, should it rise from his body to haunt us. The souls of evildoers have no rest, Mistress."

And how might Simon stop a bedeviled soul from haunting the Poynards' household? The poor old man. To be treated in death with such contempt.

Bess crossed the room to where Goodman Jellis lay. "Simon, guard the door and tell me if anyone comes."

"What mean you to do?" he asked, scampering to the door to do as she asked.

"She means to cause trouble," said the constable.

"'Tis best I not tell you, Simon," she said. "Constable, the light is weak in here. I could use the assistance of your sharp eyes."

"Is there a lantern in the shed?" he asked Simon.

"There is, but it's not lit," the boy said. "And I can't go to the kitchen for a kindled match without getting asked why I need one."

"Stay by the door then, lad." The constable joined Bess. "This is the part I have the least stomach for, Mistress."

"If possible, I will only expose the torso and arms and keep his face covered," she said. "Do not faint on me, though."

Before beginning, Bess said a brief prayer for the man. She lifted the edge of the canvas sheet. The old man was sadly easy to shift as needed, his body no more than skin and bones, and very light bones at that. She succeeded at keeping hidden his face, but not at preventing the sweet stink of death from escaping.

"Shallow breaths, Constable, are best," she said in response to his recoil. "We look for pricks or scrapes of red."

Together, they bent over the body. Goodman Jellis's skin was wrinkled and spotted with all the marks that an aging man normally bore.

"Nothing, Mistress. I see nothing," said the constable.

"Keep searching," she said, though she found no remnant of a poke or a scratch, either. "How goes it, Simon?"

"No one comes yet, Mistress."

Good. "Help me turn him over, Constable."

Gingerly, they turned the old man onto his front. But their inspection did not reveal the pricking of a thorn on his back, either.

"There is nothing," she said. "I was wrong. 'Twas a far-fetched idea that has borne no fruit."

"You were wrong about the how, Mistress," said Constable Harwoode. "But we may still be right to believe his death was no accident. Just as Anna's was not."

Simon, eavesdropping from the doorway, let out a low whistle. "'Tis true one of the Merricks' dairymaids is dead! Is that why Master Harwoode shows a witch's poppet around?"

"One of the Merricks' dairymaids has indeed died, Simon," said Bess, sliding Kit Harwoode a glance. A muscle twitched in his jaw. "But we still have no answer as to how Goodman Jellis's death was achieved, Constable."

The constable dragged fingertips through his beard and frowned at the man's body. "Perhaps Mistress Grocer *did* see an old crone at the jail. A woman Jellis confused for a witch. Enough of a fright to stop his heart."

"As I told you, Mistress Ellyott," said Simon, his eyes wide. "You see, I was right! The witch *did* come to visit Old Jellis and killed him!"

The constable lifted a brow. "Mistress?"

"I should have mentioned straightaway what the lad told me, Constable. However, the person both the boy and Mistress Grocer saw had to be merely a simple crone walking within the market square. Not a witch. Not Mother Fletcher," she added with emphasis. "The sighting of this woman may have stopped Goodman Jellis's heart, though, Constable. For Simon also told me—did you not, Simon?—that Master Poynard had gone to speak to the fellow afterwards but ran off, ashen faced. Such a reaction suggests the goodman was already deceased."

"That *is* what I saw, Mistress," the lad responded.

A scowl replaced the constable's lifted brow. "Have you any

other critical news you should have long ago shared with me, Mistress Ellyott?"

"None that I can think of," she retorted. She considered the sad, haggard vagrant stretched out before them. "Poor fellow . . . wait. What is this?"

The canvas had slid free of the back of his head, and the lantern light showed a dark discoloration upon his scalp where his sparse hair did nothing to hide it.

"What?" asked the constable.

"This bruising here. As though he'd been hit by a heavy object."

"What? What is it you look at?" asked Simon from the doorway, eager to join them.

"Please stay on your guard, Simon," said Bess. "Could anyone have gotten inside the jail to have delivered such a blow, Constable?"

"No. It's locked, and I trust those who possess the keys," the constable replied. "The blow might have been delivered the night of Reade's. Mayhap to render to render Jellis unconscious while the killer left Reade's belt and purse with the old man as supposed evidence for us to find. Jellis was weak and unwell when I spoke with him yesterday morning."

"But why did the coroner not make note of the bruising?"

"You must esteem our crowner's abilities more highly than I do, Mistress, if you ask that question."

"Mistress! Constable!" hissed Simon. "Master Jeffrey has come out into the yard!"

Hastily, she and the constable turned the dead man onto his back and replaced the cloth.

"Have you settled on our excuse, Mistress Ellyott?" asked the constable.

"But Master Jeffrey does not head this way," said Simon. "Master Howlett has walked out after him."

The constable went to peer around the door with the lad. Bess finished tidying Goodman Jellis before joining them.

"What is happening?" she asked, rising onto her toes to see.

"They are arguing," Constable Harwoode said, moving to make way for her. "Howlett is likely begging for the money his troupe is owed. They want to leave, but they can't afford to depart without those funds."

The fellow's face had gone an ugly shade of red. "His urgency seems most odd. For where would they go? There is plague still in London. Here they are fed, housed, and safe. What is the hurry?"

"I can propose an answer, and it involves two deaths," said the constable.

"Would Master Howlett have killed Anna, Constable? He has no cause, for he does not know her." Bess had not seen *him* at the Merricks' farm before the girl had died. *Although* . . . "Although Anna *did* mention encountering the master of the troupe when she'd gone to greet Bartholomew Reade the day he arrived. Master Howlett had seen her with Master Reade. However, at the time of the murder, Anna was abed, ill, and no witness to the crime. Master Howlett need not fear her."

"Perhaps Howlett had another motive we have yet to discover, Mistress."

"Might the troupe master and Master Jeffrey be fighting over the robe that has gone missing from among the troupe's goods?" asked Simon.

Bess stepped back from the doorway. A piece of clothing was gone from among the players' possessions? "What is this?"

"A black robe is missing. Trimmed in fox fur, it was," said

the lad. "They use it for their plays. One of the players blames us servants for stealing it."

"Constable, could it be the garment we seek?" she asked. A garment that might be stained with a stabbed man's blood.

"Possibly. However, our time to ponder the vanished robe is ended," said the constable. "For Howlett has returned to the house and Jeffrey Poynard makes his way to us. Simon, back to your perch." He grabbed Bess's hand. "Mistress, come with me."

★   ★   ★

"As you see, Mistress, Old Jellis has been well tended to," said Kit, loudly enough for not only the approaching Jeffrey Poynard to hear, but also for anyone walking past on the lane beyond the garden wall.

Bess Ellyott jerked her hand from his grasp. "You need not drag me about like a captured mouse in a cat's mouth, Constable."

She gave Poynard a fleeting look. She understood what Kit was about. A bit of playacting on their parts. Perhaps they should join Howlett's troupe.

"I do comprehend I need not have thought otherwise," she added as loudly as he'd spoken. "Forgive my error, good sir. I care too greatly for a vagrant accused of a horrible crime."

Overdoing it, Mistress Ellyott?

Poynard blocked their path and stared at them down the length of his nose. "Mistress Ellyott. Constable. My servant said you were in our outbuilding."

"A foolish whim on my part, Master Poynard," said Mistress Ellyott. "Forgive my impudence for trespassing on you. However, I am pleased that my trespass permitted me to see that Simon is fully recovered from his fever. And so, I must return home."

"I will speak with you later, Mistress Ellyott," said Kit.

Poynard shifted to prevent her hasty escape. "You went to see Jellis's body."

From the corner of his eye, Kit noticed the twitch of her fingers longing to ball into a fist.

"As I said, Master Poynard, a foolish whim," she replied. "I feared his body might be mistreated, but you and your household have proved me wrong."

The fellow turned his attention to Kit. "You were required to accompany Mistress Ellyott, Constable?"

"I saw her heading here. I thought she might prove troublesome."

She made a faint noise of protest, but his comment seemed to ease Poynard's suspicions.

"You were right to follow her, Constable." He inclined his head and stepped aside. "Good day to you, Mistress."

She hurried past him. At the gate, she paused to look back at Kit before slipping out onto the road.

Poynard waited for the click of the gate shutting behind her to speak. "There has been another death."

How convenient of him to mention it. "You were seen at the Merricks' yesterday, Master Poynard."

His face did not move. Nothing on him moved except the plume tucked into his velvet cap, tugged by the wind whipping across the courtyard. Would such a fop stab a fellow and risk spattering blood on his silvery doublet or fine netherstocks? Trod through a cow-byre to beat a girl and force her under the animal's hooves? Kit, however, had known other wealthy men who'd sit at table and delicately pick at their food to not soil their hands but would not hesitate to draw gore with a well-placed punch.

"I went to speak with David Merrick," Poynard replied. "Not to attack a dairymaid. The girl was trampled by a rogue cow, or so I have been told by one of our servants."

"What was your business with Master Merrick?" asked Kit.

"He spreads rumors that I murdered Bartholomew Reade. I'll not tolerate such lies."

Which agreed with Jennet's tale.

"I have heard you threatened his health," said Kit.

A muscle along Poynard's jaw twitched. "Threats are sometimes required for Master Merrick to listen, Constable. I make no serious plans to harm him," said Poynard. "Now if you will forgive me, I must arrange to make payment to Master Howlett. He and his men will be leaving soon. Thankfully."

Damn. "When do they make to depart?'

"Tomorrow morning. At dawn, if the weather allows."

Which meant Kit had precious little time to find a killer before a suspect escaped his grasp.

★   ★   ★

"Mistress Crofton arose right after you departed, Mistress," said Joan, meeting Bess at the door. "She has gone to her house."

"How did she seem?"

"In an ill humor." She collected Bess's hat and the kerchief she'd tied about her shoulders for warmth. "Your good sister snapped at Humphrey."

"That is not an ill humor, Joan. That is acting with sense," quipped Bess. "I return, though, with news we found no sign that Goodman Jellis had been pricked by a thorn. Although I did find a dark red discoloration upon his scalp as though he'd been hit."

"'Twas the blow that killed him?" asked Joan.

"No, we . . . that is, the constable suspects it was delivered the night of Master Reade's murder," she said. "As for how he died, we must conclude that Goodman Jellis's heart simply failed him. Witnesses saw an old woman near the jail. The goodman may have mistaken her for a witch and perished of fright."

"Oh, my."

"Indeed." She nodded at Joan to dismiss her and made to enter the hall.

"Mistress Ellyn has at last left her chamber, Mistress," said Joan, halting Bess. "She secrets herself away in your still room. I thought you would wish to know."

"Have you told her about Anna?"

Joan nodded. "I thought it best she hear it from me, rather than Humphrey. He would not be kind."

No, he'd not. "My thanks, Joan."

Inside the still room, Ellyn Merrick had taken down one of Bess's clay pots and removed its lid to examine its contents. She was dressed in a worn kirtle that Joan had placed in Ellyn's borrowed chamber. It fit her better than it had ever fit Bess, who'd brought the gown with her from London.

"That is a mixture of marjoram, cloves, and rose leaves, Mistress Ellyn," said Bess.

The young woman spun about, dropping the pot onto the stone flooring. It shattered into pieces, scattering the herb mixture everywhere.

"I did not hear you," she said, sinking to her knees to gather the broken pieces of the clay pot. "Forgive me my clumsiness, Mistress Ellyott. I have destroyed your work."

"I should not have startled you." Bess retrieved a broom she kept in the corner. "And I often drop pots and bowls. That mix of herbs is not as valuable as the waters I prepare or the containers of expensive spices my brother buys for me on his travels."

Ellyn straightened, and Bess swept the shards and herbs into a pile.

"What did you mean to do with the contents of that pot?" Ellyn asked.

Bess took her apron from its hook. "Hold this flat against the floor if you will," she said to Ellyn, who did as Bess asked. She swept the debris onto the apron. "They were to be mixed with civet and musk to fill a taffeta bag."

"For the pleasantness of its aroma."

"To make a sweet bag. Yes." Bess set aside her broom and folded the apron over the broken pieces. Standing, she set it atop her worktable to be emptied later. "You look well this morning."

Ellyn glanced down at herself as if to assess the truth of Bess's words. "My body is healed."

"But not your heart?"

The other woman's eyes met Bess's. "That old red cow would not ever have trod upon Anna without cause, Mistress. It was an unruly beast, 'tis true, but she was skilled with the creature. Unlike Thomasin, who makes the animal anxious."

"I meant to tell you when I returned last night what happened to Anna, but you were asleep," said Bess. "It seemed another day's wait to tell you the sad news would not be amiss."

"My thanks."

"I do not solely blame the red cow for Anna's death, however," Bess continued. "There were fresh marks upon her body. On her forearm, as though she had raised it to fend off the blow of a rod or thick switch."

Ellyn did not look surprised. "Fresh ones?"

"She had been struck before?"

Ellyn's gaze shifted to rest on the bundle holding the broken pot and herbs. Or did it rest on the nearby broom that Bess had leaned against the work bench?

"My mother can be strict with the servants," Ellyn said at last, her eyes dark with bitterness.

"And strikes them," said Bess.

"She'd not be punished, would she?"

Not even if Mistress Merrick had beaten Anna to death would she be punished, for the law required proof a master or mistress had exceeded their right to correct a wayward servant.

"Jeffrey Poynard came to your house yesterday, not so many hours before Anna Webb died," said Bess. "He was in search of your brother and was most furious."

The gaze of the woman standing opposite her revealed no more emotions than those of a woman staring out from a painting. The flat eyes brushed onto canvas in oils. Such secrets she held close.

"They mislike each other," she said with a voice as flat as her eyes.

"I must also tell you that Master Poynard says he yet intends to wed you, Ellyn," said Bess quietly.

Ellyn lifted her chin. "He may intend that all he wants, Mistress, but I will not take as husband the man who forced himself upon me. Not when it was Bartholomew I loved." Her eyes were no longer flat and lifeless. They were pain-filled. "The only man I shall *ever* love."

CHAPTER 15

Mist floated up from the river, covering the fading green-ery of the churchyard like a wealthy woman's sheer veil drawn over her face to conceal its contours. Fittingly somber, thought Bess as she awaited the burial of an aged vagrant accused of murder.

Only those who need be in attendance had assembled. The church minister. The sextant and another fellow hired to carry the bier and casket borrowed from the church. A young woman in a plain kirtle and coarse canvas apron, who looked anxiously at the minister, then to the hole that had been cut into the ground, then back again, her body taut with the need to be gone. Goodman Jellis's daughter, Bess presumed. And off to one side stood Jeffrey Poynard, who schooled his features to appear sor-rowful rather than impatient. He did not now nor had he been seen earlier that day to carry the demeanor of a guilty man. Per-haps she might be wrong about his blame.

But how I wish you to be guilty of murder, Master Poynard, for what you did to Ellyn Merrick. For that you should suffer.

Bess tugged her cloak tight about her body. The burial would take place in an unconsecrated corner of the yard, where com-mon criminals were disposed of amidst weeds and prickling shrubs and inky shadows. Hasty and ignoble, unlike a ceremony for a man in good graces with his god. For such a man, the church bells would be rung, a meal served afterward, and gifts given out to those who'd attended. Goodman Jellis merited no such kindnesses. And no townsman would feel grief for the departure of a common drunkard who disquieted any who crossed his path.

God have pity on us all that we do not come to such an end as his.

Was the loneliness of his life and death the reason Bess had chosen to attend? Because she knew no one else, besides his daughter, would?

No one except Master Poynard.

He must have felt her staring at him, for he turned to look at her. He nodded and dared to offer a tight smile, sure enough that, with each passing hour, his complicity in any crime was becoming less likely to be proved. He deflected, with the ease of a master tilter, the lances of suspicion thrust his way.

The breeze lifted, carrying the voice of the minister, who prayed over the open casket words that might appease his restless, bedeviled soul. Bess did not acknowledge Master Poynard's regard, but resumed watching the service. Overhead, crows cawed from the lone oak standing guard over the churchyard. Their cries were as mournful a noise as the sound of the wind rattling the tree's branches, shaking free the last of its autumn leaves. They drifted down like great orange flakes of snow.

Brief prayers concluded, the minister stepped back. The sextant and his helper lifted the casket and tipped Goodman Jellis into the hole. The sheet tucked about his body snagged on a splinter, unraveling to reveal the man's scrawny nakedness as he fell. His daughter cried out, and the sextant hurried to undo the snag. He and the other man quickly tossed dug-up earth over him and packed it with their shovels. Come summer, the grass would grow upon the dirt, leaving no evidence that he rested beneath it. Just like the many others whose bones occupied this yard, unmarked. Unseen. Perchance forgotten.

Goodman Jellis's daughter ran from the churchyard, ducking through the lych-gate behind the minister. The sextant and his assistant, carrying the bier and now empty casket, chatted as they made their way back to the church. The casket would be cleaned and made ready for another impoverished soul who could not afford to be buried in aught else but a sack or a coarse length of cloth.

Jeffrey Poynard doffed his feathered hat at Bess and wandered off.

Leaving her alone with a freshly made mound of dirt. "God rest you, Goodman Jellis."

"A Papist prayer for a supposed criminal, Mistress?"

The man's voice behind her gave her a start. "You walk on cat's feet, Constable. Quietly."

"An ability that serves me well." He nodded toward the grave. "You need not have come here to mourn for him, Mistress. You did nothing wrong this morning."

Mayhap penance for disturbing the peace of a dead man's body was her true purpose for attending his burial. If so, the constable understood her better than she herself did.

"Do the burgesses share your opinion of my actions, Constable?" she asked.

"I have received no complaints," he said. "As yet."

"I am not comforted by that response, Constable," she said. "I hear they bury Anna on the morrow. I expect Ellyn Merrick will attend, if she feels well enough."

Should she tell the constable what Jeffrey Poynard had done

to Ellyn? In truth, informing Kit Harwoode would benefit no one. Ellyn would likely fail to convince the law that Master Poynard had assaulted her. Her family would not want her to admit to the entire town that she'd been with child. The baby was gone.

"It's gracious of her to care about a servant," said the man at her side.

"She is not coldhearted in the least, Constable. I find her to be merely quiet and sober-minded." Desirable qualities in an herbalist. Bess glanced about the churchyard. "Where was Master Reade buried? I see no disturbed plot of ground."

"His family buried him at a church near their farm."

"Ah." Bess headed for the lych-gate. The constable followed. "I told Ellyn about Jeffrey Poynard's anger with her brother. She admitted they share a mutual dislike but nothing more."

"She protects her brother, just like their mother does," he said as they left the church behind and made their way across the market square.

"Ellyn also suggested that her mother caused the marks on Anna's body," said Bess. "Apparently, she strikes the servants."

"Not unexpected that Mistress Merrick beats her servants, but an interesting admission by her daughter, nonetheless."

"So who are we now to greatest suspect, Constable?" asked Bess.

"If you have a suggestion, Mistress, I welcome it," said the constable.

They turned onto the lane leading to Robert's house. Joan had been watching their approach from the parlor's street-facing windows. She flung open the front door. "Mistress. The church-warden is here to see you."

Bess looked over at Kit Harwoode. "Constable, you may

have spoken over-soon about not receiving a complaint. I warrant the churchwarden is at my house to deliver his in person."

★　★　★

"Widow Ellyott, it pleases me not to be required to meet with you."

It did not please her, either.

She stood in the hall alone with the churchwarden. He had insisted that Kit Harwoode return to his duties, and Bess had assured the constable that she had naught to fear from Master Enderby. Had Constable Harwoode heard the tremble in her voice as she'd spoken, though?

The churchwarden paced the room's patterned rush matting. The air inside the hall was thick with the scent of camphor that clung to his black gown, black doublet, and black hose. Bess fought back a sneeze.

"You cannot be here to condemn me for my absence from services, Master Enderby." He'd accused her before and threatened fines . . . and worse. Her prior mistake had taught her the cost of rebellion against the church she had little faith in. "My servant and I have diligently attended these past weeks."

"And I am heartened by your conformity," he said, not sounding heartened in the least. "I am not here, though, to condemn you for your laxity. I am here on another, equally serious, charge."

The door between the entry passage and the hall hung ajar, and from outside it came the sound of Joan gasping. She could not help but eavesdrop.

Bess twisted her hands together at her waist. "What is this serious charge, good sir?"

"A witch's effigy has been discovered." He halted before the bank of windows overlooking the courtyard. "I have been told that it was you who crafted the abomination."

Her stomach tightened around his words, and her senses spun. When she was a young girl, Robert would turn her around and around until she stumbled and collapsed onto the ground, her head twirling. When he did so, she'd squeal with laughter. She'd not laugh now, and she must not stumble, for the ground she would collapse upon was rife with rocks rather than the soft grass of her childhood home.

"You accuse me of being a witch," she said with more composure than she felt.

"You do not deny it."

"By my troth, Master Enderby, most certainly I deny such an accusation. I am no more a witch than you are."

His nostrils flared with a hastily indrawn breath; she'd spoken wrongly. The rocks were desperately near.

"I crave your pardon, sir," she said. "I despair that any in this village would think I had made the poppet and speak over-boldly."

Master Enderby tilted his head to stare at her. "You are a stranger in this town, Widow Ellyott. Someone not well known by those of us who have lived our lives here. A woman who dabbles with herbs."

Women like us . . . we are to be suspected. Strangers. Healers. At one moment we are salvation. At the next, we are accursed. Mother Fletcher's painfully wise words.

"I have lived here more than a year now, Master Enderby. Both my brother and my sister have lived in this town for many years. Further, my grandmother was from just outside this village. I am hardly a stranger," she replied, her composure cracking. *Martin, I am in desperate trouble.* "And I make simples for those who cannot afford the help of a physician or the apothe-cary. I vow I do not make magical potions or cast curses. I wish no harm on anyone."

Her pleas did not sway him.

"A woman was observed upon the highway yestermorn, skulking about in a mysterious manner," he said. "Then you appear in town with a witch's effigy in your possession. Not long after, the young woman cursed by that foul thing is trod-den to death by a cow."

"I discovered the poppet at the Merricks' farm. I had gone there to visit Anna Webb, only to learn that she was recovered and at her work in their dairy barn," said Bess, not the truth but a wor-thy explanation. The veracity of her tale mattered not, for it seemed her words bounced off the churchwarden's ears like raindrops bounced off stone. "As I readied to leave, I noticed the poppet near a fence and brought it with me to give to the constable."

"To deflect suspicion, Widow Ellyott. The curse had been cast, the damage done," he replied. "You ensured that you would not be blamed by supposedly discovering the thing and taking it to Constable Harwoode."

"However, Master Enderby, I have clearly *not* ensured that I would deflect blame, as someone you will not name has accused me," she said.

"I do not hide the fellow's identity. 'Twas a plowman of good standing in this town, despite his humble birth, who saw the strange woman on the highway. He claims it was you, and that you are the effigy's creator."

"If I had wished to harm Anna, Master Enderby, I would have done so when I first went to tend to her," said Bess. "It would have been sadly easy to give her a physic that worsened her illness rather than cured it. But that is not what happened, is it?"

He did not reply, and she felt a moment's fluttering of hope that she might survive.

"Further, before the morning that Mistress Merrick summoned me to heal the girl, I had never even heard of Anna Webb," she continued. "How could I have developed a hatred for her, a desire to curse her, so quickly?"

"Another paid you to craft the effigy and cast the curse on the girl."

"I vow no one paid me to cast a curse upon that gentle young woman," she said. "You may question my servants. They will attest that I have not been making poppets or cursing villagers."

He stared down the length of his nose at her. "I did speak with them before you arrived here. They could not say that they had seen you craft the poppet. But I warn you, Mistress, I watch you closely."

Before Bess could reply, the churchwarden turned on his heel and swept from the room. Joan bolted from her hiding spot to throw open the front door.

Bess rushed after him. She should be happy to see him gone, but she'd had a thought.

The churchwarden moved quickly and was many paces up the lane already. "Master Enderby, wait!"

He stopped. "Have you aught to tell me?"

She did not intend to make a confession, if that was what he hoped from her. "I have a question about the woman that the plowman noticed skulking upon the highway. Did he provide you a description of her?" *Other than to merely claim it was me.*

"A woman like any other," he said. "A countrywoman with

a clout over her face, to protect her nose against the dust and dirt of the road."

"Which I was not wearing yesterday, Master Enderby, so it could not have been me he saw."

His lips puckering, he turned and stomped off.

"'Tis ever good to see the back of him, Mistress," said Joan, who'd crept up behind Bess. "Pricking and poking me and Humphrey to confess we had seen you make that evil thing. Someone, though, must stand accused."

"Past question, if I am not responsible, then Mother Fletcher must be. Thanked be God she appears to have left the village and cannot be punished." Bess watched Master Enderby until he turned the corner onto the market square. "I also saw the curious woman he described, Joan. On the highway yestermorn as I headed for the Merricks'. A countrywoman in simple sturdy clothes with her face protected by a clout and a forehead cloth that dipped low. She walked upon a road that was not dusty that day. So why the coverings?"

"Was the woman Mother Fletcher?" asked Joan.

"No. I am positive she was not," she said. "But who?"

★ ★ ★

"You cannot mean to delay tonight's supper, Christopher."

"Good day to you, Frances," Kit said to her, unpinning his cloak to toss it over the nearest stool. He missed, and it fell to his parlor's floor in a heap.

"Tush, Christopher, this is why you need a wife," she said, hurrying to pick up the discarded garment and brush the dust off it. "You care naught for your belongings."

"I do not need a wife, Frances, when you and Gibb have so kindly pressed Alice on me. As I have said before." He gestured at the room's lone chair that was fitted out with a cushioned seat. "Prithee, take a seat."

"I do not intend to stay long," she said. "If you need sit, you are welcome to."

"My thanks, Frances. I shall." He dropped onto the hard wooden chair at his desk. Through the window above it, he could see the churchwarden's house and watch for the man's return.

Perhaps he shouldn't have left Bess Ellyott to be bullied by him. But she was clever, and Kit was not her protector.

"Christopher, are you listening to me?" asked Frances. "No, so I will repeat my question—why must you delay the supper? My friend remains not long in town. Moreover, I have already purchased all of the fish, as we were to eat this day, a Friday. If I had known you'd attempt to move the supper to tomorrow, I could have procured pheasant or venison instead."

"It can't be helped, Frances." He squinted, thinking he saw Enderby striding across the market square. "Another murder to look into."

"Another murder? I have not heard such news. Are you certain?"

"Hmm."

"I shall allow you to delay our meal until tomorrow, but not a day later."

"As you wish, Frances." It *was* the churchwarden, already finished with Bess. Enderby shoved through a clutch of school-boys who'd run into the square to play a boisterous game of blindman's buff. The grammar school master shouted profuse apologies to the churchwarden and yelled at the boys to return to their studies.

"Christopher Harwoode, can you not attend to me? What is

it outside that draws your attention so?" she asked, her tone rising with impatience.

"A minor matter," he replied.

"Dearest cousin, you weary yourself with this role you have taken on. See the distraction it causes you."

He turned to face her. "I did not take on this role willingly."

She crossed to where he sat, his cloak still folded over her arm. "Then why engage in such work if you were so reluctant? Not for pay, for I know you receive the barest of fees to cover an expense here or there. You tire yourself only to satisfy your pride."

"My pride requires a great deal of satisfaction, Frances."

Her smile slipped from her face, and she set his cloak atop his narrow desk. "Your father is not moved by your dedication, Christopher. I admire you, 'tis true, but he believes you ignore your business and risk ruin."

He now had no reason to read the letter his father had sent, as he could readily presume it was filled with complaints about his negligence.

His gut clenched hard around all the feelings he'd ever had about his father. "I do not care what he thinks or feels."

She looked at him with pity. "Bah, 'tis certain you do. What son does not?"

The front door latch clanked, and the door itself swung open. Gibb charged into the narrow entry passage, bringing with him a blast of chilly air and the noise of the square outside. Kit called to his cousin before he bounded up the stairs for the hall.

"Gibb. In here."

"I have succeeded in frightening the entirety of the village, coz," he said, dropping the basket he carried onto Kit's desk.

"Does your visage alarm them, brother?" teased Frances.

She peered at the contents of the basket. "Merciful God, what is that?"

"A witch's effigy," said Kit. "Did anyone know where it came from, Gibb?"

"To a person, they blamed a witch. A plowman I showed it to became agitated, left his plow and his ox in the field, and ran to talk to the churchwarden."

"Who has only just left Mistress Ellyott's house." *No coincidence, I'd guess.*

"Christopher, what do you think is going on out there?" asked Frances, whose attention had shifted from the effigy to the square outside Kit's window.

Kit turned to look. Villagers clustered together, staring and pointing at something east of the village that had drawn their excited interest. Some began to run that direction. "Nothing good, Frances. Gibb."

He rushed outside with his cousin. Thick black smoke curled in the distance.

"Fire!" someone shrieked.

Fire.

CHAPTER 16

Master Enderby had been gone from Robert's house no longer than five minutes when Humphrey lumbered into the hall where Bess sat by the window, idly watching the chickens in the courtyard.

"Mistress?"

Bess looked over her shoulder. "Aye, Humphrey?"

"There be a fire. Near to the highway to Avebury." His face pinched with a look she could not decipher. Distress? No . . . gloating.

"The farmers have been burning the residue of their fields," she said.

"Nay, Mistress. 'Tis a cottage that is ablaze."

"Jesu, why did you not say so immediately?" Bess leaped to her feet. "Joan! I require my ointment of honey and alum for burns."

She left Humphrey standing in the hall as she rushed to collect, with Joan's help, all she'd need to tend to anyone who might be burned. The ointment. Clean squares of linen.

Joan handed Bess her satchel. "This is a most unchancy fire, Mistress."

Bess slung the satchel's strap over her shoulder. "You sense it, too."

"Need me to attend you?"

"No. Stay with Ellyn. I will return as quickly as I can with news."

★   ★   ★

The fire flared hot, burning through the dried thatch roof and decaying cob walls with the speed of a flame racing through pitch-soaked branches.

"'Tis the crone's cottage, Kit," said Gibb, out of breath from having run with Kit to the site.

"I know whose it is," Kit replied. The old healer. The one the townsfolk thought was a witch.

"I should not have shown that poppet around," said Gibb. "It angered the villagers and made them fear. And look what they have done!"

Damn.

A handful of the woman's neighbors stood with empty buckets in their hands. One of the Merricks' male servants had also come to help; their farm was just over the rise behind the cottage. The bystanders had gone to the river for water to throw onto the flames, but had not bothered to return to it for more. The house was past help, anyway.

"Stay back!" shouted Kit to a pair of lads who ventured too near to the building. The boys scattered, laughing and jostling each other.

One of the onlookers trotted over. It was Goodman Cox. He of the witch-cursed sheep.

"She's done for," he said to Kit and Gibb, no hint of remorse or pity in his voice.

"Who started the fire, Goodman Cox?" demanded Kit.

He stepped back. "How would I know?" he asked, defiantly

throwing forward his chest. "I saw the flames from my house. Came running. It was already afire by then."

"Did you hear any screams for help?" asked Gibb. "Is there anyone inside?"

"No. I heard no screams."

"Are you certain? You had no love for the woman who lived here, Goodman Cox," said Kit. "You accused her of killing your sheep."

"I do not lie, Constable. I heard no screams."

Just then, the beam supporting the roof collapsed in a heap of sparks, prompting those assembled to cry out in alarm. One of the local plowmen ran over to stomp out the fire that the spray of embers had ignited in a close-by patch of grass.

"Anyone here see who started this fire?" called out Kit. "If any of you know and do not say, you are also guilty of the crime."

His question was met by stony faces.

"'Tis God's punishment!" one finally declared.

"Aye," echoed Goodman Cox. "You'd not attended to keeping us safe from the woman, Constable. So God had to intercede."

"My thanks for your opinion, Goodman Cox."

Grumbling, the man sauntered off to join those who loitered about, watching the cottage burn to the ground. Some of the crowd began to disperse, having lost interest in the fire.

"Any number of these people know—or suspect—who set this cottage ablaze, Kit," said Gibb. "I would wager upon it."

"Shall we torture them to gain a confession?" he asked bitterly. "I know you are right, Gibb. But what can we do?"

"Should I search for Mother Fletcher's body?" his cousin asked.

"Let the fire die down. We'll search then."

Out of the corner of Kit's eye, he spotted a familiar figure running up the road.

"No!" cried Bess Ellyott. "I am late again! Was she in there? Is she dead?"

She flew past Kit, bound for the crackling remains of the house. He grabbed her before she went too far.

"Mistress, stay yourself."

"But Mother Fletcher!" Her eyes reflected the flames that surged and subsided. "She may have returned. She may be inside."

She tried to twist free of his grip, but he dragged her close. "If so, she is long past our aid."

"No!" she sobbed, but did not struggle any longer.

★ ★ ★

The rock Bess sat upon dug its sharp edges through her skirts and into her buttocks and legs. She slumped over her satchel, clasped on her lap, and watched as Gibb Harwoode prodded the smoking ruin of the house with a long stick he'd found in the nearby woods. Flames still licked timbers, but for the most part, Mother Fletcher's cottage was a pile of ashes.

"They burned one of her houses before, Constable," she said to the man who paced in front of her. On occasion, he paused to kick at a stone or a clod of dirt. Everyone else had departed, leaving her and the Harwoode cousins to reflect upon the destruction of a helpless old woman. "The house that stands across from the ruins of the old friary. When her family had been afflicted with the plague, the townspeople did set afire their home. She lost them then. She lost everything. And now . . ."

"She was not inside when the cottage burned, Mistress Ellyott." Kit Harwoode looked at his cousin, gingerly stepping over a smoldering pile of timbers. "Gibb would have found her body by now if she had been. She is gone from the village, as you suspected when she did not answer your knock yesterday."

"Then why burn her cottage?" she asked.

"To keep her from ever returning."

And to exact a measure of vengeance for their superstitious fears, thought Bess.

"Gibb believes that his questions about the poppet encouraged them to do this," said the constable.

"The townsfolk did not need your cousin to ask questions in order for them to want to harm Mother Fletcher, Constable. They already feared her. What shall they do, though, who shall they next condemn, when their sheep persist in falling ill and perishing?" she asked. "When folk die in mysterious ways? When that mound—" She gestured toward the old fort hill that rose not so far distant. "When that cursed mound remains to loom over the road, haunting them? Will they risk some even more ancient curse and tear it to the ground, scattering the rocks and dirt?"

He turned his gaze to her, his face somber.

"Or shall they blame me, Kit, when someone's newborn child fails to thrive and withers away? Or their crops are blighted by bad weather? Shall they burn my brother's house around my head? I have already been accused of making that poppet. What next?"

She'd never called him by his given name, let alone the pet name his cousin used; he did not remark upon her overfamiliar transgression.

"We shall find the one who murdered Bartholomew Reade and Anna Webb, and the townsfolk will see it's not a curse that struck them down, Mistress," he said, his gaze kindly. Gentle. "Trust me."

"I do. I do," she replied. "But shall the townsfolk trust you? Believe you?"

He had no answer for her questions. How could he?

★ ★ ★

Bess shifted the weight of her satchel and climbed the incline to the Merricks' farmyard. She should have returned home. But many confusions remained, and their resolution would not be found by hiding in Robert's garden or near the hall hearth. However, it might exist within the whitewashed walls of a dairy barn.

She entered the yard. A servant sang inside the barn opposite the dairy buildings, his voice melodious. The youngest Merrick daughter ran across the gravel, chasing the chickens. The family's tan dog danced after the birds, tail wagging. Feathers fluttered into the air. The girl stopped and eyed Bess, who greeted the child but received no polite response in return.

Bess squared her shoulders and slipped around the open barn door. The warmth cast off by the animals was a welcome respite from the cold outside. "I pray I do not disturb you, Thomasin."

The dairymaid stood before one of the stalls located halfway along the length of the barn. She looked over at Bess, her pale eyes frosty. "Does Mistress Merrick know you are here, Mistress? You no longer have a patient to tend at this house, and I have work to do. You should be on your way."

"I require only a moment," answered Bess.

Another young woman, whom Bess recognized as the housemaid, poked her head out of the stall. "Are we finished, Thomasin?"

Thomasin hesitated, then nodded. "Go back to the house, Jennet."

The housemaid removed the stained holland apron she'd tied over her blue dress and scurried past Bess, dashing outside. Thomasin stepped into the stall, the cow within lowing softly.

Bess, her thick-soled shoes crunching through the straw scattered the length of the aisle, passed the other stalls. The one where Anna had died was empty and cleaned. The red cow was not in the barn, so far as she could tell.

Thomasin had taken the milking stool the housemaid had abandoned. "That one will not succeed. She fears the cows. Especially since Anna died. She says they are dangerous." She squirted the cow's milk into the pail set beneath the animal, a rhythmic splash created by her practiced touch. "How did you know?"

"Know?" asked Bess, confused.

"That Mother Fletcher was wed to my mother's cousin." The rhythm of Thomasin's hands did not break. "That is why you are here, is it not? Because of the fire."

"Was it you who provided for her?"

"When I could. 'Twas not much, for the Merricks are not generous masters," she said. "But if you have come to offer sympathy, I have no need of it. She was a trouble-causing woman. The village is well rid of her. And now that she is gone, I will no longer need to suffer whispers and rumors. Nor give away precious pennies."

"Mother Fletcher is not the reason for my visit, Thomasin," said Bess. "There were marks upon Anna's body as though she'd been struck by a rod." She did not allow her gaze to wander to where the cattle prod stood. "I have been told your mistress disciplines the servants severely."

The cow's milk slowed to a trickle, and Thomasin sat upright. Her gaze was steady. "It is her right," she replied, confirming what Ellyn had said.

"And Anna would attempt to ward off the blows."

"Though it would do her little good."

Standing, Thomasin picked up the milk pail and low three-legged stool. Bess stepped aside, and the dairymaid went into the next stall. She placed the stool by the cow within and sat.

"Are you finished, Mistress?" she asked, the rhythm of splashing milk beginning anew.

"I came to the farm yesterday in hopes of visiting Anna and saw you arguing with her," said Bess.

The sound of Thomasin's milking stuttered. "You spy upon us, Mistress Ellyott?"

A guilty flush heated Bess's cheeks. "I did not mean to." *God forgive me my untruthfulness. 'Tis necessary.*

"Anna was late in coming to the barn," Thomasin answered plainly. "I scolded her. 'Twas all. And I know not why you concern yourself with an argument I had with Anna. She is dead. The cow killed her."

"Do you honestly believe her death was an accident? I do not."

"What does it matter what either of us believe? 'Tis the constable's business, Mistress."

"Why had Jeffrey Poynard come here, Thomasin?" Bess persisted. "He was in a foul temper."

The cow she milked shifted restlessly, and she tutted to the animal to calm it. "He was here to shout about wanting to speak with Master David. That he would not be blamed for killing Master Reade."

The same as Constable Harwoode had learned. "He dragged you aside, Thomasin. I saw it. What did he want from you?"

"You *do* spy upon us," Thomasin accused.

"I mistrust him," said Bess. "I think you might as well."

Thomasin lowered her hands to wipe her fingers across her apron. "He sought to browbeat me. To force me to admit that I knew it was David Merrick who'd killed Bartholomew to keep him away from Mistress Ellyn. To admit I knew that he, Master Poynard, was innocent," she said. "Though how would my avowal profit a prosperous man like him? The useless word of a servant."

"Why would Master Poynard think *you* knew any such thing, Thomasin?"

"Master Jeffrey Poynard is currish and requires no good reason for what he believes." Thomasin turned back to the cow, which had been patiently waiting, and resumed milking.

A small brindled cat slinked into the stall. It meowed at Thomasin.

"Do not look to me for food. Go catch your mice, puss," she said, chasing off the animal. "'Tis Master David's cat, but it misses Anna, who petted it."

Bess regarded the creature as it meandered through the barn, its tail flicking. "Have you ever noticed a weasel near the old fort hill, Thomasin, or heard of one there?"

Though who would confuse a cat for a weasel?

Mayhap village boys intent on seeing a witch's familiar in the guise of one. Keen to see what they wished to see. To believe what they wished to believe.

"That story?" said Thomasin. "The lads like to frighten the girls with such tales."

"But not only girls are frightened, Thomasin. And now your kinswoman's cottage is burned to the ground."

Thomasin pressed her lips together. "She was troublesome."

And deserved to have her home destroyed?

"A witch's effigy *was* left in the yard here," said Bess. "I, for one, do not think Mother Fletcher is responsible for putting it there, however."

"Cook thinks her responsible, and this morning she made certain to tell this to any who'd listen," said Thomasin, exhaling sharply. "What is done is done. Now please go."

"I have one more question, Thomasin; then I will leave you be," said Bess. "Do you know a woman, a countrywoman, who walks the highway and covers her face all about with a clout and a low forehead cloth? I saw her upon the road yesterday, but I did not recognize her."

"There are many countrywomen hereabouts, Mistress."

Bess tried to recall any feature that might produce a name. "She was of a typical height, but walked with a hunched back. Her dress was unremarkable. Grayish brown, I think."

"Perhaps the farmwife at the cross road. Though she has a large nose you'd not miss," she said. "It could be anyone. Anyone." She rested a chapped hand against the cow's flank and looked over at Bess. "Why do you ask?"

"A plowman claims it was *she* who made the poppet, Thomasin," said Bess. "And I must find her."

★ ★ ★

"She is not the countrywoman I saw," Bess muttered, moving away from the low shrubs that marked the boundary between the Merricks' farm and the farm at the nearby crossroads.

After many minutes of waiting, Bess's patience was rewarded when the wife of the farmer came outside to retrieve stockings she'd left to dry atop a row of bushes. Thomasin had been right; her nose was quite prominent, and Bess would have noticed the feature.

She headed back for the roadway. *So who was it I saw?*

Bess trudged homeward, studying the traffic that she passed on the road. Today was not a market day, which brought folk from near and far to town, so the highway was not as busy with people as it could be. A shepherd's boy guided a wandering sheep along the verge and through a break in a hedgerow. A girl plodded by, pulling a cart laden with straw behind her. A farmer walked along the inclined edge of the road and inspected the low shoots of winter wheat poking through the soil of his fields.

But no countrywoman wearing a clout and a low forehead cloth limped past.

Why did she trouble herself with this matter? 'Twas the constable's concern, as he often reminded her. Had it not been for Ellyn Merrick arriving at her gate, bleeding from the loss of her baby—Jeffrey Poynard's baby—on the same day Bess had been called to tend to a sickly Anna, she'd have had no cause to even think upon Master Reade's murder. Other than to mourn the sad wastefulness of a young life cut short.

You have always cared about justice, Bess. Ever trying to right the wrongs of the world.

"And so I have, Martin," she said to the voice inside her head that might never cease to speak to her. I'faith, she did not wish that voice to ever cease. When it grew silent, would that not mean she had forgotten him, the man whose love had given warmth to her days and meaning to her life?

I will never forget you, Martin.

She neared the lane that led to Mother Fletcher's cottage. The acrid smell of smoke hung over the road. Three boys rummaged through the smoldering ruins.

Bess charged forward. "Get away from there!" she shouted. "Leave her things in peace!"

One waggled fingers at her before they turned and ran across the field with howls of laughter.

Bess scowled, tears of anger burning in her eyes. The old woman had not ever harmed anyone. Her only sin was that she'd come from elsewhere and had kept to herself. However, being a stranger, an outsider, was enough of a sin. As the woman had been aware.

Her steps dragging, Bess eventually arrived at Robert's house and went inside.

"Joan, I have returned at last," she called out, untying her cloak and hanging it on the nearby hook. "Joan?" she called again after receiving no reply.

Shouts echoed in the courtyard. Bess hurried through the hall to the rear door, which hung open. Joan and Humphrey stood in the center of the garden, trampling the herb beds. Quail barked and pranced about in a frenzy of excitement. Ellyn Merrick stared at them, her arms clutched about her middle.

Humphrey waved an item he held at her. "You put it there! Admit you did!"

"I did not!" Ellyn shouted, stumbling over Quail as he bounded beneath her legs. The dog yelped and leaped aside.

"What is this?" asked Bess, rushing across the courtyard. They did not hear her.

Joan grabbed Humphrey's arm and tugged. "Leave Mistress Ellyn be!"

"You *would* defend her, Joan Barbor," he answered, shaking off her grip. He prepared to say more but spotted Bess. His mouth clamped shut over his unspoken words.

"Quail, come away," Bess ordered the dog. He loped to her side. "What is this?" she asked again.

Joan dipped a brief curtsy. "Mistress, Humphrey accuses Mistress Ellyn of making this horrid creation and leaving it in the garden."

"What creation?"

Humphrey tossed what he'd been waving at Ellyn onto the ground at Bess's feet. "That."

Quail lunged for it, but Bess retrieved the item before the dog's teeth closed around it. The item was a straw-stuffed figure in the shape of a person. A square of cloth had been wound about its body, the material of rust-red linen. And from the center of the figure protruded a single thorn.

"'Tis the color of your dress, Mistress," said Joan, her voice shaking.

"Yes." Bess pressed her hand to her stomach, her fingers curling over the madder-dyed linen of her gown. "So it is."

CHAPTER 17

"You must not accuse Mistress Ellyn of leaving that poppet in the garden, Humphrey," said Bess.

They were closeted together in the front parlor Robert used for his office. Joan no doubt lingered outside the door, her ear pressed to its thick oak. Quail's nose poked through the gap between the door's bottom and the flag floor, betraying his presence.

Humphrey stood with his thick shoulders back. He gripped his wool cap in his hands, the only sign of deference to Bess's position as the mistress of the house in her brother's absence. His thinning dark hair lay plastered onto his skull, and the pockmarks his cap normally concealed formed an array of dots across his forehead. If she were to encounter him in London, she'd believe him to be a cutpurse or a bullyboy. Instead, he was her brother's trusted servant. The fellow who had nursed Robert back to life when his wife and her maid had fallen ill from fever and perished.

Were Bess to fall ill, she had no confidence that Humphrey would offer *her* such care.

"I accuse Ellyn Merrick because I saw her there," he answered at last.

"She is welcome to be in the garden," said Bess. "And sitting among the fading flowers and ripening quince is what she should be doing to recover."

"She was not sitting. She was looking about. In your herbs."

"She is welcome to do that, as well."

"I say she pretended," he said. "Because it was after her being in the garden that I spied it. Sitting in the bed of winter betony. 'Twas not there this morn when I planted out the cabbages. I'd have seen that . . . that thing."

He jabbed an elbow in the direction of the poppet, which lay on the table between Bess and Humphrey. She had removed its lone thorn—only one for her, as opposed to the other poppet, which had been stuck throughout with many—and tossed it onto the hall hearth.

"Joan tells me she was with Mistress Ellyn shortly before she went into the garden, and that Mistress Ellyn did not have the poppet with her then," said Bess.

"Joan defends the woman, for she pities her. 'Poor Mistress Ellyn. She has been treated right poorly,'" he mimicked. He screwed up his mouth as though he might spit, but thought better of it. "Joan blames a man for bringing Ellyn Merrick to harm, and needs must champion her to one and all. Joan does so because she hates men. 'Twas a man what gave her that nasty scar on her face. I know 'tis true. So she would pity any female with a sorrowful tale. *I* have no pity for Ellyn Merrick. She is not what she seems, Mistress. There. I have said it."

"And so you have, Humphrey Knody." They were the most words he had ever spoken to her. It was unsurprising they would be words full of bile. "Joan may be sympathetic of Mistress Ellyn, but she would not lie to me to protect her."

"I do not say Joan lies, Mistress. I say she is wrong," he

answered. "The woman put that thing in the garden. And she made the other like it."

"Ellyn cannot have left that poppet in her family's farm-yard, Humphrey. She was in this very house all of yesterday, recovering."

Humphrey sniffled loudly and twisted his lips into a cynical grimace. "You were at the Poynards', tending to that servant of theirs, that Simon. She slipped out, as she did the day before when she went to the river."

"You saw her leave?" she asked.

He did not answer, which meant he could not prove his claim.

"Mistress Ellyn would not wish to lay a curse upon me," she said. "I have given her no cause. I have tended to her and allowed her to stay in this house, and she has been grateful."

"She killed her lover, who wanted another. She killed her servant, the one he wanted," said Humphrey, providing a terse summary. He slanted a look at the poppet. "A curse can kill, Mistress. And now one has been cast upon you."

* * *

Kit had just taken a bite of warm manchet bread when he heard Alice scurrying to answer a knock, followed by heavy footsteps outside the hall.

He looked over at the doorway. "Timely, Gibb. If you want a meal." He nodded toward the empty stool near the table. "Sit. I'll have Alice bring you a mug of ale."

"I am not here to eat, Kit," he said, ducking into the room.

For once. "What then? Another fire?" he asked lightly, his stomach souring at the thought.

"No, not a fire. There is a brawl at the Cross Keys. Between the players and some townsmen," he answered. "I could not stop them."

Kit cursed. "Can we not have just a moment's peace?"

He stuffed the remainder of the bread in his mouth, and hurried from the house. From the step outside his front door, he could see that the brawl had spilled out into the square.

Three men took turns swinging at one of the players, who parried their blows with astounding ease.

"Part them, Gibb!" he called as he ran. "I shall deal with those inside."

A crowd clustered around the door. Men, women, children. A few apprentices, cheering on the fighters. One of the burgesses stood there as well. Apparently he felt no need to interfere and looked to be enjoying himself. Several onlookers placed bets on who might win.

"Stand aside!" Kit shouted, shoving at them to give him a path.

"Those players be nothing but trouble, Constable!" a fellow called out unhelpfully.

"As we have been saying," exclaimed the matron at his side, her wrinkled cheeks flushed from the excitement.

Kit made his way into the tavern. Inside, there were five spectators for every man involved in the scuffle. Stools and tables had been overturned, ale spilled onto the rushes covering the floor, and broken pieces of furniture snarled men's feet. Shouts, curses, and cheers rose in a deafening roar. The air stank of sweat.

Master Johnes tugged at a pair of men wrestling on the floor. "Stop, you reckless idiots! Stop!"

For his efforts, he was knocked to the ground. His wife, who hid behind the counter where drinks were served up, cried out. Marcye, covering her face with her apron, huddled next to her mother.

"There, Constable." The town barber, a comb stuck behind his ear, leaned through the tavern's wide window. "That be the one who started the fight."

He pointed at a red-haired player in a bright-green doublet and trunk hose. It was Willim Dunning. Blood streamed from his nose. The man he pummeled, one of the local traders whose name escaped Kit, looked just as bad. One eye was swollen shut, and his mouth was split open.

"You, there!" Kit shouted, reaching the nearest set exchanging blows. "Stop now, or I'll see you all arrested!"

A stout fellow, his back to Kit, swung wildly at his opponent. His fist collided with Kit's shoulder. Kit grabbed the man's arm and yanked him backward. "I order you all to stop!"

A gunshot rang out. Silence instantly fell. The burgess, smoke still streaming from his snaphance pistol, grinned at Kit from where he stood inside the door.

"My ceiling!" cried Master Johnes, who'd scrambled to his feet and now stared aghast at the plaster where the ball had broken a sizable hole.

Someone howled with laughter. Two others decided the shock of the moment was over and resumed scuffling.

"Stop! Immediately!" Kit shouted, bringing their fight to an end. "All of you are to leave before I find room for you in the jail. Everyone leave, except for the players and you, Master Trader."

A few trooped off. The rest, reluctant to miss the diversion that was now to follow, shuffled their feet and sniffled back blood.

Master Johnes, still bemoaning the damage to his ceiling, straightened stools and tables.

"Mistress Marcye," said Kit. "See the door barred behind these good fellows once they have departed."

Muttering, the remainder of the curious left, the burgess who'd blown a hole in the ceiling the last to go. Marcye scurried over and barred the door and the window shutters, closing them upon the faces of the curious who'd reassembled outside the opening.

"Now, gentlemen," said Kit, rolling his aching shoulder. The man who'd accidentally struck him owned a thick fist. "Tell me the cause of this fight."

The three players, Master Howlett not among them, stood in a line, gazing at their feet or sucking the cuts on their knuckles.

The trader pulled a nose cloth from beneath his tunic and held it to his bleeding mouth. "That one," he said, wincing as his lips bled afresh with the speaking. "He is a cheat."

"I am not," said Willim Dunning. "The robe *is* of good brocade."

The other two players sidled away, putting distance between themselves and their accused friend.

"What do you say to Master Trader's statement that you have cheated him, Master Dunning?"

"I am *no* cheat."

"You are," shot back the trader. "You promised finest brocade and a trimming of fox fur upon the robe. But it is not fox fur, and the robe is ruined. Stained, it is! I'll not be able to sell it now!" He stepped up to Dunning, his nose but inches from the player's. "I paid you a goodly fifteen shilling for naught! Further, it has a tear my wife cannot mend!"

A stain and a tear?

"You sold the robe, Willim?" said one of his fellows, just as tall as Dunning but with a soft, cultured voice. "No wonder that

I could not find it. And I blamed the Poynards' servants for the theft when it was you! 'Fore God, Howlett will have your head!"

"He no longer wants the thing. Were you not aware? He calls the robe accursed," Dunning answered him with a sweep of one long-fingered hand, a gesture fit for the stage. Except this was not the stage, but a blood-spattered, ale-soaked tavern, its owner moaning over a shattered stool and a hole in the ceiling. "He had tossed it aside to be disposed of."

"Accursed?" asked the trader, his lower lip splitting wide again, blood dripping from it. "You sold me clothing that is not only ruined but accursed?" He stuck out his palm. "I would have my fifteen shillings back. At once."

Dunning jutted his chin. "You shall receive your money in full, sirrah."

"I shall receive that money, or you"—the trader jabbed Dunning's chest with his forefinger—"*you* shall be hung from the gibbet as a lesson to one and all!"

Dunning blanched, his pallor revealing the freckles that dotted the bridge of his nose.

"What is the stain, Master Trader?" asked Kit. Blood? And would the tear match the scrap of black material Kit had found snagged in brambles near the old fort hill?

The trader shrugged. "I know not. All I know is that the robe will not fetch the price I paid for it, with such a mark."

"Do you have it now at your shop?" asked Kit.

He nodded, mopping his lip with his nose cloth.

"I would have you show me the robe." He looked at the players. "And you are to go with my assistant to the stocks. Save for Master Dunning. I will meet with you at my house."

"What have we done?" the one who hadn't yet spoken wailed.

"Caused a brawl," said Kit. "Master Johnes, I shall speak with you later about the fine you are to pay for this fight today."

"But my ceiling!" He gawped helplessly at the hole.

"The town shall pay for its repair," said Kit, uncertain the burgesses would agree to do so, even though one of them had caused the damage. He turned to the trader. "Come, Master Trader. Show me this robe."

★ ★ ★

"You saw no one toss a witch's poppet over the garden fence?" Bess asked the servant of the family whose property adjoined Robert's.

A fine drizzle had begun to fall, and she and the girl huddled together on the strip of land behind the houses' garden walls. The servant had been given charge of the family's youngest, an infant but a few months old. She jiggled the tiny red-faced boy, swathed in tight linen swaddling bands except for his arms, who made ready to release a wail.

"A witch's poppet?" she asked, her eyes wide. "No one, Widow Ellyott. Not a soul. When think you someone did toss it into your garden?"

"Today, mayhap this afternoon." No earlier than then, thought Bess, as Humphrey had been at work in the garden that morning.

"I was out in the courtyard. Some of this day," said the servant. She hunched over the baby in her arms, protecting it from the dangerous rain. The infant reached for the strings of the girl's coif and tugged. "Scrubbing linens clean afore the clouds came and the rain began. I made no note of any person in particular. I did hear your manservant moving about in your yard." She screwed up her face as she sought to recall. "Lads walked by, chattering, though they ought be at their classes or their work. I cannot remember others."

"Not any of those players who are in town?" asked Joan, who stood in the muck and weeds that lay behind the brick wall of their garden.

"Nay, not them, for I'd have marked them most certain," the girl said. The infant she carried let out a feeble whimper. She tucked her finger into the child's mouth to suck, quieting it.

"What about an old woman who covers her lower face with a piece of linen?" asked Bess.

"I saw no such woman, Mistress, but I did have this one to keep my attention upon."

Bess looked over at Joan. "'Twas *not* Mistress Ellyn," said Joan.

Bess's gaze shifted from Joan's face to the upper floor of Robert's house, visible over the top of the garden wall. A woman's face showed in one of the chamber windows. Ellyn watched what they did.

"My thanks. Hurry into your mistress's house with the babe," said Bess to the servant girl, sending her back through the opening in her neighbor's fence.

Bess scanned the area behind the garden wall, though the daylight was fading and the rain clouds hung heavy in the sky. As she'd observed when she searched the afternoon Ellyn fled, the ground was well trampled by the feet of all those who chose to make it a path. 'Twas a narrow stretch of land, unusual in that no one in particular laid claim to it. In the summer, the townsfolk's children often played with their whirl-jacks and their hobbyhorses behind Robert's property and the houses alongside. Someone who'd passed by had lost a brass pin from their clothing. Not far from the pin, a worn fragment of leather lacing was tangled in a patch of taller grass.

Joan came over to her. "What hope you to find, Mistress?"

"A clue I'll not discover, Joan."

"Mayhap one of the boys that girl heard did toss the poppet over the wall."

Bess stopped her futile search. "In jest out of cruelty?" Up at the house, Ellyn had withdrawn from the window. "We can be certain of one fact. 'Twas not Mother Fletcher who left the poppet for me."

"Can we be certain, Mistress? We know not to where she has gone."

Sighing, Bess lifted her face to the mist of rain; her skin prickled where the droplets landed. "I wish I could once again be a child in Oxford, Joan. Where I felt safe and protected. Where murders and danger did not consume me. Before I understood the evil in this world."

Before her father had died. Before Laurence had taken her beloved husband from her. Before her hope of sanctuary here in Wiltshire had become a false hope, as unreal a thing as the draperies hung about a players' stage to offer the pretense of other times and places. Before. Before.

Alas, she could not return to the safety of her youth, though.

And evil pressed all around.

★　★　★

"They are safely secured in the stocks, Kit. Full of complaints, the two of them," said Gibb, slipping into Kit's hall. "The other one, Willim Dunning, waits below. I have paid the butcher's boy to keep watch over him for us."

The lad was strong from hefting slabs of meat. Dunning would not escape his guard.

"My thanks, Gibb." He glanced at the purpling bruise beneath his cousin's right eye. "You need to duck next time, coz."

Gibb smirked. "So should you." He nodded at Kit's shoulder, which Kit rubbed to ease the stiffness that ached.

"A minor blow."

"If you insist," said Gibb. "But what have you learned from the robe?"

Kit had spread it atop the narrow table set near the hall window. The lantern he'd lit revealed the raised pattern woven into the black brocade.

"I warrant the stains are blood." They were not easy to see on the material. Held up to the light in the proper manner, though, dark streaks showed across the front of the robe as though it had been spattered. "Also, do you see this rip?" Kit pointed out the tear along the hem. "It is a curious thing."

Kit retrieved the scrap of black material from where he'd stored it alongside a bloodied knife and broken reed pen. Setting the scrap adjacent to the tear, he moved it into place where the edges of one matched that of the other.

"I found this torn bit in brambles near the old fort hill," he said.

Gibb whistled between his teeth. "We now have the robe worn by the fellow who killed Reade. And all this while that I searched for it, it's been amongst the goods in a trader's shop."

Kit drew his fingers down the length of the fur—rabbit, not fox—trimming the edge of the robe. Long enough to reach the ground and of deepest black, it would be a fitting disguise against the dark of night. The fur beneath his fingertips was luxuriously soft, except for where dried blood caked it.

"Bring Dunning up here," said Kit. "And have the butcher's boy wait."

Gibb departed, his boot heels rapping against the staircase treads. He returned with the player. His nose no longer bled from his fight with the trader, but his green doublet had been ruined by the pummeling.

Gibb closed the hall door and leaned back against it, his hand resting on the long dagger at his hip.

"I know not why you hold me, Constable," said Willim Dunning, shooting a look at the robe.

Kit dragged his fingertips through his beard. "Tell me again about this robe, Master Dunning."

"Howlett had tossed it aside to be given to one of the Poynard servants after we departed. That is what he told me," he said. "When I learned we might not receive our pay, I decided it wasteful to give away the robe when good money could be had for it."

"When did you make this decision?"

"The morning after our planned entertainment," he said. "The morning after . . ."

"Yes, yes." The morning after Bartholomew Reade had been murdered.

"You said, Master Dunning, that Master Howlett thinks the robe accursed," said Gibb. "Why does he make such a claim?"

"Howlett believes it brings us ill luck," Dunning answered. "We entertained a lord in Reading and made use of the robe for our play. The fellow who wore it tripped and fell that very night. Broke his arm. And lateward, when we traveled through Gloucestershire and the weather was most foul, I took it from our trunks to wear over my own doublet and cloak. 'Twas but a moment later that the horse I rode unseated me." He looked over at the robe. "Damned thing. We would do well to be rid of it."

"Further, it *has* been the cause of a brawl," said Gibb.

"Aye. That is so! The robe *is* accursed!" exclaimed Dunning.

Kit rolled his eyes. "The morning after Reade's death, you, still intent upon making a penny off Howlett's mistrust of the robe, decided to sell it. Most cool-headed, Master Dunning."

"Not so cool-headed, Constable. Petty and greedy," he said. "But I was free to take it from our properties and sell it to the trader. No crime."

"Your fellow player claims the robe was missing the day of the play. He'd gone to look for it, meaning to make use of it. Despite its cursedness."

He fixed his gaze on Kit's face. "All I know, Constable, is that when I went to fetch the robe the morning after Bartholomew died, it was where Howlett had tossed it."

"And where was that?" asked Kit.

"In the corner of the room where our other properties were stored. The storage room that is next to the Poynards' massive kitchen." He paused, his reddish-yellow brows meeting above his nose. "A room any in the Poynard household could access, Constable, as we were not allowed to lock the door. They mistrusted us and would not honor us with a key."

"Did you see anyone with the robe the evening of the performance, Master Dunning?"

"Nay, I did not," he said. "But I was out searching for Bartholomew. And then . . . and then I found him."

Kit eyed the fellow. Were they any nearer the truth of what had occurred that day?

"Why do I not believe your tale, Master Dunning?" he asked.

Though the room was far from hot, Dunning began to sweat. He blotted his forehead with the back of his sleeve. "I know not, Constable."

"Yes, you do," he replied. "Tell me the truth, or I shall wring it from you."

Gibb looked over at Kit, alarm in his gaze.

"As you will," croaked Dunning. "I did find the robe and hide it."

"It was not in the Poynards' storage room?" asked Gibb.

"No. 'Twas alongside the highway," he said. "Near to where Bartholomew died."

CHAPTER 18

Gibb cursed under his breath. More profanity than Kit had ever heard his normally gentlemanly cousin utter.

"Alongside the highway," repeated Kit.

"I was searching for Bartholomew, calling out to him. Telling him to stop his dalliance with his fair lady and come to play his part," he said, suddenly keen to unburden himself of the secrets he'd been holding. "Then I saw the robe, tossed beneath a thicket of brambles and grasses. I recognized it instantly as the one Howlett thought accursed. In a trice I gathered it up and searched around for who might have left it there. 'Twas then I noticed the hillock through a gap in the brambles. Saw the figure reclined atop the mound. At first I thought the person asleep. I might have walked on, but I did not."

He paused to swallow and blot more sweat off his forehead.

"Continue, Master Dunning," said Kit.

"I was struck with terror to realize the murdered man was Bartholomew," he said. "And that someone might discover that the black robe belonged to the troupe. One of us would be accused of the crime. In my panic, I made haste to hide it away."

"Yet you sold the robe the next day to the trader, Master

Dunning," said Gibb. "'Twas stained with your friend's blood. *You* would be the one accused."

"In the weak light that evening, I'd not noted the blood staining the black brocade, Master Harwoode," he said. "Overnight, ideas crept into my troubled brain. The robe was worth a great deal of money. I am in debt. I decided to retrieve it from where I'd stashed it and sell the robe to one of the town traders. Be rid of any evidence that might link the troupe to the murder."

Kit considered Dunning. "Could Howlett have taken the robe from the Poynards' storage room without any of the players noticing?" They had vouched for each other but not for Howlett the afternoon of Reade's murder.

"'Twould not have been difficult," said Dunning. "But he would not ever choose to wear the robe. He was terrified of it, and the troupe has other equally suitable garments to make use of. Unless . . ."

"Unless?" asked Kit.

"Unless he plotted to make use of the robe all along, Constable, and merely did pretend to be fearful of it." Dunning's eyes widened. "God's blood! Howlett!"

"Take Master Dunning to the stocks to join his mates, Gibb, with the help of the butcher's lad."

Gibb threw open the hall door, grabbed Dunning's elbow, and dragged him out of the room.

"What? I have committed no crime!" shouted Dunning, his voice echoing off the plaster walls beyond the room. "You seek another! Why not question Howlett?" He continued to shout as Gibb pulled him down the steps. A boot kicked at the staircase wall to slow their descent. "I saw him this morning. Searching

Bartholomew's trunk. He means to flee with that manuscript!
The one he craved! Howlett wanted Bartholomew gone!"

★ ★ ★

"Why are my men in the stocks? We depart on the morrow! At
dawn!" shouted John Howlett. Gibb had brought him to Kit's
house, and he paced the office. "Forsooth, I would we'd not
come to this town."

In the kitchen at the rear of the house, a pot clanged to the
tiled floor. Howlett's shouting must have startled Alice. His
shouting startled Kit. Within the confines of the ground-floor
office, the man's volume was loud enough to make Kit's ears ring.

Gibb opened the door and leaned around it. "Kit?"

"Master Howlett is distraught but means no harm."

Gibb nodded but remained standing within the door's
opening.

"Your men are in the stocks for brawling, Master Howlett,"
replied Kit. "Therefore, you do *not* depart on the morrow."

Howlett dragged in a breath, his nostrils flaring. "I shall
speak to Master Poynard about this. To the burgesses. For—"

"   sooth. Yes. As you say," said Kit. "You are welcome to
speak with them."

Kit unfolded the brocade robe. "What have you to tell me
about this robe, Master Howlett?"

"It is accursed," he said firmly.

Kit tossed the robe over a nearby stool. "Why dispose of the
robe now, Master Howlett, when I hear you have long thought
it unlucky?"

He hesitated before answering. "I had a bad-boding dream.
A warning."

"Your dream spoke the truth, as the robe is stained with blood. Reade's blood."

Howlett recoiled. "I know naught of how blood got upon it!"

"One of your players has said that he searched for it the day of the intended performance but could not find the robe among the troupe's belongings," said Kit. "Where might it have gone, do you think?"

"'Tis certain, Constable, that Dunning had already taken the robe, intending to sell it to a local trader."

"How intriguing, then, that he admits to finding it along the highway not far from Master Reade's dead body," he said.

"He has confessed to killing Reade? Then why question me?" cried Howlett. "Accuse Dunning, who had the robe in his possession and sold it. *He* murdered Reade!"

"What motive had he?" *Give me a credible one, and I might consider the truth of it.*

But Howlett did not present a motive, credible or otherwise. Instead, he sputtered and mumbled.

"This morning, you were seen searching the room Bartholomew Reade shared with Willim Dunning," said Kit.

"Who makes this claim?"

"More than one person," answered Kit. Unwilling to trust Dunning's word alone, he'd had Gibb question the other players. "You had broken open his trunk. What did you want? The play he'd refused to give you? Did you mean to flee with it?"

Howlett exhaled. "I did search. I confess. And why not? Reade had no more use for it; he is dead. But I did not find the manuscript, and I ceased looking."

Kit leaned back against his writing desk and folded his arms. "The problem remains, Master Howlett, as to where you were when Bartholomew Reade was being knifed on a Wiltshire hill. No one can account for you."

"I have told you. When Reade was not at the Poynards' at the proper time to prepare, I went to search for him along with the others. But I went the wrong direction, did not find him, and had to return to beg forgiveness for the delay," he said, his voice shaking. "That is what happened. Nothing else. Nothing else!"

"I much prefer the tale that you followed Reade to retrieve that damned play," said Kit. "He'd told you and the other members of your troupe that he'd give it to a friend for safekeeping rather than see you take possession of the manuscript. You reasoned that the friend he meant was the woman he intended to meet on that hill."

"No!"

"In a passion, you killed him and his blood spattered this robe, which you wore to conceal your elegant pearl-colored doublet and trunk hose," said Kit. Howlett wore the pieces of clothing now, his peasecod-bellied doublet shimmering with the silver aglets that hung from the tips of its many laces. "I must say that stabbing the reed pen into his throat was a theatrical touch, Master Howlett."

"No. No!" He glanced at the door, but Gibb barred exit with his body. Howlett might be taller than Kit's cousin, but he was not likely stronger. "Forsooth, that is *not* what occurred!"

"Where were you late yester afternoon, Master Howlett?" asked Kit. Around the time when a young woman was trampled to death in a barn. "Near to sunset. Your men cannot account for you then, either."

Gibb had also questioned them about that.

Howlett had begun to sweat as much as Dunning had earlier. "I went for a walk along the river. I was restless and thought
to clear my head."

"Did anyone see you there?"

"Some boys who had gone to fish. Servants of the Poynards,
I think," he said. "I walked past them and saw no others."

"So you did not go to a nearby farm in search of that trea-
sured manuscript, which might have been in the possession of
the young woman you believed Reade had planned to meet the
afternoon he died?" asked Kit. "A young woman you saw with
him the day he arrived in the village with the troupe." According to Bess Ellyott, who'd learned of the encounter from Anna.

"No. No! To the river! I went to the river!"

Howlett might be telling the truth. Or he might not.

Witnesses. I need witnesses.

"Take him to the stocks to join his fellows, Gibb."

The man howled protests. Gibb hauled him through the
house and outside, the closing of the front door silencing
Howlett's bellows.

★   ★   ★

The doors to the hall were shut to the world beyond. A low fire
crackled, the thorn long ago consumed by the flames that
snapped the stems and branches Humphrey had stacked upon
the hearth. The dreary rain that had begun to fall soured Bess's
mood, and she'd had Joan draw the curtains tight against the
weather. The paneled and decorated walls and low-beamed ceiling seemed to press down around her. Quail lounged upon the
tiles before the hearth, warmed by the fire. He twitched his
brows at her, his eyes following as she sat, then rose, then sat
again on Robert's chair. The poppet itself . . .

"The poppet," she murmured, eyeing it where it lay, face-down on the stool that always stood near the fireplace. She had thought to toss the entire poppet into the flames as she had the thorn and watch it sizzle. Was it dangerous to burn such a thing, though, or was that the proper way to destroy it? Would it be better to bury the object along the highway or drop it into the river?

"Am I so superstitious as to grant it powers over me I know it does not possess?"

But still . . .

It oozed evil, the hole torn through the red fabric by the thorn that had poked its body a menacing wound. Bess pressed a hand to her stomach just below her pair of bodies. *Martin, what have I done by concerning myself with these matters?*

The hall door to the entry passage opened and closed, and soft footfalls crossed the room's rush matting. Bess had no need to turn to see that Joan's feet made the noise.

"Here, Mistress." Joan handed her a heated posset of milk and wine spiced with nutmeg. "Are you certain you do not wish to take some food?"

Bess had decided against supper, her appetite failing her. When was the last time she'd hungered for a meal? Before Anna had died? Before Robert had departed for London? Before that awful dream she'd had?

"My thanks, Joan, but I am certain." She took the earthen-ware cup and sipped, the drink's warmth insufficient against her chill. "Could Ellyn have placed that creation in the garden, Joan, without our seeing?"

"She would never have done so, Mistress," said Joan. "'Twas those lads that the servant girl heard, I warrant. That is the answer."

"Humphrey says Ellyn wishes to frighten me, but I only wish to help her, and she knows that," said Bess.

Joan dismissively clicked her tongue against her teeth. "Humphrey mislikes Mistress Ellyn. He'd spew no end of vileness and false claims against her."

Bess lowered the earthenware cup to her lap. "He also says you sympathize with her because of the fellow who gave you your scar."

Joan, her fingertips lightly brushing the edge of her coif where it covered the jagged red line on her face, dropped her gaze.

"What happened, Joan?" Bess asked, for her servant had never revealed the whole of the story. "Will you not tell me?"

Silence spun out, and the only noises were that of the fire, the rattle of wagon wheels upon the road beyond the house, the bark of a town dog that pricked Quail's ears. The church bell tolled curfew. Soon would come the sound of the watchman's staff rapping against the broken cobbles and scattered gravel of the road.

"I befriended a whip-jack, Mistress, believing his tale that he was a sailor without a ship and in need of food and money," Joan answered, her face blank as an unused slate upon which any emotion—or none—could be written. "In return for my kindness, he assaulted me. My friend came to my aid."

"The friend who watches Laurence for us? Who sent us that message?"

"Aye," said Joan. "We made certain that whip-jack would not assault another woman again, and vowed to protect each other ever after."

"That is terrible," said Bess softly.

Her gaze met Bess's. "Which, Mistress? The ease with which sweet words did gull me, or our revenge?"

Both. "I am sorry for what you have suffered."

"It is over and past, Mistress. Naught to be done now save not think 'pon him."

"I will not mention this again."

Her servant inclined her head in gratitude and resumed staring at the poppet. "We should take that thing to the constable, Mistress. As you did the other."

"I no longer know what he can do to help us, Joan," said Bess. "I no longer know what anyone can do."

★ ★ ★

"The family still sits at supper, Constable," said the Poynard servant who answered Kit's knock. The hall, which lay to Kit's right, was visible through the entrance cut into the screens passage. The Poynards ate in subdued silence around their table. "We be most busy at this hour."

"I'll not keep you long from your work if you take me to Simon now," said Kit.

If Howlett had indeed passed some of Poynards' servants along the river, it was as good a guess as any that Simon had been among them.

She wiped her hands across her apron and pointed to the doorstead at the opposite end of the passage. "He be in the kitchen. Come along."

He followed her down the passage and into the corridor that led past the various service rooms, now empty, that had housed the players and their belongings. Where a black robe had been tossed aside and a manuscript of a three-act play had been searched for and—if Kit believed John Howlett—not found.

The kitchen was a massive room fitted with a vast hearth. Buckets and brass cauldrons were stored beneath the stone washing slab, and on the walls were hung racks and cupboards to hold plate. The aroma of cooked meat and onions and herbs filled the air, as did the noise of servants bustling to prepare the final dishes to be sent to the table. A tawny dog, gobbling scraps that had fallen from the trestle-supported plank at the center of the room, snapped and growled at an orange cat that ventured too near. Among the servants, Kit did not notice Simon.

"You took long enough, Pitts," growled a heavy-jowled fellow, his face shimmering with sweat from the heat of the blazing fire at his back. He did not look up from the tart he'd drawn from the oven, set upon the trestle table, and sprinkled with sugar. "This is late to be served. They will be wrathful."

"I'm not Pitts," said Kit. "I would like to talk to Simon. Where can I find him?"

The fellow lifted his head. He jerked back when he realized it was the constable who stood in his kitchen. "What has the boy done?"

"Nothing criminal," he said as Simon walked through the door that led out onto the courtyard.

"Well, there he be." The man nodded toward the lad.

Kit strode across the kitchen. "Come outside, Simon," he said to the boy, taking his elbow and pulling him out of the kitchen.

"What is it now, Constable?" Simon asked once Kit had shut the back door behind them.

"I want to ask you about the master of the players," said Kit. "I thought you might know the answer to my question, as you're so very watchful."

The lad grinned at the compliment, revealing his chipped front teeth. "They are all in the stocks for brawling. Even Master Howlett! Out in the rain!"

"Aye, just so."

Kit scanned their surroundings to see who might be listening. A torch, tucked into a holder next to one of the outbuilding's doors, sputtered in the drizzle. A man who'd been cleaning a bucket beneath its light ducked back into the stable and out of the rain. Leaving them alone.

"Yesterday afternoon, did you notice Master Howlett anywhere that might not be usual for a visiting player like him to be wandering?" asked Kit.

"I saw him near the river," he answered. "Me and the boy who works in the stable went to fish. We be allowed, Constable!" Simon hastily added.

"I am not here to arrest you for fishing on Poynard land, Simon. Continue."

"I saw the fellow, walking along the path that goes near by the river," said the lad. "An hour or so before the sun began to set."

"Did he look anxious or in a hurry?"

"Not much," he said. "He just kept on his way." He pointed away from the grounds surrounding the house. Away from town.

"Howlett was headed that direction?" asked Kit. "Are you sure?"

"Certes, I am."

Kit gazed into the dark, the rain as it fell winking like jewels in the torchlight. That direction would have led Howlett toward the eastern road that passed the old fort hill. And the Merricks' farm.

A simple walk along the river, Howlett? I think not.

And the noose is closing about your neck.

CHAPTER 19

"The bruise on your face looks worse this morning, Gibb," said Kit.

"My thanks for the compliment, coz." Gibb touched fingertips to his cheekbone. "It feels worse as well."

They strode across the market square, splashing through puddles. The sun had risen barely a half an hour earlier, but already a gaggle of onlookers had collected where the traveling players, including Howlett, remained locked in the stocks, their hands and feet protruding through the holes. Out of curiosity, Kit had once asked to be locked there. The jailer had humored him, and then, chuckling, had fastened the lock and walked off. Not long after, Kit's legs had begun to tingle, then lose all feeling. Shouts and threats of seeing the jailer placed in the stocks himself had brought the fellow running back to free him.

"Why think you Master Howlett would need to kill Master Reade?" asked his cousin, his attention on the crowd. Even the priest from All Saints, in his long dark gown and severe black cap and coif, had joined them. The wife of the tailor, whose shop was located hard by the stocks and pillory, stood with her arms folded in the entrance to the business. The rabble blocked any customers from reaching her door. "Why not simply steal the manuscript from Master Reade and refuse to return it, if that play was what he most desired?"

A roar arose from the crowd. The more boisterous among them shouted obscenities at the players, making the rest laugh over their increasingly creative insults. Dunning flushed with anger. Howlett hung his head.

"Because Howlett failed to locate it," said Kit, stopping to watch the crowd in case matters spun out of control. "Otherwise, he might have done just that."

"He *would* have been most angry to not find the manuscript upon Master Reade's body," said Gibb. "But why harm Anna?"

"He must have concluded that Reade had managed to give the manuscript to her just before Howlett arrived at the hill," said Kit. "He did not know that she hadn't met Reade because of her illness, though."

"But the witch's effigy?"

"A warning. Mayhap he pinned a note to the poppet, threatening her if she did not return the manuscript."

"Ah." Gibb's brows tucked together. "But I still do not understand why he sought to kill Anna, if he did."

"She did not respond to his threat, and he panicked," said Kit. "Intent upon departing the village as quickly as possible, he went to the Merricks' farm. One of the Poynards' servants spotted him walking that direction the day Anna died. Once there, he confronted the girl, attempting to get her to hand over the manuscript. The cow became agitated—"

"And trampled her!"

"Before she died, she must have protested that Reade hadn't given her the manuscript, for Howlett continued to search for it yesterday morning," said Kit. "Unsuccessfully."

The crowd looked uninterested in doing more than taunting

the players, so Kit continued on. He turned his steps toward the lane that would head away from town and toward the Merricks' farm. He had one final broken thread to tie in his investigation. He needed a witness to confirm that Howlett had been near the barn when Anna died. Then all would be concluded and the man could be charged with the crime.

"I must say that Frances will be happy we near a resolution. You shall have no more excuses to delay her supper," said Gibb, a grin lifting the corner of his mouth. "Tonight, then. And I vow you will find Beatrix pretty."

"That is the name of Frances's friend? Beatrix?"

"Aye," said Gibb. "She will be happy, too. She tires of idling in wait for you, the handsome and most agreeable Constable Christopher Harwoode. Or so Frances would have her believe." He dodged Kit's fist with a laugh, then sobered. "'Tis time you put the memories of Luce to rest, Kit. She would not wish you to mourn her forever. It has been five years now. There are other women. Worthy women."

Kit pulled up short, his spine, every muscle, stiffening. Gibb's intentions were good. But his freehearted cousin could not comprehend the pain he felt, which burned and itched like a scar.

"You needn't accompany me to the Merricks', Gibb."

"I meant no harm, Kit."

"Nonetheless," he said. "Keep a watch on those people. I'll return soon."

He strode off, his cousin staring after him.

★ ★ ★

"All is concluded, Constable?" asked David Merrick, stretching his neck above his ruff. "I am most pleased."

They stood together in the farmyard, where Merrick had

been watching one of his family's cowherds move cattle from their barn out toward the fields.

"Not quite yet, Master Merrick." Kit's gaze tracked the herder in his dun-colored tunic and sagging wool hose as he poked and prodded the animals toward an opening in the woven fence that separated the farm buildings from the meadows beyond. "We have found the black robe the killer wore while stabbing Master Reade, though."

Merrick recoiled at Kit's bluntness. "Then what remains unfinished, Constable?"

"The matter of how Anna Webb died."

"We have paid the fine for the red cow causing her death. And sold the animal, to be rid of it. None of the dairymaids would work with the beast," he said. "My father will be angry. Though old, the cow gave good milk. It could not be helped, though. He will understand."

Merrick did not sound certain about his father's understanding.

"The master of the troupe of players was observed walking this direction, not so long before Anna died," said Kit. "Did he come here, Master Merrick?"

David Merrick blinked. "John Howlett? I think not. I have been occupied with dairy accounts, though. They keep me in my office most hours of the day."

"I would like to speak with Thomasin, then," said Kit, as the woman herself appeared at the entrance of the barn, a pail of milk in each hand. Sparrows that had settled nearby flew off as Thomasin closed the barn door. She carried herself with a straighter back than provided by a tightly laced kirtle. A confident stance that Kit associated with fearlessness. "If you do not mind."

Merrick squared his shoulders and jutted his chin. His stance was never confident, Kit realized.

"Thomasin, come here," Merrick called to her.

Her brow furrowing, she set down the pails and walked to where they waited.

Thomasin dipped a brief curtsy. "Master David?"

"The constable would talk to you."

Her pale-eyed gaze skipped from Merrick's face to Kit's. "Aye?"

"Thomasin, you are an observant woman," said Kit. "Jennet has told me she noticed no strangers near the farm when Anna died. Can you say the same?"

She shot Merrick a glance before answering. "I may have noticed a stranger, Constable. I should have mentioned this to Mistress Ellyott when she was here yesterday, nosing about. But she did not ask what I might have seen, and I did not say."

"What saw you?" asked Merrick.

"I am certain 'twas just a shadow," she said. "A trick of the fading light, but I imagined I saw a person. In the trees, there."

She pointed at a copse at the base of the hill upon which the Merricks' house and barns had been built. If Kit could see through the trees, he'd spy a grassy vale, a lane where the remains of Mother Fletcher's cottage smoldered, and another stand of trees, beyond which rose the mound where Reade had died.

Merrick stepped nearer to her. "Was it the master of the troupe?"

"Master Merrick, I shall question her. If you will," said Kit. "Could you tell if this person was a man or a woman?"

"I did go over to look," she explained. "But when I reached the woods, no one was hiding there. I did not hear the sound of running. I did not see fresh-trampled footprints in the mud. I returned to the house and put the event out of my mind. 'Twas just a shadow."

"What think you, Constable?" asked Merrick.

That I wish I had proof this specter in the woods was John Howlett.

"Thomasin, did Anna ever mention the master of the troupe to you?" asked Kit.

"She talked at supper about Bartholomew's return," said Thomasin. "On and on she spoke about him, 'til we tired of her chattering. She said nothing about the others, though. I cannot say if she knew this fellow."

"One of the players," said Merrick. "Of course 'twould be one of them! Any one of them would hurt a pretty young woman like Anna! He hid in the trees. Seeking the right time to attack—"

"David!" shouted Mistress Merrick, stepping into the yard. "David, there you are. Come now. Your brother is most violently ill."

Merrick headed for the house, and his mother moved aside as he passed by her.

"This house is accursed, Constable," she cried out to Kit. "We have a curse upon us!"

★   ★   ★

"Mistress Ellyn will hopefully be staying with us for some time, Humphrey," said Bess. She knelt in the kitchen garden, a cloth beneath her shins to protect her skirt against the wet ground. She dug up leeks and parsnips for the evening meal, enjoying the aroma of the soil, the sight of worms wiggling away from her spade. She usually left the task to Joan, but today it was one that felt needful. A task that might soothe her unquiet mind. "I intend to train her as an herbalist, so you must accept her presence in the house."

Robert's manservant, his head and face sheathed in gauze, worked at the great woven-straw beehives occupying the corner of the garden. He prepared the bees for their winter rest and would take the weakest hive to be gradually merged with the stronger so that all would survive the coming weather.

She sat back upon her heels and looked over at him. "Did you hear me, Humphrey?"

He made a grunting noise that might signal he had heard but continued peeping through the opening of the nearest hive. A handful of bees buzzed around him. "I did."

Bess shook dirt off the parsnip bunch she'd pulled from the ground. "We must not continue to suspect Mistress Ellyn of any part in the crimes that have occurred," she said, laying the parsnips alongside the leeks in her basket.

He did not reply; 'twas certain Humphrey would continue to suspect her all he wished.

"She also did not leave that poppet for us to find," said Bess. "A band of mischievous boys tossed the thing over the wall. The servant girl next door heard them."

"Town lads may have done." Humphrey straightened and carefully swept a bee off his sleeve. "The village folk mistrust you."

A statement he delivered with untroubled ease, as though the townspeople's opinion was only to be expected.

Oh, Robin, what am I to do with your manservant?

"Then I must win back their trust," she said, standing up.

The gauze netting concealed the look on his face. "Aye, Mistress."

Must he sound so doubtful of the success of such an endeavor?

Bess collected her basket and returned to the house. Joan met her at the back door.

"Mistress. The Merricks have sent a servant to bring you to their house again," she said. "'Tis their youngest son this time. He has been struck strangely ill. Like Anna."

★ ★ ★

Mistress Merrick, her hand upon her protruding belly, met Bess at the door. The gaunt house-servant—Jennet—who'd brought her to the Merricks' darted off. A rush of anxious voices greeted the girl as she disappeared into the house's service rooms.

Lips pinched tight, Mistress Merrick glanced toward the noise. Unwelcome gossip to be punished later.

"I regret that I have had need to call you here again, Widow Ellyott. This time, my youngest is ill," she said. "He purges like Anna did. Come this way."

Bess, gripping the strap of the satchel that held her physic, followed the woman. They passed through the ground-floor rooms and up the stairs to the chambers above. In the upper parlor, the other Merrick children huddled together like a cluster of unhappy and frightened puppies. They had defensively set their backs to the wall of the room, through which Bess had walked that first day when she'd been called to tend an ailing dairy-maid. The children silently watched her and their mother, their quietness a measure of their unease.

Bess entered a chamber set off the parlor, the woman with her pausing halfway across the room.

"He is in there," she said, pointing to a smaller chamber to her right. "I dare not enter, to protect the babe in my womb."

"I understand, Mistress Merrick," said Bess.

She went ahead without the woman and entered a cramped room set all around with low bedsteads. This must be where the youngest children slept with the servant tasked to watch them.

Someone had opened the sole narrow casement window to freshen the stinking air within the space. The ill Merrick boy, green faced and moaning, lay atop a bed in the corner. At his side stood Constable Harwoode, his arms crossed.

He inclined his head. "Mistress Ellyott."

"Is a sick child a concern for the law these days, Constable?" she asked, setting her satchel alongside the boy's bed. Furnishings were sparse—a handful of trunks, the bedsteads, a woven rush mat frayed about the edges that had likely been used elsewhere at one time—the whitewashed plaster walls empty of all decoration. Somber but adequate for children.

"It is if the cause of his illness is the same as what sickened Anna Webb," he said.

"She had a stomach sickness." Bess drew over the only stool she noticed in the room. "An illness that occurs with sad regularity, Constable. Without question you have suffered from it yourself, as have I."

"Any sickness of mine, however, has never kept me from a planned meeting with a man soon to be murdered, Mistress Ellyott," he said.

Indeed.

She smiled down at the lad, whose eyes were the same shade of cinnamon brown as his sister Ellyn's. He was a handsome little boy, far more so than his brother David. "How do you feel, young sir? Are any of your siblings sickly, also? Or any of the household servants?"

She'd asked Anna a similar question, and she received a similar response from the boy. Afraid to open his mouth for fear the nausea would return, he shook his head.

"Then mayhap you alone have eaten something foul, which has tortured your stomach," she said, resting the back of her hand against his forehead. No fever to speak of, same as with Anna. Bess reached for her satchel and untied the strings binding it closed. "Is that what has happened? Bad food?"

Strangely, his eyes began to water. "I did not mean to."

"What did you not mean to eat, hmm?" she asked.

Bess retrieved the jar of boiled organy and mint leaves that had been diluted into wine. The same physic she'd used to treat Anna and Ellyn. Disquiet shivered across her skin as she poured out a quantity into the pottery cup she had brought.

"I drank it. I shouldn't have done," he said, crying openly now.

The shiver became a prickle of gooseflesh. "Drank what?" she asked. "What did you drink?"

"From that bottle," he said, swallowing hard. Bess wiped the tears off his cheeks. "Out by the rubbish pit. Where I saw Jennet with that cloth poppet."

Bess shot a look at Kit Harwoode. "Where is this pit, lad?" he asked.

"Behind the front barn."

Not far from the fence where Bess had retrieved a witch's effigy from a patch of thistle.

"I will go look, Mistress," said the constable. He ran from the room, calling for Mistress Merrick.

"Boys like you can be most curious, I know. 'Tis understandable." Bess smiled again at the lad, wishing to calm him. "Tell me about Jennet and the poppet."

"I saw her with it. She tossed it into the weeds." He sniffled. "I went to look at the poppet, but Little screeched that it was evil."

"'Little'?" asked Bess, straining to hear Kit Harwoode's voice.

And there it was, along with Mistress Merrick's. So far as

Bess could tell, they were headed outside. One of the Merrick children came to peep around the doorstead, while the footfalls of the rest pattered across the warped floorboards of the parlor and down the steps, chasing after the constable and their mother.

"'Tis what we call her," said the boy. "The little sister."

"Ah," said Bess. "Did you also see Jennet with the bottle you drank from?"

"No," he said. "It tasted foul." He squeezed his mouth shut.

Bess grabbed the bucket one of the servants had placed nearby and set it by the bed, but the lad's nausea passed.

"The physic I have brought for you will help your queasiness," she said.

Boot heels rapped across the floor in the outer room, and the constable entered. He held a vial of mottled mustard-colored glass, which he held out to her. The bung that would have sealed the long narrow neck was gone. "The bottle was still by the pit—near to another empty one just like it—but there's not any more liquid within. He drank it all."

The boy gazed apprehensively at the constable.

"A residue might remain for me to taste," Bess said, taking the bottle.

"Do not risk your health, madam."

"Do not fret, Constable. 'Tis too small an amount to cause me harm." She slipped her little finger into the neck, swiped it around the glass, and raised it to her tongue. Bitter but not overmuch. She sniffed the vial. A faint aroma greeted her. "Artemisia, I believe. Known commonly as mugwort. Possibly mixed with savin to increase its effects. A strong enough solution would grieve anyone's stomach. And this appears to have been strong enough. A mistake, by whoever prepared the simple, to have added so much. No wonder you are ill, young sir."

Bess patted the boy's hand and gave back the vial to the constable.

"What is its use?" he asked.

"Artemisia by itself can calm the fits that come with ague and ease inflammations," she said, staring at the glass. In the room's dim light, it glowed an evil yellow. Her gaze moved from the bottle to the constable's face. "More importantly, and mayhap more relevantly, at the right concentration it may start a woman's monthly flows."

And thereby, perhaps, remove an unwanted child from her womb.

CHAPTER 20

"Why did you not tell me before about finding the witch's effigy, Jennet?" asked Kit.

They stood in the Merricks' low-ceilinged hall. The room had recently been strewn with a large quantity of meadowsweet to scent the space, its pungent smell so overpowering Kit longed for an open window. Mistress Ellyott had left the sick boy in the care of one of the other servants—the lad's mother would not be convinced that his illness was not catching—to stand near the unlit hearth. Her unhappiness read in every line of her face.

"I was affrighted by it." Jennet squeezed her work-worn hands together. "I went to toss a broken cup in the rubbish pit and saw it by the barn. I thought the poppet was for me. I did not want to tell you, Constable, lest the curse strike me too for speaking about it."

"Why might you think the poppet was meant for you, Jennet?" asked Bess Ellyott.

"Foolishness." The girl shook her head, the strings of her coif flapping beneath her chin. "I was affrighted. I sought to be rid of it. I threw it toward the fence. I should not have touched it."

"Did it have a note attached to it?" he asked.

The girl tucked her brows together. "No."

"The boy"—Kit didn't know his name—"drank from this bottle." He held the vial up to the light coming through the broad window. "He found it near the rubbish pit. Did you notice the vial when you went to discard that broken cup?"

Jennet eyed the bottle he held. "I cannot say, sir. The poppet scared me so greatly I'd not have seen anything but it."

Kit set the vial on the table at his side.

"The young master's illness is similar to what Anna suffered from," said Mistress Ellyott. "Might she have also drank from that bottle?"

"Anna would not make herself sick wittingly, Mistress. 'Twould keep her away from her work," she said. "Not a one of us would do so."

"Think carefully, Jennet," said Mistress Ellyott. "Did Anna mention a strange taste of food or drink the day she fell ill?" She looked over at Kit. "I did not ask Anna when I tended her, for I'd presumed she had simply eaten something spoiled."

"She misliked the ale we'd been served with our dinner that day," said Jennet. "She said she could not fathom how I had swallowed it all so happily. I did not think it untasty, though."

"No one else said it tasted foul?" asked Kit.

"No one, Constable, that I remember."

"And this bottle, Jennet." Kit tapped the vial with a fingertip. "Have you ever seen one like it in this house?"

"There are bottles the same as it in the mistress's workroom," she replied. "Where she makes her simples."

"Do you mean Mistress Merrick?" asked Mistress Ellyott.

"Nay. Mistress Ellyn," said the girl.

"Can only Mistress Ellyn access her workroom?" asked Kit.

"Most usually, yes, but the key has been lost some weeks now," answered Jennet. "Master Merrick was too busy to attend to its replacement before he left for the cheese fair in Burford."

"So anyone could have gone into Mistress Ellyn's workroom and retrieved one of those bottles and mayhap even made use of the simples she'd prepared?" asked Bess Ellyott.

"Might be possible, Mistress," said the girl. "Though who would dare? 'Twas Mistress Ellyn's room, and she is most protective of it."

★   ★   ★

"You suspect Ellyn Merrick of poisoning Anna," said Bess. She shifted the strap of her satchel and gathered her skirts to attempt to match the constable's lengthy strides. All she succeeded in doing, though, was kicking up mud and grit from the road and onto her stockings.

He looked over at her. "Have I said that?"

"I attempt to extract your thoughts from your head, Constable, where you keep them so carefully stored."

They rounded the curve in the road. Soon they would pass the lane that led to the blackened remains of Mother Fletcher's cottage. And farther along, the mound, its evil yet spreading its tentacles across the village and the surrounding countryside.

"I have not concluded Ellyn Merrick was the one who tainted the girl's drink," said the constable. "It could have been someone else in the household, wanting to keep Anna from her tryst with Reade."

"Ellyn most likely prepared the simple, however, since she had a specific reason to consume artemisia," said Bess.

The lane to Mother Fletcher's cottage came and went. But the old fort hill, the supposed druids' mound, loomed ahead.

The constable took Bess's elbow and drew her nearer to him. A comfort she was grateful for.

"If Ellyn also drank the mugwort, to be rid of her child, why did she not vomit the physic harmlessly away like her brother and Anna?" he asked.

"She did, some," said Bess, recalling the mess streaking the front of Ellyn's bodice the night she'd collapsed at the garden gate. "Mayhap she'd been taking sips for days, waiting for it to take effect, and finally became desperate to drink more. When finished, Ellyn discarded the vial at the rubbish pit. Then her blood began to flow, and she became alarmed and ran to me."

"Very reasonable thoughts, Mistress," he said. "I should inform you that a bloodied robe has been found. It belonged to the troupe of players."

"One of them murdered Master Reade."

"Possibly the master of the troupe, Mistress."

They passed the hillock. Constable Harwoode did not release his hold upon her arm, though. She also did not beg him to let go.

Bess rolled her lips together. *My next question will not please him . . .*

"What, though, do we make of the second poppet?" she asked, once the mound was far behind them and the cottages at the edge of town drew near.

He halted. "A second poppet?" he asked, his brows lowering.

"Yes," she said. "The one left for me."

★　★　★

"Mistress Ellyott. Your servant woman said you would return anon, and here you are." Jeffrey Poynard made a long leg. "But was that the constable I heard shouting outside?"

Alerted by Joan to his presence in the hall, Bess had entered to find him inspecting the painted designs of vines and flowers that framed the room's street-facing window. Mayhap he was jealous of Robert's good taste.

"Constable Harwoode accompanied me from the Merricks', where I had attended to their youngest boy. Upon our approach into town, he received a piece of news that greatly distressed him," she said, handing off her satchel and cloak to Joan, who'd accompanied her into the room.

"News about his investigation of Master Reade's murder?" he asked. "Rumors swirl that bets placed at the Cross Keys indicate Master Howlett will be accused."

Gossip flying faster than birds upon their wings. "Do any at the Cross Keys place bets upon the name of the one who set fire to Mother Fletcher's cottage?"

He smirked over her question. "Why might they?"

Indeed. Why might they. "I am not free to speak on such matters as concern the constable, Master Poynard," said Bess. "Joan, bring ale for our visitor."

"No need, Mistress," he said. "I shall not stay long."

Joan departed, closing the door only partway. She'd not leave Bess utterly alone with the odious fellow.

"I pray that young Master Merrick is not too ill," he said.

"He suffers from the same sickness that afflicted Anna Webb. Curious, think you not?"

"Children and servants. I understand none of them."

His smile was apologetic. She did not trust the veracity of it.

"What brings you to my home today, Master Poynard?" she asked, as he'd not bothered to previously attend to the woman he should be there to visit. "Assuredly you did not come to inspect the decorations on the walls of my brother's house."

His gaze wandered to the nearest painted flowers. "They are most fine, Mistress Ellyott."

"I can recommend to you the painter who did the work." Were they to dance about the topic all the day? "But such trifles are not why you are here."

"You are bold indeed," he said. Boldness he'd likely be pleased to tell Robert all about once her brother returned. "I have come to fetch Ellyn."

"To where?"

"To my home, Mistress. Where else?" he asked. "My father is prepared to welcome her. And soon we will wed."

"She will not go with you."

"Nay, Mistress Ellyott. You are mistaken," said a voice from the doorway. Ellyn stepped into the hall and looked over at Jeffrey Poynard. Her eyes had gone hard as glass, and the line of her jaw was stiffly set. She would not ever cower. "I will go with him."

★ ★ ★

"A second poppet, Gibb," said Kit.

He stared out the window of his office, his hands folded behind his back. Overhead, tables and chairs scraped across the hall floor. Tonight was Frances's supper—Gibb had relayed that his sister had sworn she'd arrive at Kit's house with her friend Beatrix whether he liked it or not—and Alice was in a frenzy of preparation. Outside in the market square, the usual commotion of townsfolk about their daily tasks was reaching a midday peak. Servants were at the well. A horse and rider trotted toward the inn. A pair of merchants in their embroidered robes, thick ruffs, and velvet caps strolled together, deep in conversation. The poulterer carried a brace of flapping chickens into his shop. One of the carpenter's apprentices paused to spit at the players in the stocks.

"A second poppet?" asked Gibb.

"Left in Mistress Ellyott's garden yesterday."

"Marry, what ill news." The stool his cousin sat on creaked as he shifted his weight. "Does Master Howlett know her?"

"Not that I can say, which troubles me. What reason has he to threaten her with a poppet?"

"He is not our murderer, then," said his cousin, disheartened.

"Do not presume we're wrong about him, Gibb," he said. "But what have I missed?"

"Are you asking me, Kit?"

He glanced over his shoulder at Gibb. "Is there someone else in the room?"

"As often as you mutter to yourself, coz, I can never be certain," he replied.

Kit dragged over the chair by his writing desk and sat facing Gibb. "As you are here, perhaps you can help."

"Gladly I would." His cousin sat forward. "Anything to avoid my father, who wishes to review the accounts I drew up for Michaelmas. He claims I have erred and would like to correct me."

"In that case, I'll save you from my uncle's wrath." *Where to start?* "Let us set aside Howlett as our murderer for the present and return again to the beginning. When a troupe of players arrives in the village, brought here on Bartholomew Reade's suggestion. To be hosted by the Poynards."

"Jeffrey Poynard accepted the offer, though he knew Master Reade to have once been Ellyn Merrick's suitor."

"So mark that as the first of many irregularities in this tragedy, Gibb," said Kit. "Reade and Howlett have argued on the journey here. Over a play that Reade has written. His great work. The one that shall make his name, but which he'll not let the troupe perform. A troupe that has lost its patron and is in dire need of funds. His fellow actors already despise Reade's arrogance. His unwillingness to help only adds to their resentment."

"Master Howlett is furious with him."

"Just so," agreed Kit. "Howlett hopes, though, to profit from the visit to the Poynards."

"Upon arriving here, Master Reade arranges a meeting with Anna Webb," continued Gibb. "Possibly to give her the manuscript for safekeeping . . . we have covered this before, coz."

"Humor me, Gibb." More scraping across the floor over Kit's head was followed by a thud as Alice knocked over something heavy. "They may, in truth, have only meant to whisper together over their plans to go to London. Reade, though, has boasted of this meeting."

"If Reade meant to hand off the manuscript to Anna Webb, Kit, why be so bold as to speak his intentions aloud and risk Master Howlett learning of his plans?"

"He did not care if Howlett knew. Or Reade simply enjoyed boasting." Kit buffed his fingers against his beard and realized it had grown long and required a trim. Time for such niceties later. "Meanwhile, Ellyn Merrick learns that the man she loves has returned to the village. Unfortunately, she carries Jeffrey Poynard's child, and she undoubtedly presumes Reade will not want her if she bears another man's bastard. She plots to be rid of it. And quickly."

"The contents of the vial that sickened the young Merrick lad," said Gibb. "You should arrest her for killing the child."

"We have no witnesses to state they observed her actually drinking the physic, Gibb. Without witnesses or a confession from Ellyn Merrick, we cannot," he explained. "Ellyn Merrick overhears Anna chattering about Reade. She might assume the girl hopes to go with him to London. She can't have been happy."

"So *she* poisons the girl with some concoction to stop her?"

"Ellyn Merrick had the greatest reason, although the fellow appears to have charmed many women in this village. Marcye's eyes grow soft when she speaks of him. Mayhap he charmed other women at the Merricks' as well." Kit folded his arms atop his stomach. "Here now we arrive at the afternoon of interest. Reade heads to his tryst at the old fort hill. He may have taken his valuable play with him."

"Do not forget, Kit, that the very morning of the day Master Reade died, he was observed arguing with David Merrick. Over a woman Master Merrick wished Master Reade to stay away from," said Gibb.

"I asked Merrick about that argument," said Kit. "He says he was warning Reade to stay away from one of their dairymaids. But would Merrick bother to protect a dairymaid's reputation?"

"He might if they were lovers, Kit," said his cousin. "If David Merrick meant Anna, did he know the time and place of her tryst with Bartholomew Reade?"

"Servants gossip. Masters overhear," said Kit. "Meanwhile, a killer plots his crime. He has obtained a fur-trimmed black robe from among the troupe's belongings to hide within."

"Wait." Gibb held up a hand. "How did the killer obtain the robe? Only the players, Master Howlett, and the Poynards had access to the room wherein it was stored."

"Agreed. Thus Howlett remains our uppermost suspect," he said. "But let us continue. Reade is at the mound, waiting for

Anna Webb, who doesn't arrive. In the trees nearby sleeps a drunken old man. The killer approaches Reade—"

Gibb interrupted again. "Could this fellow have done so without Master Reade hearing his approach?"

"Reade must have dozed while he waited for Anna and was inattentive, for his own weapon lay at his side, unbloodied," said Kit. "He had drawn his knife but not used it. Suggesting to me that Reade was taken by surprise. He was stabbed repeatedly, the final copestone of the act to be the thrust of a broken writing pen into his throat. The work of a very angry individual."

Gibb's stomach grumbled, and he pressed a hand atop his doublet. "Do not scowl at me, coz. I'll not request food. You may go on."

"Perhaps Jellis stirs at this point, alerting the killer to his presence," said Kit, resuming his tale. "The killer strikes the old man, knocking him senseless, and the murderer strips Reade of his belt and purse and places it with the drunkard. He rushes toward town, discarding the knife into a ditch. He also tosses aside the bloodied robe."

"The knife . . . Master Howlett had one with him when we took him to the stocks, as did the other players," said Gibb. "Would he or the others own two?"

"Add that observation to our list of irregularities," said Kit. "At the Poynards', the time for the entertainment approaches, but Bartholomew Reade is absent. Howlett sends the players to search. A while later, he steps onto the stage to introduce the play."

"Could Master Howlett have returned to the Poynards' hall from the druids' mound so quickly and with time to spare to apply cosmetics to his face and pull on the clothes he wears for the play?"

"Beneath the robe, he may have already been dressed in his attire," said Kit. "I continue. Dunning finds Reade's body. He dashes for the Poynards' and alerts us. We go there, find Jellis, and arrest him."

"Poor old sot."

Another crash overhead was accompanied by an unhappy cry.

Gibb winced. "Think you Alice means to destroy your hall so she need not prepare supper?"

"As long as my gittern is not among the victims of her recklessness."

Alice pounded down the steps and popped into the parlor. "Fret not, sir. Naught of import is broken, I promise," she announced, dropped a curtsy, and hurried off again.

"I fret more now than before, coz," said Gibb.

As did Kit.

"Back to Jellis," he said, determined to head up to his hall once he'd finished with Gibb. "He tells me he saw a woman near the mound, but is she real or a phantom? Then, not long before he's found dead in the jail, the old man receives a visit from both a shrouded crone and Jeffrey Poynard."

"He was frightened to death, was he not?"

"That is our only explanation," said Kit. "Who was the shrouded crone, though?"

"The woman who left the poppet Mistress Ellyott found in the Merricks' farmyard," said Gibb. "Marry, Kit. Mayhap there *is* a witch!"

Kit sighed. "A few hours before Anna Webb is trampled to death by a cow, Mistress Ellyott spies Jeffrey Poynard at the Merricks', incensed. He explains he was angry that David Merrick was bruiting about that he is Reade's killer."

"If so, I would expect Master Poynard to attack Master Merrick, to mend his honor," said Gibb.

"Perhaps Poynard is not the rash fellow we imagine him to be, or his anger was a ruse," said Kit. "Also on the day of Anna's death, Thomasin notices a shadow in the trees. Anna's killer lurking, perhaps. This shadow has vanished, though, when she goes to inspect the woods."

"If there is no witch, who would threaten Mistress Ellyott with this second effigy?" asked Gibb. "The players? Master Poynard? David Merrick? Marry, I cannot fathom *him* threatening the woman who has taken in his sister."

Too many pieces out of place in the mosaic Kit was attempting to construct. *Damn.*

"Do we have any fresh ideas now, Gibb?"

"A great Gordian knot of confusion, coz." Gibb frowned. "Am I to release the players from the stocks, or do we yet suspect them of a hand in these murders?"

"Their punishment for brawling is not concluded, Gibb."

"But it is to end on the morrow."

"Leaving me scant hours to identify the killer," he said, "and the person who has thrown a second poppet, enwrapped in red cloth, into Bess Ellyott's garden, if they are not one and the same."

Gibb was watching Kit with a puckered brow. "Want me to keep guard over her, Kit?"

"Aye, Gibb," he said. "But discretely."

CHAPTER 21

"You vowed, Ellyn, that you would not agree to wed him," said Bess from the doorstead of the chamber the young woman had borrowed.

"I have given thought to that vow, Mistress, and find it was ill judged of me to make such a profession," said Ellyn.

She collected what remained of the clothing she'd been wearing when Bess found her—her pair of bodies, a thinly padded waistcoat, her woven-tape belt. All the rest had been ruined, her kirtle and petticoats and chemise stained by blood. She'd not even had a coif covering her hair. A spare gown went into a satchel Bess had gifted her with, along with netting and pins for her hair, an old quilted petticoat.

"Do not do this, Ellyn. Prithee, stay with us awhile. Until you have had time to think further on your decision."

Ellyn looked over. Wrinkles had formed on her skin as if by magic, the weight of her decision marking her face.

"Do not think me ungrateful for all you have done for me, Mistress Ellyott," she said. "The healing you have given. The concern and advice you have offered. These items you have gifted me."

Bess crossed the room to her.

"You have told me how much you despise him. I have seen the pain on your face when you speak his name," she said. "Do not punish yourself by now agreeing to marry the man who violated you."

Ellyn wore but a sheer net over her hair, and the strands were black as night against her chalk-pale cheeks. She appeared nearly as wan and frail as the day she first arrived. "No one else will have me, Mistress Ellyott."

"That is not so!" Bess exclaimed. "Other women have found husbands after . . . such a misfortune. You will also."

"Other women in *this* town? Where gossip and slander are traded like wool or cheese?" asked Ellyn. "I will find no good man willing to overlook my misfortune, as you name it, Mistress."

"Do not go with him. I beg of you."

Ellyn's chin trembled from withheld emotion, but she could not prevent tears from springing to her eyes. "'Tis too late to undo what I have done. What I have declared."

"It is not too late."

"But it is," she replied. "I have been forced to realize I have nowhere else to go than with Jeffrey Poynard. For 'tis certain I cannot remain a woman without a husband, mistrusted and disdained."

"Oh, Ellyn," whispered Bess, unable to deny the truth of Ellyn's words.

"Forgive me. I beg you, forgive me. I hear your promises to help me, Mistress, but what can you truly do? My choice is marriage to him or try to return to my family, who will not take me back if I do not agree to wed Jeffrey. My mother sent a message yesterday telling me as much. If I were to try, she has vowed she will send me to my aunt in Salisbury, a most cruel woman," she said. "So you see? No choice at all."

"You can find a place elsewhere. I am certain. You could find solace in becoming an herbalist. 'Tis a worthy occupation."

"At my age, who would take me in?" she asked. "Even were I to study at your side, who would entrust me with healing them? And I am too old to be a household servant, Mistress Ellyott, or to become apprenticed to a mantle-maker. Too stained by sin to be welcomed into a godly home."

"I cannot change your mind?" asked Bess.

"I am sorry, but you cannot. At least marriage to Jeffrey Poynard will offer a measure of safety and respectability I sorely need." She swiped away the tears that had fallen and gathered one final item—an ivory comb missing a tooth—to place inside the satchel. "And now my family will be happy with me again. I shall ask Jeffrey to take me to my house and beg forgiveness of my mother. She will be delighted," Ellyn added bitterly.

"So be it," said Bess, heart weary. "At least take my simple of organy and mint with you for your little brother. He drank from that yellow bottle out by the rubbish pit, Ellyn. Near to where Jennet also found a poppet."

The other woman looked over at her. "He is unwell?"

"He will recover. Do not fret," said Bess. "Its existence explains Anna's sickness, though."

Ellyn turned aside, busying her hands by picking up the satchel and pulling upon its strings to close it.

Bess stepped around her in order to best observe her face. "Before you leave this house, Ellyn, I must know this. Did you poison Anna, then drink the physic yourself to be rid of the babe?"

"No."

"Ellyn, honor me by giving me the truth."

Her chin rose. "As you will, Mistress Ellyott," she replied. "I did go into the servants' hall and slip a small dose of artemisia into Anna's ale to keep her from meeting Bartholomew. But I did not go in her stead, intending to strike him down. I would not ever wish to hurt him. I loved him."

"Though he had hurt you by choosing her?" asked Bess softly.

"My heart will recover." She grabbed the satchel. "I vow my heart will recover."

She stormed from the chamber, calling out to the waiting Jeffrey Poynard her readiness to depart.

★ ★ ★

"Father will not be pleased you have turned our house into an extension of your offices," said Frances, her hands folded primly over her heavily embroidered stomacher.

She gestured at the parlor, which was all that Kit's workaday space was not—elegantly furnished, warm, and spacious. Frances's touch was everywhere. In the embroidered cushions. The selection of Turkey carpets tossed over tables, kept there until called into service to shield genteel feet and bottoms from cold floors, should a need arise to sprawl on the tile. She might have even chosen the painted cloths upon the walls. The one depicting the story of the prodigal son was similar to a painted cloth Kit's father had on display. The image had long succeeded in chastising Kit; not enough, though, to cause him to hurry home and act the part of the repentant child.

"You were the one, Frances, who sent me a message to come without delay to speak with one of the Merricks' servants."

"I'd hoped you might take her elsewhere," she replied. "The girl is in the kitchen having a bite of food. A startled bird of a creature and thin. Do not the Merricks feed their servants?" She cocked her head to one side. "I believe I hear her coming now."

She leaned toward him to whisper, her movement wafting the spicy scent from her silver pomander. "I shall not tell Father you are here conducting interrogations. Our secret, Christopher."

Jennet entered the room, and Frances departed, softly closing the door behind her. The girl briefly scanned the space, her eyes wide with awe. A servant like her would not ever acquire the wealth of a Harwoode, or the more modest yet still enviable prosperity of a Merrick.

"What have you to say now, Jennet?" asked Kit.

"I must be quick, sir," the young woman said. She pressed her bony hands against the coarse holland safeguard she wore over her kirtle. Her thick shoes had left a trail of mud across the floor. "The Merricks will note I am not in the house."

"I will not delay you."

"I must tell you what I know, but could not say earlier out of fear that one of the Merricks would hear me," she said. "'Tis news about Master David."

"Go on."

"Master David left the house late the afternoon that Bartholomew died. To attend the play," she said.

"His mother, your mistress, says he did not attend the play," interrupted Kit. "That he turned back and sat with her at supper."

Jennet shot a glance around the room, as if a Merrick might have suddenly appeared to eavesdrop on them.

"He might not have gone to the play, sir, but he did leave the house, only to return near to sunset. I was in the yard tending to the wash and saw him go," she said. "Not so long later, I was preparing the table for supper and spied him rushing through the entry hall. Shaken, he was."

"Was that why you thought the poppet you found near the

barn was meant for you? Because you'd observed him behaving oddly and believed he'd left it to frighten you?"

Her nod was sharp. "When I heard of that player's death, I did wonder."

"Did Anna also spot Master David that afternoon, Jennet?" he asked.

Tears trembled. "I should have told you that also, but I was scared the Merricks would learn I spoke against Master David," she said. "Since Anna died, I have had no chance to leave the house until now. All is in an uproar there, for Mistress Ellyn has returned with Master Poynard and plans to wed him."

Now this *is an interesting turn.* "They will not learn what you say here, Jennet. You are safe."

She pulled in a long breath. "Anna saw him from the window of the chamber she'd been given during her illness," she said. "She'd arisen to make water and noticed him upon the house path. When news came of Bartholomew's death, she was convinced that Master David had killed him. She told me so the next morning and would not be persuaded elsewise."

"Did he realize she'd seen him?"

"Anna told me he looked up at the house and espied her in the window."

Providing Merrick a reason to either frighten Anna into silence or eliminate the threat of her knowledge completely.

"You're very courageous to tell me this, Jennet."

"I had to, for guilt haunts me. I cannot sleep for it," she said. "But if the Merricks learn I have come to you, I will be punished for my disloyalty."

"I will protect you as best I can," he answered. Although how well could he protect *any* servant from a master intent on punishment? "Mayhap you can answer me this, Jennet. Was

Master David wearing a long black robe when he left the house that afternoon? Think carefully."

"I need not think carefully, sir, for he was wearing his crimson-lined short cloak atop his puce-colored doublet and trunk hose," she answered. "The attire he favors when he ventures out on a visit."

"Did he return in the same outfit?"

"I am certain he did."

Damn. He'd thought himself close to the evidence he needed. Although it was possible Merrick had secreted away the robe, retrieved it for the crime, then discarded it.

"Jennet, do you think Master David could also be responsible for Anna's death?" Kit asked. "That is why you sent for me, isn't it?"

Jennet chewed her lower lip. "It may be so, sir. Because of the cat."

"The cat?"

"Aye. His brindled cat," she answered. "The one which follows Master David everywhere. Much like a dog might do. It did not come into the kitchen when we prepared supper that day. I know not where it was. Unless it was outside the house. With Master David."

★ ★ ★

"Mistress, how can we let Mistress Ellyn wed him?" asked Joan.

"We cannot stop her, Joan," said Bess, dipping her needle in and out of the linen of the shirt she sewed for Robert.

She sat by the hall's street-facing window, where the light was strongest. Strong enough to easily read in Joan's eyes her troubled thoughts.

"Harm will come," said her servant.

Am I not aware of that possibility?

"At least Mistress Ellyn is safe from Humphrey's grumbles that she should be punished for making those poppets," said Joan when Bess did not reply.

Bess set down her stitching and stared out the window. A cold wind had risen, scattering leaves along the road that startled the neighbor's orange cat.

"Yet we cannot name who *should* be punished for making them, Joan."

"The clout-covered woman you saw upon the highway before finding the first one, Mistress," said Joan. "She must be the maker of that one. And the lads who wish to play imitators and frighten you, the second."

"Aye." Bess narrowed her gaze and set aside Robert's shirt. "My sister approaches, Joan. See her inside and bring warmed wine for us."

Joan made for the entrance and hustled Dorothie into the house, who made a great ado about entrusting Joan with the hood she'd secured atop her coif.

"Elizabeth?" she called.

"In here, Dorothie. Come into the hall."

Dorothie swept into the room, causing Quail to leap up from where he'd been sleeping beneath the window to bark at her.

She scowled at him. "Hush, now. Hush!"

"Quail." Bess signaled for the dog to sit at her side. Quail padded over. "What brings you here, Dorothie?"

"The curse a witch has placed upon you." Dorothie went to the settle and perched on its edge, her black skirts spilling across the seat. "My servant girl heard the news from Humphrey."

"Ah."

"First a fellow is murdered the day before my return, then

one of the Merricks' dairymaids is crushed by a cow, and an old widow's cottage is burned down," listed Dorothie.

In her list, she had omitted the death of a vagrant locked within the jail. However, Dorothie would give Goodman Jellis little thought beyond her story of a cottager and a hawthorn.

"And now this poppet!" her sister added.

"I can assure you I am not cursed by a witch."

"Someone seeks to have you believe you are." She exhaled, and it was then that Bess realized her sister was trembling. "At least that Ellyn Merrick has gone."

More gossip she had gained from Humphrey? "She went home and plans to marry Jeffrey Poynard."

"She has yielded and agreed to wed him? I am surprised. I assumed she was like the rest of them. Strongheaded." Dorothie tutted. "I recall when Agnes Merrick had just delivered her fourth—or was it her fifth?—child, yet she chased an escaped sheep and wrestled it into its enclosure. She risked the health of her babe. For what? To prove her fortitude? Bah. All the Merricks are unsensible."

"I pray the Poynards treat Ellyn well."

"They will treat her as she deserves, Elizabeth."

Joan returned with two cups of warmed and spiced wine, which she handed out.

Dorothie waited until she'd gone to continue. "And what intends the man who watches this house from across the way?"

"A man watches the house?" Bess peered through the window and marked the fellow Dorothie meant. He hid himself poorly, if he meant to not be observed. "'Tis Master Harwoode, the constable's cousin."

"God be thanked for that, then." She paused to sip her wine. "Does he spy on you because of the poppet?"

"To protect me, I suppose." *My thanks, Kit Harwoode, for your care and concern.*

"From a witch's curse," said Dorothie. "See? I did tell you."

Bess caught Gibb Harwoode's eye and smiled at him. He hastily crouched behind barrels stacked alongside the street gutter.

"I trust you have disposed of the poppet," said Dorothie.

"I have locked it inside a box stored within Robert's parlor. I know not what else to do with the thing." She glanced over at her sister. "Dorothie, have you seen a clouted countrywoman upon the roads of late? She is secretive in demeanor."

"Secretive? No, I have not, Elizabeth," said her sister. "You trouble yourself with matters you should not. If Robert were here, you would behave with more propriety."

"But Robert is not here to scold me."

"Which leaves *me* the unenviable duty of taking charge of you in his place."

Jesu.

★　★　★

Alice pranced anxiously outside the door to Kit's house. "They are all of them in your office, sir."

"Who, Alice?" he asked. Beyond the panes of wavy glass moved the shapes of men.

"The coroner," she said. "Other important folk."

"Ah. If the crowner has come, I can imagine what this is about," said Kit. "Go back into the house, Alice. And my thanks for the warning."

He waited for her to dart inside before entering the house himself.

Squaring his shoulders, Kit pushed wide the door to his office. The coroner in his dark gown towered over the others—merchants and burgesses of the town—who'd packed themselves into the room, awaiting Kit's return from his uncle's house. A vulture among the ravens.

"Gentlemen," said Kit, untying his cloak and tossing it aside. "Is the guildhall no longer a suitable location for meetings so that you must crowd into my meager office?"

He knew them all, a choice selection of the most prominent men of the village. The same men who'd chosen Kit to serve as constable. By the dark looks in their eyes, their opinions on that matter appeared to have changed.

"Master Harwoode, we have come to speak to you about the recent deaths," said the coroner.

Master Harwoode, is it.

Kit closed the door behind him. The air in the room was already stale from the hot breath of a dozen men, and stank from the scents they used to perfume their clothing or to fend off fleas; shutting the door would only make the space more uncomfortable. Mayhap they'd then hasten to leave.

"Have you gentlemen information you'd like to share?" he asked. "I find myself to be all ears."

"We informed you after Old Jellis perished that your queries and investigations were to be ceased. Yet you persisted. We are here to repeat that you are finished, Master Harwoode." The coroner had clearly been chosen as spokesman by the rest, who nodded their agreement.

"Am I, Crowner?" asked Kit.

"Indeed, so," he replied. "The old man accused is now dead and buried. The Merricks' dairymaid died from misadventure, not any other cause. The witch has been driven off. The players, who have brought us all . . ." He paused to look at the assembled men, his glance gathering them. ". . . who have brought this

town many troubles, will conclude their punishment for brawling on the morrow and thankfully depart. There is naught else
to consider nor further actions to pursue. Surely you comprehend this."

"A tidy summary, Crowner."

"You are to question no one else, Master Harwoode, nor
make any more demands upon anyone's time."

A comment that implied complaints had been made about
those demands. "I have a difficulty with your request, however.
I am not satisfied that my investigation is concluded. No more
than the first time you informed me I was done."

The coroner glared. "You are finished, sirrah. Should you
continue, you will be removed from your position. A most
shameful situation for a man of your standing to endure."

Was the situation most shameful? Kit had endured worse.

"My cousin, the lord of the manor, proposed my name for
this position," said Kit. "You'd go against his wishes, Crowner?"

"I expect he would agree with the decision, should it be
required," he replied. "Good day to you."

The coroner yanked open the door and swept from the
room, his companions marching out with him.

Alice scuttled into the entry passage from the service rooms.
"Are you to lose your position, sir?"

"Do not fret, Alice. It's not as though I am dependent upon
the miserable fees I receive as constable to pay your wage."

"But, sir, your work contents you."

He looked over to where she stood. "You think my position
contents me, Alice?"

She flushed. "Aye, sir! Certes, it does! Else you'd not devote
such time and care to it."

He'd thought her a silly, anxious mouse; she might be made

of more substance than that. "Alice, I may have been wrong about you."

The front door clacked open, and Gibb stepped inside. Kit dismissed Alice.

"What are you doing here?" asked Kit. "I instructed you to keep watch on Mistress Ellyott."

"I was uncareful and she spied me."

"Well, go back anyway, Gibb," said Kit, returning to his office. "And send someone to keep an eye on David Merrick. I don't want him leaving the village."

CHAPTER 22

"Where go you, Elizabeth?" asked Dorothie, frowning from the doorway of Bess's bedchamber.

"To a supper at the constable's home."

"Which explains the gown you wear," said her sister.

Joan bent over that gown, of a lustrous peacock color, examining it for any sign that all was not perfect. She'd found an embroidered ivory stomacher and matching forepart to complete Bess's attire, items that had belonged to Robert's late wife. Bess skimmed her fingers across the parti-colored stitching, recalling the gentle young woman who'd owned the stomacher and forepart before disease had taken her life. If Robert were here, would he be displeased to see them on Bess? Or happy that another had found use for them?

"I would look my best," said Bess.

"For the constable," said Dorothie. "Hmm."

"Read not more into this invitation than is warranted, Dorothie," she said. "The evening is a mere diversion from the troubles that have recently affected the village."

"The constable has a fine income from his lands, I understand," her sister said, apparently undeterred by Bess's response. "He would make a good husband."

Blushing, Bess shot a glance at Joan, who fought a grin as she adjusted Bess's skirts where they draped over a bum roll. The pad of horsehair strapped to Bess's waist would make her gown dip and sway with each movement. Joan had tried to convince Bess to wear a larger farthingale, but Bess had refused that extravagance. As it was, every time she turned, she expected to knock against the wall or bump a piece of furniture and send it crashing.

"I do not seek a husband to replace Martin," said Bess.

"Well, you cannot live in this house forever, Elizabeth. Robert will return from London with a wife and that will be that." Dorothie paused and considered Bess. "You could live with me in my great, empty house. Margery would welcome you."

"And you would be jealous of your daughter's welcome."

The skin around Dorothie's mouth tightened. "I would *not* be jealous."

Joan settled Bess's cloak about her shoulders and tidied a strand of hair that had escaped the pearl-encrusted net secured upon her head. "You look most fair, Mistress."

"I trust I also look uncomfortable. The stomacher is very stiff, and I cannot draw in a full breath."

"What need have you for breathing, Mistress?" Joan teased.

"You do look most fair, Elizabeth," conceded Dorothie. A compliment from a woman who guarded praiseful remarks like precious sugared comfits to be handed out on the rarest of occasions.

"My thanks, sister."

"Shall you return before curfew, Mistress?" asked Joan.

"I might not return until well after sunset, but do not fret for me, Joan. Or you either, Dorothie," said Bess. "The constable's cousin waits for me outside and will see me safely home afterward."

"Nonetheless, watch for a clout-covered crone, Mistress. She means harm."

Bess rubbed a hand down her servant's arm. "Tut, Joan. I shall be well with Master Harwoode at my side."

"If you say, Mistress," she said. "But trust that I shall be waiting right here, impatient to learn of Constable Harwoode's true intentions for wishing you to attend tonight."

"As am I," said Dorothie.

As am I, thought Bess.

★ ★ ★

In the market square, the day's activities were reaching their close, shutters being set over shop windows and links and lanterns being lit at entry doors.

Gibb Harwoode strolled alongside Bess, humming as he walked. He had been abashed to admit that his cousin had set him to the task of watching her house, but her profuse thanks had stripped him of his embarrassment that she'd exposed him at his task.

"Master Harwoode, you have a bruise upon your face," she said. "You should have had me tend to it. I make a simple of honey and black soap that works well."

"'Tis nothing. A penalty for helping my cousin, Mistress," he replied.

"Dangerous business, sir."

"Indeed so."

"Might I ask a question of you?"

He bowed over his outstretched arm. "Proceed."

"Why have I been invited to this family supper?" she asked.

His mouth twitched with a grin. "To meet my sister."

To meet his sister?

They drew near Kit Harwoode's home, and Bess paused. The first-floor windows of his hall glimmered with candlelight, and the shapes of the other guests moved within. Bess shivered with anxiety and expectation.

Gibb Harwoode stopped when he realized she no longer walked at his side. "Mistress?"

"I hesitate so that I may collect myself, Master Harwoode."

"My sister is not half as fearsome as Kit imagines her."

He opened the door and ushered her inside. They were met by the constable's house-servant, who curtsied repeatedly and whose hands trembled as she removed Bess's cloak.

Gibb Harwoode bounded up the steps, squeezing past his cousin on the way down them.

"Welcome, Mistress." Kit Harwoode gave a brief bow and gestured toward the door open at the head of the stairs. "Come up and join the others."

His servant scurried off with Bess's cloak. Bess hiked her skirts and climbed the steps. Voices—Gibb Harwoode's and those of two women—echoed in the enclosed staircase.

She turned into the hall, awash in candlelight. The table in the center of the room had been lain with a linen cloth and set with pewter dishes, spoons, and good glass cups. Bottles of wine stood in readiness atop a court cupboard.

"Mistress Ellyott has arrived," announced the constable.

The heads of the women turned as one. Bess did not recognize them, beautiful in silk gowns that glimmered in the candlelight. Three women and two males; Dorothie would tut over the irregularity of uneven numbers.

So why am *I here?*

"See? I have brought her safely," said Master Harwoode.

"I'm proud of you, Gibb. Come meet the others, Mistress," said his cousin.

One of the women stepped forward, her hands extended, a painted fan swinging from one slim wrist. "Welcome, Mistress Ellyott."

"This is my cousin, Frances Harwoode Westcote," said the constable. "Gibb's sister."

Bess could see the resemblance in her even features and fair eyes. She took the woman's fingers, which were strong and assured. Mistress Westcote kissed Bess upon both cheeks, a pleasant sweetness rising from her silver pomander.

"And what Christopher does not say in his meager introduction of me is how much he adores me, Mistress Ellyott." She smiled at him before steering forward the woman who waited patiently behind her. "This is my friend Beatrix Pollington. She visits us from Gloucester."

Mistress Pollington did not move with Mistress Westcote's confidence, and her gaze kept dancing over to Kit Harwoode's face. A young woman as pretty as she was—her skin free of any blemish, her blonde hair the color of ripened wheat, her waist nipped tiny beneath a rose stomacher embroidered with more elaboration than Bess's—should never be unconfident. Bess envied Mistress Pollington's waist, though; hers would never again be so small after having borne children.

"Mistress Ellyott," she said, her voice more forceful than Bess had anticipated. She also kissed Bess's cheeks, but hastily, eager to retreat.

"Well, then. Ladies," said the constable. He cleared his throat.

"Christopher, honestly," chided Mistress Westcote. "I will tell Alice to serve supper, lest you stumble about in your awkwardness and discomfort us all!"

"If you would, Frances," he said.

The constable caught Bess's eye and walked over to join her. Mistress Pollington's gaze traced his progress across the room.

"My thanks, Mistress, for attending," he said quietly. "This may not be the most pleasant of evenings for you."

"No, Constable?" she asked. "Why not?"

"My cousin and her plots."

Plots? "Your cousin told me Mistress Westcote wished to meet me."

"He did?"

"Was that not the reason for this supper?" asked Bess.

He cast a subtle glance at Beatrix Pollington.

Ah, then. Mistress Westcote plotted to draw an unmarried friend with wheat-pale hair into acquaintance with an equally unmarried man, thought Bess. *And I am but a piece in this game of chess. But what sort of piece? One meant to block Mistress Pollington's acquaintance or one meant to encourage it?*

"Before our meal begins and I lose the opportunity, I should tell you that Mistress Ellyn has admitted she gave the dose of artemisia to Anna that sickened the girl, but maintains she did *not* meet Bartholomew Reade that night and kill him," Bess said, mispleased by the unhappy jealousy that had stung at the thought of Mistress Pollington and Kit Harwoode together.

The change in the direction of the conversation visibly relaxed the taut edge of his jaw.

"And I should tell you, Mistress, that around the time of Reade's death, Jennet observed David Merrick rushing back to the Merricks' house looking distressed," he said. "She didn't see him wearing the bloodied robe we've located, however."

"Most intriguing, Constable," she said. "However, I cannot comprehend how he might have obtained the troupe's robe to begin with."

"He *was* at the Poynards' that morning, arguing with Reade."

"Yet to slip inside their house to retrieve it from the troupe's stores?" she asked. "Could the reason for David Merrick's distress instead be that he had stumbled upon Master Reade's dead body?"

The constable narrowed his gaze. "My cousin calls these mysteries we face a Gordian knot, Mistress. You present a plausible explanation for Merrick's actions, but I seek a proper sword to cut that knot fully in twain."

Mistress Pollington strolled over to join them.

"Forgive the interruption, Constable Harwoode, Mistress Ellyott," the young woman said with a smile that revealed a full set of even, white teeth. Mayhap she was confident after all. "But I would have you help me find my place at the table, sir, if I may trouble you with that task."

"Later, Mistress Ellyott. We have much to speak of," he said before leading Mistress Pollington away.

★　★　★

Kit's restless mood deepened. He itched for the meal to conclude, though he couldn't fault the food Alice and Frances's kitchen maid had prepared. Not the salad of lettuce and leeks and mint dressed in sugared oil and vinegar, nor the herring in mustard or the ling pie. Not even the fricassee of eggs and sweet roots. It had all been delicious. Gibb had said a proper grace over the meal. The clove and cinnamon spiced claret had—so far—been dispensed without Alice spilling any onto the tablecloth borrowed from his uncle's supply. The conversation had been lighthearted, Mistress Pollington providing her impressions of Wiltshire and the sites she'd seen in Frances's company. She'd proven to have a ready wit and a willingness to laugh.

As for Bess Ellyott, she'd been quieter than usual, saying little, complimenting the meal, though she ate sparingly. She had dressed with great care that evening, with pearls in her warm brown hair and silver threads sparkling on her bodice. Had the effort been for him? Aside from their brief conversation, though, she'd paid him scant attention, her evening spent focused on Beatrix Pollington.

Alice bustled in to remove the remnants of the first course and refresh the wine. Frances covered Kit's hand, resting on the table, with hers.

"If you continue to glower so, Christopher, I shall be forced to apologize to Beatrix for your ill manners," she whispered to him.

"She is pleasant, Frances."

"I knew you would find her so." Her eyes slanted to peer at the woman seated across the way. "But who is this Mistress Ellyott?"

"Gibb has not mentioned her to you?"

Frances's brows made the slightest movement upward. "Should he have done?"

"Bess Ellyott is a local herbalist, a healer, and a friend," he replied. "And I do not mean to glower, Frances. However, my mind is preoccupied by my work." Despite what the coroner and burgesses and merchants wanted.

"Must you always think about your work? Gibb does not hesitate to enjoy himself," she said. He'd engaged both Mistress Pollington and Mistress Ellyott in a conversation that made the women laugh. "Rest your mind for once, cousin."

"My apologies."

"I do not require apologies, Christopher," she said. "I want your good humor restored to that of the man I used to know."

"When did I ever have good humor, Frances?"

"I have not forgotten, even if you have," she answered.

Frances's servant and Alice, red-faced and sweating from her labors, returned with groaning platters. Frances had planned a second course of trout stewed in herbs, sturgeon cooked in a vinegar sauce, fried sole, an apple tart, and quince cakes. After this supper, Alice would either quit or request she never be asked to prepare so much food again.

"Delicious, Frances," said Gibb, saluting her with his glass of wine. "Delicious."

"My thanks, brother. I only wish we had some pleasant diversion to look forward to after supper."

"We could play at maw," offered Mistress Pollington.

"You are too skilled with cards, Beatrix. You will beat us all as you did Father this afternoon," said Frances. "Or perhaps we could have some music." She looked over at Kit. "Would you play upon your gittern for us after supper, Christopher?"

"I have not ever heard you play, Constable," said Bess Ellyott.

Mistress Pollington reacted to her comment by smiling all the more coyly at Kit. "Do you play, Constable Harwoode?"

Bloody . . . "Not well enough to give anyone here pleasure, Mistress Pollington."

"He is being humble, Beatrix. My cousin is most talented," said Frances. "Mayhap I should have hired the town waites to play for us tonight, though. They are quite competent."

"We endured their squeaking enough the night of the Poynards' entertainment, Frances," said Kit.

"I did hear you have a troupe of traveling players in town," said Mistress Pollington.

"Unhappily, Mistress Pollington, their play was rudely interrupted by a murder," said Gibb, who'd drunk too freely of the spiced claret.

Beatrix Pollington, her mouth falling open to form an O,

lifted a hand to her ashen face. Across the table from her, Mistress Ellyott's knife paused midair, the morsel of sturgeon balanced on its blade readying to fall off.

"Master Harwoode, you distress your sister's friend," said Mistress Ellyott, carefully lowering her knife. "Do not fret, Mistress Pollington. You are safe here."

"Forgive me if I have disquieted you, Mistress Pollington." Gibb inclined his head, the feather tucked into the band of his velvet hat dipping dangerously close to the candle on the table. "We had succeeded in keeping the news from your delicate ears. But now I have been a fool and blurted it out."

She blushed prettily. "I am made of sterner stuff than to faint away over such news, Master Harwoode."

"Well done, Mistress," he said, and Frances turned a speculative gaze upon her brother.

"I doubt the lack of a performance was a great miss, Gibb," said Kit. "The players can't have much talent, if they're wandering through Wiltshire."

"'Tis not so, Constable Harwoode. I am familiar with this troupe," said Mistress Pollington. "They did stop in Gloucester last month. They are a most excellent group of players, truth be told. There is one among them who transforms into a most believable woman. I initially imagined they had hired a female as a member, which would be scandalous."

Bess Ellyott abruptly set down the knife she'd once again lifted. It clinked against the edge of her pewter plate.

"What was it about the transformation that made it so believable, Mistress Pollington?" she asked.

"Why, his manner, Mistress Ellyott," she replied. "He changed his voice until it was soft as a young girl's, and the linen coif he wore cleverly concealed the line of his masculine jaw."

"How would you describe this player?" asked Kit. For if the fellow could imitate a young girl, he could also imitate an aged crone.

Mistress Pollington paused longer than necessary to nibble a bite of trout. Pleased, perhaps, to have everyone's eyes on her.

Finished, she daubed her mouth with her napkin. "He was just an ordinary fellow of ordinary size, Constable, from what I saw after he removed his disguise at the end of the play."

"Christopher, what is your interest in this fellow?" asked Frances. "He is but a player who can dress and act as a woman does. 'Tis common enough. Every troupe requires such skills."

Before he could respond, Mistress Pollington interrupted.

"That is indeed a requirement of every troupe, Frances," she said. "However, I dare say no one is as convincing in such a role as Master David Merrick. *He* is fully astonishing!"

CHAPTER 23

*J*esu. Mistress Pollington blinked at them, unwitting of the effect her otherwise unremarkable observation would cause. If she had shot a cannonball through Kit Harwoode's hall, Bess believed the impact would hardly have been greater.

"Why do you all stare at me in such a fashion?" She looked from one to the other. "Frances, what does this mean? What did I say?"

"I find myself as perplexed as you, Beatrix." Mistress Westcote arranged her eating utensils upon her plate and calmly lowered her hands to her lap. "But I feel the stares have to do with the murder my brother mentioned."

Mistress Pollington blanched, and she blinked faster.

"David Merrick then, Kit?" asked Master Harwoode.

"But how can that be, Constable?" asked Bess. "You just told me he was not wearing the robe that afternoon."

The constable removed his napkin from where he'd hung it over his left shoulder and tossed it onto the table. "You know David Merrick well, Mistress Pollington?"

"You ask as though such familiarity is ill-advised," she said. "Frances, prithee tell me, whatever is the matter?"

"You might wish to answer my cousin's question, Beatrix. I assure you, all will be well."

"If you are certain, Frances." She composed herself. "Certes, I know David Merrick, Constable Harwoode. My family and I used to live in these parts, which is how I am also acquainted with Frances. Do you not recall us?"

"I'd not been living here long, Mistress, before you and your family removed to Gloucester," he said. "I'd not had the privilege of being introduced to you as yet."

"I am the one being forgetful, it seems," she replied. "However, as I said, I am well familiar with the Merricks. My father sold them a portion of our property, land they now use to graze their cattle. But it has been at least seven or eight years since I have spoken with any of the Merrick family. I did not renew our acquaintance while I have been here. Our families no longer occupy the same circle, now that we make our home in Gloucester."

And have undoubtedly become wealthier than dairy farmers, thought Bess.

"When did you observe David Merrick's excellent ability to playact the part of a woman?" asked the constable.

Mistress Pollington looked around again, as though seeking an ally to whisk her away from his discomfiting queries. She found none.

"I observed his ability not long after my father made the sale of the land," she said. "As a celebration of that event as well as our imminent departure, Master David and Mistress Ellyn did provide an entertainment. They often did act together. That even, they performed a short play he had written, during which he was attired as an old crone, wrapped in aprons and cloaks, and hunched like an aged creature might be. It was most amusing."

"Did he include a clout over his face as part of his habit?" asked Bess.

By now, though, she perceived what the woman's answer would be.

"Indeed so," said Beatrix Pollington. "Like a countrywoman would do."

Silence fell, its weight dragging more heavily on Bess than all of her skirts and petticoats. The constable rose slowly from his chair before turning to his cousin, who scrambled to his feet.

"We go to the Merricks', Gibb," he said with an icy voice. "David Merrick has questions to answer. From the inside of a jail."

★ ★ ★

They found David Merrick in only a linen shirt, loose doublet, and hose, preparing to retire. Two of the men Kit had brought hauled Merrick from his house without giving him the chance to throw on a cloak to cover his undress.

Mistress Merrick, clutching her belly, watched from the doorway while younger Merricks huddled behind her skirts. "No, Constable! He has done nothing wrong!"

Dairy workers, including an ashen Thomasin, assembled to shake their heads and whisper among themselves.

"Constable!" cried Merrick. The torches the onlookers carried lit his face. It was dirty, and one eye was swelling shut. Someone had been free with their fist as they dragged him out into the yard. "Of what am I accused?"

"You killed that player fellow and yer dairymaid!" shouted the town baker from the safety of the horde that had trailed behind Kit and Gibb and their men. His breath misted in the damp air. "Merricks! They be not worthy of trust!"

"Not murder!" Merrick protested. "Not Anna. An accident! Not murder! None of them."

The men holding his arms yanked him, and he stumbled.

Ellyn Merrick appeared at the doorstead. She shoved past her mother and grabbed one of the men who held Merrick. "What are you doing to him? Let him go!"

"He be a murderer," called a townsman from the depths of the mob.

"No!" she shrieked, and began to strike the nearest fellow. "He did nothing! Let him go!"

Gibb ran forward, seizing her about the waist and pulling her backward. "Come now, Mistress Merrick."

"Leave me be!" Ellyn Merrick slapped away Gibb's hands. "He is innocent!"

"Ellyn, stop," said her brother.

"You despised Bartholomew Reade," continued Kit. "Resented his success. An actor tripping upon the stage. A life you'll not ever enjoy, trapped here at your family's farm."

"No," he whimpered.

"And then there is the marriage between your sister and Master Poynard," said Kit. "Bartholomew Reade's return cast that event in doubt, didn't it?"

"He would not," cried Ellyn Merrick.

A fellow bolted from the house, knocking aside the youngest Merrick girl, who'd been standing in his path. "I found 'em, Constable!" He held aloft a crumpled gown and kerchief. "At the bottom of a trunk in his chamber."

The outfit of a crone.

The gathered crowd murmured.

Kit, his hand gripping the pommel of his dagger, turned to Merrick. "A clever disguise, sir, to conceal yourself as you crept about. The poppets were also clever. To throw suspicion upon a witch."

"What?" he sputtered. "What?"

"David would never . . ." Ellyn Merrick tried to break free of Gibb's grasp, but he held her fast.

"And to frighten Old Jellis to death." Kit shook his head. "He would have swung in your place, Master Merrick."

"I did visit Old Jellis in that garb, not wanting to be recognized," he admitted. "But only to ask what he might have seen. I . . . I suspected Poynard. I did! But Old Jellis took one look of me dressed so, gasped and clutched his chest, then fell straight dead. I vow it! I did not intend to harm him!"

"No!" cried his sister. "Say nothing more, David!"

"Then Anna," continued Kit. "She saw you coming back from having killed Reade. She had to be silenced."

"No," he wailed. "'Twas not like that. No."

"Then what was it like, Master Merrick?" asked Kit.

He didn't answer. Ellyn Merrick sobbed but ceased struggling.

Kit frowned, his stomach twisted and taut. "Take him away, gentlemen."

★   ★   ★

"Your good sister did weary of awaiting your return, Mistress, and had Humphrey see her home. She vowed to return on the morrow, though, at first light," said Joan, taking Bess's cloak from her. "How was the constable? How was the meal?"

"Well enough and well enough." Bess worked her feet free of her tight leather shoes and stepped into her soft slippers. "But I am overwearied from the night's events."

"Should I help you out of your gown, Mistress?"

"In a moment, Joan." Bess looked over at her. "The constable means to charge David Merrick with the murders."

"Mistress Ellyn's brother?"

Bess padded through the entry passage and into the hall, relaying what she'd learned. Quail tapped after her as she crossed to the fire burning upon the hearth.

"He was the clout-covered woman!" exclaimed Joan. "He scared Old Jellis and left poppets for Anna and for you!"

"Marcye Johnes was correct about him, it seems." Quail dropped to his haunches by the hearth, and Bess reached her hands toward the flames. Why did the fire not warm her, though?

"But to have harmed Anna, one of his servants . . ." said Joan. "He is evil, Mistress. Poor girl."

Bess stepped nearer to the hearth and rubbed her hands together. "The constable concludes that David Merrick took advantage of Anna's sickness to meet with Master Reade. Master Merrick was envious of Master Reade and sought to keep him away from Ellyn. He may have wished as greatly as his mother did to see her wed to Jeffrey Poynard, a most beneficial union."

"Such a wish required Master Reade's death?" asked Joan.

"Perhaps David Merrick did not mean to kill him," said Bess. "Perhaps he only sought to warn him again—recall Simon telling you he'd seen a man shouting at Master Reade to 'stay away from her'—but Master Merrick's passions overwhelmed his self-command."

Quail jumped to his feet and barked at the street-side hall window. A flare of orange lit the diamond panes of glass. Joan hurried over to look out onto the road.

"Men with torches come down the lane, Mistress. And they drag David Merrick behind them."

Bess joined her at the window. Rain had begun to fall, and the torches spat and smoked in the dampness.

"How much sorrow could have been avoided if only Bartholomew Reade had not returned to the village," said Bess. The men's angry voices caused candles to be lit in windows and noses to press to glass so their owners might gawp. "Poor Anna. An innocent victim caught in a tangle of jealousies. I wonder if Master Reade truly meant to take her to London, or if his gifts and promises were but sport to him."

Of a sudden, she recollected a snippet of a conversation that seemed from a distant time instead of a mere few days ago.

He even gave me a gift that proved his regard, though it was taken from me.

Bess's thoughts tumbled, like checkstones tossed about in a child's game. She had never been as nimble as Robert at catching the pebbles. She still felt slow.

"Think you not, Mistress?" asked Joan.

"What is that?" asked Bess, her attention fixed upon a notion that pained her.

"I was saying, Mistress, that Master Merrick's guilt means I need not fret over that missing scrap of cut material."

Bess looked over at her servant. "What cut material?"

"While you were at the constable's, I set myself to mending your madder-dyed gown. The hem is raveled at the back," she said. "We store the ells of spare material in the trunk in Mistress Margery's chamber, the room she uses when she is here."

The chamber Ellyn had also made use of. "And?"

"The length of madder linen has been cut. A small piece hastily trimmed from one edge."

The tremor that sped across Bess's skin had naught to do with the night's chill. *No. Not her.* "Did Margery make use of any of that material when last she was here, Joan?"

"No, Mistress. I am certain she did not."

"Which means . . ."

"Which means that Mistress Ellyn cut it," said Joan.

"To make a poppet for me."

"Aye, Mistress."

I have been blind. Caught up in sympathy for a woman who'd seemed pitiable, but may have deserved no mercy, no compassion at all. The realization made her heartsore.

She lied to me. And I was so easily gulled.

"Joan, I need my cloak again," said Bess, stepping back from the window. "For I go to the constable's."

★   ★   ★

"What do I with the food, sir?" Alice gave the hall table, only partly cleared of platters and glasses, a forlorn look. "Your good cousin, Mistress Westcote, had no thought but for her unhappy friend and did not take what remnants she ought to give to her servants."

"You are welcome to it," said Kit, dropping onto the chair he'd drawn over to the fireplace.

"But there is so much!"

"I care not, Alice." Shouts echoed outside, men heckling David Merrick. Kit should have demanded the watchmen enforce the curfew and clear the square. The watchmen were probably among the hecklers. "Take what you want and give the rest away. Whatever you see fit."

A knock sounded on the house door, and Alice hastened off to answer it. A female voice echoed up the staircase, and the woman soon crossed the threshold of the hall.

"If you still have an appetite, Mistress Ellyott, plenty of food remains," he said, standing.

She lowered the hood of her cloak, scattering raindrops that had collected on it. "I have no appetite, Constable, for I have an admission to make," she said. "One that gives me no pleasure."

★ ★ ★

"You think Ellyn Merrick made the poppets, Mistress Ellyott?" asked Kit.

She hurried through the rain at his side. He'd sent a message with the watchman to have Gibb meet them at the Merricks' farm. If Bess Ellyott was correct about her suspicions, they might need his cousin's help.

"The one found in my garden for certain, though likely both. Made with fabric she'd found in the chamber she borrowed, stuffed with straw and feathers easily collected from our outbuildings," she replied, the hood of her cloak drawn low over her face. She'd not listened to his arguments for why she should stay at her house. She never did listen to his arguments. "How it will gall me to admit to Humphrey he was right."

"How could she have left the one at the dairy barn?" he asked, his grip firm on the pommel of his dagger to keep the weapon from slapping against his hip. "She was at your house, recovering."

"Ellyn, not so weak as I had thought her, may have slipped out," she said. "My brother's manservant thinks she did."

"Ah."

"'Tis my fault she left that poppet for Anna." She peered at him around the edge of her hood. "I told Ellyn I thought the girl had witnessed something important, something that had frightened her. Not many hours later, a witch's effigy was tossed into the farmyard."

"Ellyn Merrick needed to keep Anna quiet to protect her brother."

"Or protect herself," she replied grimly. "Anna had told me of a gift given to her by Bartholomew Reade when he first arrived in town. When she mentioned the item, I'd presumed it to be a trinket. But what if it had been a robe from the troupe's stores?"

"A substantial gift."

"And not easy to conceal," she said. "Anna told me it was taken from her, though. She would not tell me who had done so, but she may have meant Ellyn."

"She'd have a reason to seize the gift from Anna—bitter jealousy." His grip tightened on his dagger. "However, did she keep it or give that robe to her brother?" The garment black as the shadows Merrick had hidden within while he waited for the perfect moment to strike Reade down.

"I pray she tells us the truth. I confess I no longer have faith she will."

Gibb waited for them at the edge of the Merricks' land. Though the hour was late, a lantern glowed inside one of the ground-floor rooms of the house.

"Kit?" asked his cousin, the brim of the hat he'd slapped atop his head drooping in the rain.

"Go to the courtyard, Gibb," said Kit, a firm grip on the hilt of his dagger. "I want Ellyn Merrick stopped if she attempts to flee."

"Ellyn Merrick . . . Marry, Kit!" His cousin dashed off.

"You think she will try to escape?" asked Mistress Ellyott, her cloak clasped tightly against the wet weather.

"We have arrested her brother. Locked him in the jail. But yet we come here once more," he said. "She'll understand what our arrival means."

"I suppose she shall." She looked over at the outbuildings

and dairy barns, rainwater dripping from her hood, then to the house. "I suppose she shall."

"Stay behind me, Mistress," he ordered, and strode up the pathway.

"Ellyn is not going to jump out and attack me, Constable."

Someone within the house marked their approach, for the door opened before Kit could rap upon it.

Jennet stood upon the threshold. "Constable?" Her voice wavered on his name.

Kit raised the lantern he'd brought. The girl had been crying. "Where is Mistress Ellyn?"

"She is in the cow shed. With Thomasin. Or she was there." She sniffled. "They were fighting. Screaming at each other." Jennet wiped her nose with the sleeve of her gown. "Thomasin was fiercely angry. Shouting, 'It was you!' Horrible it was!"

"Why was Thomasin so angry?" asked Kit.

"She . . . he . . . they . . ." She sniffled again and shook her head.

"I understand." *Damn.* "Stay here, Mistress Ellyott," he ordered.

Kit jogged to the side of the house where the drive led to the rear of the property and the yard. Bess Ellyott hurried after him, her skirts lifted high above the thick grasses.

"I told you to stay behind."

"I cannot lend you help by standing upon the entrance path, Constable."

Stubborn woman.

More candles and lamps were set ablaze in the Merricks' house. An unseen hand twitched aside the rear chamber window curtains, and the faces of Merrick children appeared behind the panes of glass. A servant called for them to get back.

In the courtyard, Gibb waited for Kit and Mistress Ellyott. "Where is she?"

Kit, nodding at the barn to their right, set his lantern next to the back wall of the house. "Jennet says she and Thomasin were fighting in the cow shed."

"I have heard nothing," said Gibb. "All is silent."

Not good.

"The shed is at the side of the barn where the hay is kept," whispered Bess Ellyott.

Kit gestured for Gibb to circle around the back of the building. "With me, Mistress."

He crept toward the shed, which was carelessly attached to the tall whitewashed barn as though it had been an afterthought of construction. Behind him, Bess Ellyott's footfalls were soft upon the gravel. They reached the shed door, and he inched it open. The sweet-warm scent of hay filled the air, and mice scurried across the clay floor, disturbed from their evening meal.

Light from a small lantern flickered at the far end of the shed. An untended flame in a shed full of hay, but at least he could make out the bales, the beams, and the loft that stretched overhead on both sides. Bess Ellyott pointed at three enclosed pallet chambers, reached by a ladder. They'd been timbered from oddments of wood, and cloth had been nailed up to hang over their openings in place of doors. Crude and drafty sleeping spaces. Kit would have preferred a corner of the barn, which was warmed by the cattle. David Merrick's lover and the other dairymaids apparently did not deserve warmth.

He paused to listen for any sound besides the scamper of mice. Nothing.

"So quiet," murmured the woman at his side.

"Too quiet, Mistress."

He set a toe on the first rung of the ladder and climbed, Bess Ellyott watching his ascent from the aisle of the shed.

"Be careful," she mouthed.

Beneath his boots, the rungs creaked. What would he find at the top? A dead Thomasin? A waiting Ellyn Merrick?

I do not want to have to kill her. I do not want her to attack me. Or hurt Bess. Damn, he should have demanded she go back to her house.

He clambered onto the plank that fronted the pallet chambers and crouched, alert to any movements. Not hearing any, he withdrew his dagger from its scabbard and swept aside the cloth at the opening to the first cubicle. Unused. As was the next. Which left the last.

Using his dagger's tip, he eased back the curtain. The space held a pallet and chamber pot and a stool. Not unused, then. Knife extended, he slipped around the edge of the opening. And saw her, slumped upon the ground, one arm outflung as if reaching . . .

"Bess! It's Thomasin!"

An angry red bruise swelled her cheek where she'd been struck hard. The girl was insensible but breathing.

The ladder rungs creaked beneath Mistress Ellyott's feet, and she hurtled into the cramped space to drop beside him. "Thomasin?"

The girl's eyes opened, and she moaned. "Mistress?"

"I believe she will be all right, Constable. But where is Ellyn?"

"Elsewhere."

He sheathed his dagger and retreated down the ladder as fast as he could, jumping to the pounded-earth floor.

Out in the courtyard, Gibb shouted. Kit ran for the door. He skidded around the corner of the shed in time to see Ellyn Merrick, astride a horse, bolt from a stable.

"Stop!" yelled Gibb, jumping into the animal's path.

The horse shied, lurching sideways. Ellyn screamed and kicked its flanks to spur it on. The horse bucked and charged, slamming into Gibb and knocking him to the ground.

"Gibb!" cried Kit.

He clutched his lower leg. "I am fine, coz. Get her!"

Kit chased after the woman. She struggled to control the horse pelting across the yard toward the side path, her rain-wetted kirtle tangling about her legs.

"Ellyn, stop!" He lost his footing and slipped. *Damn.* "Stop!"

She looked back over her shoulder at him. In that instant, another voice joined his command to halt. Jennet stepped into the path and shouted at the horse. It reared wildly, tossing Ellyn Merrick from its back.

With a scream, the woman fell, her head striking the ground with a sickening thud.

Chapter 24

The shriek, the whinnying horse, shouts and running . . . *something horrid has happened.*

Bess pressed her hand to Thomasin's shoulder. "Do not move. I will return as soon as possible."

Bess clambered down the ladder and out into the yard. Gibb Harwoode sprawled in the muddy courtyard.

"Master Harwoode!"

"Is she dead?" he asked between clenched teeth, twisting to reach for his lower limb, his foot bent at an unsightly angle.

"Thomasin?" she asked.

"No." He shook his head. "Ellyn Merrick."

"Dearest God."

Bess collected the lantern the constable had left near the house and ran for the path. "Constable!"

He had hold of the reins of a horse. The animal snorted and danced, his breath clouding the air in bursts. At the edge of the path, Ellyn lay unmoving. Her siblings had gathered, and Jennet came to herd them back inside the house. She gave her young mistress the briefest glance before shepherding the children away.

Bess dropped to the ground next to Ellyn and set the lantern nearby. Blood oozed from her nose and ears, the rainwater streaming down her face and neck running in thin rivulets of red.

"Constable, attend to your cousin," she said, slipping a hand behind Ellyn's head to feel for a fracture. Her fingers met more blood and the depression where the woman's skull had cracked against a jagged stone. "Master Harwoode has broken his ankle."

"Is she alive or dead?" asked a female voice behind Bess.

"Thomasin, I told you to not move. You risk your own health."

She had followed Bess from the shed. Water dripped from her unbound hair and soaked through her night rail. "I pray God she is dead. She would let David hang for her crime!"

She lunged toward the woman on the ground. Constable Harwoode grabbed Thomasin and dragged her back. She slumped weakly against him, her strength spent.

Bess leaned close to Ellyn Merrick's face. "She breathes, but barely." She withdrew her hand, easing Ellyn's wounded head onto the muddy ground. Bess probed her throat for a pulse. Weak. She looked up at Kit Harwoode through the rain that collected upon her lashes. "She may not ever awake again. She has not long to live."

Thomasin cried out, a sound both triumphant and pain-filled, and crumpled to the earth.

★   ★   ★

"She killed him, did she not, Constable?" asked Thomasin.

The young woman—a mere dairymaid who smelled of cattle and manure and soured milk—had been allowed to rest in the Merricks' parlor while Agnes Merrick shrieked and howled her anguish elsewhere in the house. Bess Ellyott accompanied Gibb to her brother's house, where she could tend his ankle.

"I believe you know the answer to your question, Thomasin," he said, standing across from the stool she occupied.

The bruise upon Thomasin's cheek was already turning from red to purple, and she momentarily pressed her fingertips to it, wincing.

"The black robe. David—" She caught herself in her familiarity. "After your visit this morning, Master David kept muttering about a black robe. That you had found one. He was distressed, and I presumed the item was connected to Bartholomew's death."

"Why think that?"

Her pale gaze was clear-eyed and intelligent. "Because I saw her with it the day he was murdered, Constable. Mistress Ellyn," she replied. "At the time, I had no care for where she might be headed wearing the black robe she had taken from Anna. In truth, I hoped she might be leaving. She'd threatened to, often enough."

"You did not like her."

"Should I have done?"

"Was she cruel to you because of your relationship with her brother?" he asked.

She blushed. Difficult to imagine a woman with Thomasin's pluck strapping herself to man with so little. Marriage to him, though, would have brought her creature comforts beyond her grasp as a dairymaid.

"She was cruelest of all to Anna," she said.

Because of Bartholomew Reade. "I didn't realize you were friends with Anna Webb."

"We were not friends, 'tis true. But I vow I did not mean to hurt her," she said. "It was an accident, what happened with the cow."

Kit leaned against the wall at his back and folded his arms. "What did happen with the cow, Thomasin?"

"Anna had seen him. Da . . . Master David." She twisted her hands together. "After he had come upon Bartholomew's body and rushed home, distraught. 'I saw her,' he said to me. 'She killed him.'" Thomasin exhaled. "In my stupidity I thought he meant the witch, my kinswoman."

"Mother Fletcher."

"Aye," she answered. "But I feared what Anna had begun to suspect. That she would accuse David. I tried several times to get her to tell me what she'd said to Mistress Ellyott, but she refused." She stared down at her hands. "That night in the barn, I tried again. I was scared. David had told me you had confronted him outside the church. I feared you thought he was guilty. I demanded Anna tell me, but she was obstinate. I had the prod in my hand and I hit her." She shook her head fiercely. "She jumped up and grabbed it. We struggled. The prod struck the red cow, startling it. Anna stumbled and fell beneath its hooves. I could not control the animal. It hates me. So I ran, screaming."

"And David Merrick helped you concoct a proper story about the events that night," he said. "Including spying a shadow in the woods."

She lifted her eyes to meet his. "Master David did not kill Bartholomew Reade, Constable. Mistress Ellyn did. She was jealous he would take Anna to London instead of her. She'd found the note Anna had sent saying she could not meet Bartholomew because she was ill. She knew what they planned."

So powerful an emotion, jealousy. "Why did David Merrick visit Old Jellis dressed as a crone, Thomasin?"

"He did not explain to me," she said. "I suppose because he wondered if Old Jellis had recognized Mistress Ellyn."

"He hadn't recognized her, though," said Kit. "He only said he had seen a woman." However, the old man's feeble eyes hadn't deceived him, after all.

"What will happen to David, Constable?"

What will happen to you*, Thomasin?*

He shrugged. "A justice might decide he meant no harm to Old Jellis." And no one would bother to waste time amending the already stated cause of a drunken vagabond's death. "But he did shield his sister, a murderer, from suspicion. I think he knocked Old Jellis senseless, placed Reade's purse and belt near him, then went to dispose of the knife."

She squeezed her hands until her knuckles went white. "Will he hang for helping her?"

Kit straightened; he could not lie to her, soften his words. "Aye, Thomasin. Just so."

★ ★ ★

Joan buzzed around Bess and the constable, who'd just returned from the jail. She brought warmed rugs to lay over their laps and warmer wine to drink. Gibb Harwoode stretched upon the settle, his ankle wrapped securely, a second glass of wine in his hand. With a wagon and male servant borrowed from the Merricks, they had transported Master Harwoode to Robert's house, where Bess could treat his injury.

"My father will not ever permit me to assist you again, coz," said Master Harwoode, downing his wine.

Joan promptly hurried over to refill his glass, earning a smile from him, which made her blush. As ever, she tucked her face behind the protective cover of her coif so that the scar upon her cheek was hidden. Would that she could find a man who'd see beyond the mark.

"Given the coroner's opinion—and the burgesses' as well—about my work, Gibb, I doubt I'll require your assistance in future," the constable replied.

"Ha!" exclaimed his cousin. "Who else will do the job? No one."

"Constable, 'tis too late in the evening for you to fret over what might occur on the morrow," said Bess.

"Evening is the best time to fret, Mistress," he said. "Were you not aware?"

Joan curtsied and left them to their discussion, softly closing the hall door behind her.

Bess leaned into the cushion Joan had placed between her and the chair, burrowing into the comfort of the bolster. The scent Robert wore upon his clothes lifted from its fabric, and she longed for her brother's consoling smile. They'd not received any news from him as to when he might return from London. In truth, they'd not received any news from him at all.

"Should we not have comprehended all along that the killer was Ellyn Merrick?" asked Gibb Harwoode, the color restored to his face by the three glasses of sweetened wine he'd consumed.

Servants had carried Ellyn to her bedchamber at the Merricks' home, and the priest from All Saints had been summoned to provide last rites. Bess could do naught else for her, except mourn the desperate folly that had led to the deaths of a young man and an innocent servant.

"I confused matters, Master Harwoode," said Bess. "I would not allow your cousin to accuse her. I believed her innocence too greatly. Even though I suspected from the very beginning that she'd rid herself of her unborn babe, I trusted her. I remained convinced she'd had naught to do with Master Reade's death. The blood upon her skirts solely her blood, not any of his."

"Come now, Mistress. Don't blame yourself for being deceived," said Constable Harwoode. "We all were. Master Reade had many enemies, and it was easy to suspect others."

"However, Anna would still be alive if I had seen more clearly," she replied.

"You do not know that for certain." He bent to ruffle Quail's ears, the dog lolling at his feet. If Robert did not soon return, he'd find that his dog had chosen a new master. "Merrick did warn Reade to stay away from Ellyn, but the advice didn't save him. In the end, her jealousy struck him down," he said, reclining in the chair again.

"She may not have intended that outcome when she departed for the old fort hill that night, Constable," said Bess.

"You think not?" he asked. "She'd brought a knife with her and had gone wearing the perfect garment to conceal herself— the troupe's long black robe, which she'd earlier taken from Anna."

Gibb Harwoode propped himself on his elbows. "She might have meant to cast blame upon one of Master Reade's fellow players by wearing the robe and by thrusting that pen into his neck."

"She had accused Jeffrey Poynard, not any of the players," said Bess. What did all that matter now, though?

I will never understand how love can turn to such fierce hate.

Laurence had loved Martin, yet had poisoned him to flee the queen's justice. And now Ellyn had killed Bartholomew Reade to keep him from the arms of another woman.

"What new did you learn from David Merrick, coz?" asked Gibb Harwoode.

"He admitted to hiding the knife—which had come from

their house—and to delivering the blow that stunned Old Jellis." He finished his glass of wine before setting it aside. "By this point, Ellyn had fled, and he rushed back to the farm, where Anna spied him from the window."

"As I unintentionally informed Ellyn," said Bess. "It was only a few hours later that I found the poppet at the Merricks'."

Master Harwoode raised himself into a seated position to better listen. "With so much recent talk of a witch and curses, Ellyn Merrick meant the poppet to frighten the girl, tossing the thing into the yard. Right, Kit?"

"Even you believed there was a witch, Gibb," said his cousin.

"Fie on you, Kit."

"Anna was already affrighted by what she'd witnessed," said Bess. "I'faith, there was no reason to threaten the girl with curses if she spoke out."

"Ellyn Merrick was desperate to protect herself. Who would not be?" asked the constable. "Her brother did help the tale of a witch's curse by visiting Jellis dressed as a crone."

"Poor Mother Fletcher," said Bess. "To be accused of being a witch." *God keep you safe, wherever you are.*

"Did Master Merrick mean to frighten the old man to death?" asked Master Harwoode.

"I think not, Gibb."

"He had gone to the jail whilst we all searched for Ellyn," said Bess. "I wonder . . . had she meant to kill herself, or had she meant to escape?"

"We'll never know her intentions now," said the constable. "Merrick also admitted that he next donned his disguise to search for the black robe his sister had worn and tossed aside. Evidence to be disposed of."

"Which is why I passed him so attired upon the highway two days after Master Reade's death," said Bess, finishing her wine and setting her empty glass on the stool at her side. "However, Master Dunning had already collected it, which Master Merrick did not know."

"But who killed Anna Webb, Kit?"

"Thomasin," he said, and described the argument she'd had with Anna in the barn.

"Thomasin could not admit to causing Anna's death, could she? For that would require her to confess what they had fought over," said Bess.

"So she and David Merrick created a story about a shadowy figure in the woods," said Constable Harwoode. "A stranger who might have come into the barn and killed Anna. I could find no one else to support the tale, though."

"And the second poppet?" asked his cousin.

"Ellyn again, I am sad to admit," said Bess. "A warning to me, for she dared not threaten you, Constable."

"It could have been an attempt to ensure we kept our attention upon anyone else as the murderer," he replied.

Ellyn had been calculating from the start. *And I was a puppet whose strings she pulled.* "I trusted her, Constable. Dearest God, I trusted her. Defended her to you."

He reached over to squeeze her fingers, his kindness lessening chagrin's sting.

Joan returned with freshly warmed wine to serve around.

Gibb Harwoode accepted another glass. "Marry, Kit, I still cannot fathom why Master Reade sought to bring the troupe to town to be the Poynards' guests. He endangered himself."

"Poynard gave us that version of the tale. Howlett only knew they'd been in communication with each other," he said. "I suspect the invitation was actually Poynard's idea from the first. To show to Reade that he'd taken possession of Ellyn Merrick."

An apt description, thought Bess.

Joan departed, and Master Harwoode sank into the settle's cushions once more. "But Master Reade had lost interest in Mistress Merrick. He had chosen to take Anna Webb to London with him."

"If that truly was his intention, Gibb, it just proves what a fickle fellow he was."

Bess released a lengthy breath, the muscles and tendons that had been taut for so long relaxing. "All is hence resolved, if sadly."

Kit Harwoode lifted his glass, the wine glowing from the firelight captured within its burgundy depths. "To you, Mistress Ellyott, without whom we'd yet be wandering in the dark."

His cousin raised his glass as well. "Well done!" he cried. "To our Mistress Ellyott, the cleverest woman there is!"

"Nonsense, gentlemen!" She blushed, not so much at Gibb Harwoode's effusive praise but at the esteem and compassion in Kit Harwoode's eyes.

God save you, Bess. You have gone and fallen in love with him.

★   ★   ★

"One of the Merricks' servants has come, Mistress," said Joan. "Ellyn Merrick's soul passed away before sunrise."

Bess sat back on her heels. Last night's rain had ceased, and fog crept across the garden, a sheer netting of white to soften the harsh angles of autumn's barren branches. When she was a girl, she'd imagined that spirits lifted from their dead bodies in filmy trails of snowy white. After becoming a healer, she would catch herself waiting, hoping to see such proof of eternity. All she had ever observed was the flicker of life departing dying eyes, heard the final breath sigh through lips that would not again speak.

"God rest her," said Bess. A Papist's prayer, as the constable would point out. A habit she'd not ever shake.

"There will be no rest for a murderer," said Joan.

Bess finished cutting the rosemary, tossed the last snippet into her willow basket, and got to her feet. "I suppose not."

"Simon tells me the players have been sent off, Mistress," said Joan. "They departed the Poynards' before sunrise, as well."

With Bartholomew Reade's play in their possession, for a more thorough search of the room he'd occupied in the Poynards' house had exposed the manuscript secreted beneath a loose tile in the floor.

"And Mistress Crofton sends a message she awoke with head pains and begs you visit her with a physic," Joan added.

Dorothie and her head pains . . .

"A busy morn, Joan," said Bess. "At least peace is restored to our little village."

"Peace?" Joan looked dubious. "I would that we had received word your brother, Master Marshall, is safe in London. Then we might have peace."

"He is occupied with wooing his ladylove," said Bess. Humphrey bustled out of the shed with a bag of feed for the chickens. She knew he must be counting the days until Robert returned. "And do not pull a sour face, Joan. I know you fret over Laurence, but my brother is not so incautious as to be taken unawares by any of his schemes. Robert shall be safe."

"As you say, Mistress."

Robert shall be safe. He must *be safe.*

And oh how angry he shall be to learn that we harbored a murderer beneath his roof.

Bess strode toward the house, the basket swinging from her arm. "Joan, do you think I should ever admit to Humphrey that Ellyn indeed made those poppets?"

They entered the house, and Bess handed the basket to Joan.

"You should admit that only if you wish him to smirk at you from now into forever, Mistress," she answered.

Grinning, Bess shook clinging rosemary leaves and garden dirt from her apron, untied it, and handed it off as well before stepping into the hall.

Through the street-facing window, Bess noticed the constable out on the lane.

She went outside. "Constable," she said.

"Good morrow, Mistress," he answered, tipping his hat.

Quail heard his voice and trotted, tail wagging, out onto the lane to greet him.

Kit Harwoode crouched to accept the dog's friendly licks. "My cousin sends his thanks for tending his ankle, Mistress." He looked up at Bess. "Mistress Pollington has delayed her departure for Gloucester to oversee his recovery. Gibb, I must say, is enjoying the attention."

"Ah."

He stood. "Have you learned the news?"

"I have," she said. "Sorrows upon sorrows."

And what of Laurence and the sorrows he might bring?

"But for us, Mistress Ellyott, another successful resolution," the constable replied.

"I most sincerely hope we have no need, in future, to resolve any other unpleasant affairs, Constable Harwoode."

"As do I, Mistress, but what are the chances of that?"

She smiled, and they stood together in companionable silence watching the town stir fully to life and the fog dissolve into the brightening sky.

Author's Note

"Double, double toil and trouble." The lore surrounding witches and witchcraft long predates William Shakespeare writing about them in Macbeth. The objects we now call voodoo dolls, known as witches' effigies in Bess's day, are also ancient. They were just one of the many tools supposedly used to place curses. In a time of limited scientific understanding, a sense of helplessness led people to blame the devil and those perceived to be in his employ for everything from disease to drought to failed business ventures. Publishing treatises on how to identify and destroy witches was a profitable occupation. Women, especially elderly women, were most commonly accused. The peak of the frenzy occurred between 1550 and 1650 in Europe, but the most famous cases in America happened late in the 1600s. Because of the fear, many thousands of innocent women—and men—would die.

Though the particular mound where Bartholomew Reade was murdered is a creation of my imagination, Wiltshire is a county filled with iron and bronze age sites. Stone circles, of which Stonehenge is best known, barrows (burial mounds), and hill forts dot the countryside. People have always sought to explain who built the monuments and why. At one time, it was popular to link them to the legends of King Arthur as well as to the druids, which I mention in the book. Scientists continue to study the sites, trying to gain an understanding of the people who expended so much effort to create these works that still fascinate us.

Lastly, a word of gratitude goes to the team at Crooked Lane Books. Your tireless efforts whipped this novel into shape. "I can no other answer make but thanks, and thanks."